SARAH McCARTY

Shadow's Stand

Recycling programs for this product may not exist in your area.

ISBN-13: 978-0-373-77705-1

SHADOW'S STAND

This edition published by arrangement with Harlequin Books S.A.

For questions and comments about the quality of this book please contact us at Customer_eCare@Harlequin.ca.

www.Harlequin.com

Printed in U.S.A.

Praise for Sarah McCarty's
Hell's Eight series

"Sarah McCarty's new series is an exciting blend of raw masculinity, spunky, feisty heroines and the wild living in the Old West...with spicy, hot love scenes. Ms. McCarty gave us small peeks into each member of the Hell's Eight and I'm looking forward to reading the other men's stories."
—*Erotica Romance Writers*

"*Caine's Reckoning* is a can't-put-it-down adventure story... This exceptional first-in-series book has this reader eagerly anticipating future stories. A hands-down winning tale that is not to be missed."
—Named Best Historical Romance
by *Romance Reviews Today*

"Intense, edgy and passionate, this is old-school historical romance at its finest."
—*RT Book Reviews*

"If you like your historicals packed with emotion, excitement and heat, you can never go wrong with a book by Sarah McCarty."
—*Romance Junkies*

"Readers who enjoy erotic romance but haven't found an author who can combine it with an historical setting may discover a new auto-buy author...I have."
—*All About Romance*

"Fantastic American-West historicals that bring action and adventure to what could have been just plain old romance. Super good job on characters and situations... you can't wait to see what happens next."
—*Night Owl Romance*

Also by Sarah McCarty

Hell's Eight

Tracker's Sin
Tucker's Claim
Sam's Creed
Caine's Reckoning

And coming soon
Caden's Vow

To my sister,
a woman who can crack a joke in the face of adversity
and has always been there for everyone.
May your future be full of love and happiness, and
shine with your own personal "happily ever after."

CHAPTER ONE

July 1859, West Kansas Territory

IT HAD TO BE DONE. Fei Yen Tseng stood in the doorway and stared through the gloom at her father sitting at the table, his head down, his back bent by years of manual labor. His long queue draped listlessly over his shoulder, the end dangling in his untouched bowl of porridge. The silk overcoat he insisted on wearing morning, noon and night was stained and torn. It was hard to believe he was once the commanding head of the family. Always well dressed. Always scheming. In charge of a hidden empire he'd built out of nothing. The man who'd taught her so much, good and bad. He looked up then and, for a moment, she saw the man Jian Tseng used to be before the blankness came over his eyes and the scowl settled between his brows. A scowl that would have sent everyone running just two years before.

"You! What do you do there in the doorway?" he rapped out in Chinese. The force of the words couldn't cover the fear behind the question. But the shoe was on the other foot, as the Americans said. Now, it was he who lived in fear. But the fear was not contained in this room.

"Nothing. I am just leaving," Fei Yen whispered, slowly pushing closed the heavy door that last inch before dropping the wooden bar across it. So many things needed to be done. So many wrongs needed to be righted. She was but a female, it was not her place to make decisions or take action. In China, she never would have. But she was no longer in China and there was no large family to take over, to tie up loose ends left by her father's illness. It was just her and the dragon that stalked her luck. She could feel the fire of its breath on the back of her neck; feel the weight of its claws on her shoulders. It wanted her to fail. Expected her to fail. She was not even a son. Just a worthless girl child of mixed ancestry. Or so it thought.

Beyond the door, she heard her father begin his ritual of pacing and prayer. Soon it would switch to ranting and threats. Nighttime was always the worst. She touched the bar. Rough slivers bit at her fingertip. The shouts were heavily muffled by the thick dirt walls of the cellar and the solid planks of the wooden door, but the anger and sense of injustice swelled through the barrier and wrapped around her, joining the dragon on her back. Once, she'd been the prisoner. Now, she was the guard. Life went in circles. The debts her father had gathered in his life were now hers to pay. His path was now hers.

Turning, she climbed the ladder out of the storm cellar to the barn floor. Lowering the trapdoor carefully, she pushed dirt back around it to disguise the opening and sprinkled hay across the surface. No one could discover this secret. Discovery meant the end of everything. The dragon's paw got heavier.

Their old horse, Grandfather, nickered a greeting. Fei's pockets were empty. She had no carrots for him, so she gave him a pat and a promise. "Later."

She sighed. She was always saying later. Always making promises. Always doing the impossible, hoping to make the dragon surrender, but it was the way of dragons to accept challenges and she was no closer to succeeding than she had been eight months ago when she'd started on this path. Eight months during which her ancestors frowned and her beliefs died.

But she was stronger than they thought. Stronger than even *she* thought, and this time she prayed to her American ancestors for help. They were brash and fearless, without centuries of culture to honor. So maybe this time help would come. The sun slanted through the open window in the loft. Squinting against the late-afternoon light, she tucked her hands into the wide sleeves of her flowing robe and hurried across the yard toward the house. She needed to change. Some things were better done in Western clothing, though it was heavy and cumbersome. Getting married was one of them.

FOR A MOMENT, FEI YEN thought she'd arrived too late. Such shouting usually indicated the end of a hanging, not the beginning. Then the crowd of men parted and she could see what caused the excitement. The thief was fighting, and well, despite the fact that his hands were tied behind his back. Excitement flared. He even looked as though he was winning. With a speed that made her blink, the thief spun around and his moccasined foot caught the sheriff on his jaw. Blood and spit flew as the heavyset man stumbled to the side. His friends caught him, tossing him back into the fray with a laugh. And he went. The thief was ready, balanced on his toes, his dark eyes narrowed, watchful. Seeing all. Fei bit her lip. He didn't look as though he needed rescuing.

The men laughed with a force not warranted by the situation. They were drunk. Not surprising. Every time the residents of the railroad camp got together, they got drunk. And fought. And, sometimes, killed. The thief stood straight amidst the rabble, daring them to accept his challenge. He was big, much bigger than she'd anticipated, with broad shoulders that were barely contained by the torn cotton of his black shirt. The muscles in his thighs bulged against his broadcloth pants. Everything about the man shouted challenge, from his lean hips to his strong features, which appeared to be precision carved by a well-honed knife.

Dragon.

For a moment her resolve wavered. She had enough dragons on her back. She didn't need another one, but she definitely could use one guarding her claim. For herself, for her father, for her cousin, Lin. And unlike someone she could hire—assuming she could find someone of honor—this one would owe her the debt of his life. No small thing. And it would also be no small thing that his continued life would depend on her goodwill, for the law said if he did not please her he would be hung immediately.

The thief slammed his head back into the face of a man who'd grabbed his arms from behind and, as they stumbled, leveraged their grip to bring his legs up and wrap them around the neck of the man who held the noose. She had no doubt he would have snapped the man's neck with the same ease with which he'd kicked the sheriff if one of the crew, Damon, she thought his name was, hadn't chosen that moment to smash the butt of a pistol against the side of the thief's head. The thief slumped to the ground, his long hair falling across his face.

Maybe not so much a dragon.

"Hell, Damon, if you went and killed him, I'm going to fire a load of buckshot in your ass," the sheriff said, spitting out a brown stream of tobacco juice. "We haven't had a good hanging around here in a month."

Fei shuddered. There was never a good hanging in her opinion. Suffocating the life from a person was ugly and horrendous.

"That man's head is too thick to be dented by a pistol," Damon sneered. "Somebody get a bucket of water and wake him up."

Fei sat on the fringes, watching. Folding her hands sedately in front of her, she focused on calming her urge to run in and interfere. Frustrated, drunken men would not see a half American, half Chinese girl as someone to be respected. She stood very still, hoping her tan dress blended with the tall grass in the shadows. Not for the first time, she debated her decision. The law on the books was not necessarily one that would be respected, either, but there were very few men in the camp not under the sheriff's thumb. If word got out about her find, claim jumpers would come like ants swarming sugar. The new law making it illegal for a Chinese to own a claim tied her hands. There was too much at stake to lose her gold. Too much at stake for her to lose her life. She wasn't a foolish woman. She understood the risks, but she also understood her responsibilities. In her father's country this would never be required of her, but here she was a woman with no country and ancestors who straddled two worlds. Her mixed blood was either going to weaken her or strengthen her. Her mother had predicted the latter. She wanted to believe her mother. Her too-soft mother who'd often whispered foolishness, who had died when fever had swept the camp. Fei had been only eight, but time had not diluted the memory. It lived in her mind as clearly as if it were yesterday.

She had sat beside her mother's body that night long after she'd passed, watching for the rise of her chest, listening for the gasp that signaled the return of life. Praying for it. In the small hours after the moon had set, Fei had accepted reality and begun the process of lighting the candles for her ancestors. When her father had come into the tent, he'd looked at her mother's freshly washed body with tears in his eyes. Then he'd looked at her with disappointment. It was then, amidst death and despair, that she'd felt the first touch of the dragon. Maybe her father's disappointment was because, unlike her cousin, her features were more American than Chinese. Her skin was too white. Her eyes not so almond shaped. Her nose was too pointed and her face too long. Or maybe the disappointment was because she hadn't been able to keep her mother alive. She'd never known what she'd done to lose her father's love, but she'd done her best to be the dutiful daughter she'd promised her mother she would be.

After her mother's death, her father had taken her back to China. There, she'd taken care of her father's house and his business. Fei had taken care of her cousin, Lin. She'd done everything she could for as long as she could, but nothing she'd done had stopped the plummet of their lives. A few years ago, he had brought them back to America and his flagging business. Lin had stayed in San Francisco. This last visit was the first time Fei had seen her in three years.

Last week, when she'd come home and found her cousin gone, taken as payment on a debt her father owed, she'd done the one thing she had never thought she would. She'd revoked her father's heritage.

Water sloshed and splashed as it hit the man who lay unconscious, bringing her back to the present. They'd fetched the bucket.

"He's awake," Damon called.

The thief spat and sat up. He was more than awake.

He was furious. His glance collided with hers. His lips twisted in a sneer. She shivered and wrapped her arms around her stomach, as if the gesture could ward off the stranger's disgust. The thief stood, shaking his head. Water dripped down his face. His blue-black hair flared around his shoulders. With his eyes narrowed and his lips drawn back in a grim smile, he had the look of a lion about to pounce. The men guarding him took instinctive steps back before catching themselves.

Fei had no trouble understanding the reason. The thief had a personality as big as his size and he wielded intimidation well. This was not a man who would be easily controlled. He would not be easily intimidated, either. And that ranked high on her list of requirements. Gratitude and greed were powerful motivators. If she saved his life, hopefully that would motivate him to do her this favor. And it was not as if he would not have a reward. She stood and straightened her skirt, then pushed her way in just as the deputy put the noose around the thief's neck.

"Any last words, injun?"

With a smile cold enough to freeze water, he answered, "Yeah. You're a dead man."

Damon wasn't impressed. "I'm not the one with the noose around my neck."

The thief's smile held. "Not yet."

The smile sent shivers down Fei's back. Even the men with weapons looked uneasy.

"Get him up on the horse," the sheriff snapped.

Fei took another breath. It was now or never. "Wait."

All the men turned to look at her. "Son of a bitch, Fei Yen. What are you doing here?"

No "Miss" or any other courtesy preceded her name. That did not bode well. To the left, a man she didn't know bundled in a dirty coat, despite the heat, took a swig from a flask. Keeping her eyes down, feigning submissiveness, she murmured, "My father insists I invoke the law and take this man to husband."

"I told you last time, you don't get the man without making it legal."

She had not married the last one. There had not been that much fight in him. She had let him die for his crimes.

"I understand."

"Goddammit, Sheriff, you can't be considering this. We get little enough fun around here, and this injun was caught red-handed stealing a horse."

"Shut up, Damon."

"I don't want to shut up. I want a hanging."

"Yeah!" Damon's friend Barney chimed in. "A hanging would liven up the evening."

This was getting out of hand. She raised her voice to be heard. "I am aware of the price."

"Horses don't come cheap," the sheriff countered her offer.

"It is my understanding that he did not succeed in the theft."

"Doesn't mean he wasn't giving it a hell of a try."

She squared her shoulders and set her chin. "But no

theft means no compensation." She couldn't afford to give up any coin.

"That's true," Barney cut in, "but you'd be better off waiting on some white boy or drunk Chinee. This one will kill you and Lin without blinking an eye. Maybe worse. Indians ain't got no honor."

And Chinese had no worth. She'd heard the slurs too many times before to believe them valid. Especially coming from Barney. Just last week he'd tried to capture her along the way back from the claim. If the stench of his body odor hadn't warned her of his presence, the fate he predicted might already have been hers. At his hand. She glanced at the sun sinking on the horizon. Night would arrive soon. Night meant suffering. She needed this man, now. Lowering her eyes, she folded her hands and resumed a properly demure stance. "I cannot go against my father."

"None of you Chinese can, which makes for some nice recreation for us," Damon sneered.

She could feel the thief's gaze upon her. The stares of the other men didn't bother her, but his did. Those brown eyes, so dark they were almost black, seemed to see all the way to her soul, to the secrets she was trying to hide. She would have to be careful around him. This man was discerning.

"Do you wish me to go back to my father and tell him the marriage was not possible?"

"Jian sent you?" Damon asked.

"Yes."

"Shit!"

"This is not to your like?" Fei Yen asked.

"I'd like you to tell him to shove it up his ass, and if it weren't for his ways with explosives, I'd do just that," Barney growled.

Jian Tseng had a talent with explosives and the railroad needed a tunnel. His skill bought them better quarters, more consideration, favors. It would hopefully buy her this one.

Barney stepped closer and touched his finger to her cheek. "But as soon as we get that tunnel through the mountain, it's going to be a whole different game, little girl."

Disgust whipped down her spine. She didn't lift her gaze or move away. This man would not see her run. "I'll tell my father of your decision."

The fact that Jian would be unhappy was heavily implied and the men were not too drunk to pick up on it. Her father had a reputation for being quick to anger, and when he was angry, he didn't work. Or he worked in ways that caused accidents for those with whom he was displeased. Barney dropped his hand. "You won't be telling your father squat."

No she wouldn't. But only because it would serve no purpose. Jian Tseng was not the man he'd once been since the madness had taken him. The thief was still studying her with those dragon eyes that saw more than a person wanted. Again, she wondered if this was a mistake, and again she knew she didn't have a choice. The situation was getting too dangerous. The game too complex. The delicate web of her deceit too fragile. She needed an ally. At the very least, a guard dog. She waited.

There was swearing, but nothing from the thief.

"Someone go fetch the padre."

Padre was a loose term for preacher, that she understood. But if the man of God who served this camp had ever known the inner peace that came from greater wisdom and a connection to his ancestors, it was long gone. He drank to excess and always smelled of urine and vomit and was rarely coherent. Yet they still called him a man of God.

There were many things she didn't understand about this land. Her father had raised her in the way of his people, separate from the world, trained in obedience and duty. Until he'd decided to leave their home in China where he was but a third son and return to America with her and Lin to take up work on the railroad and make his own fortune. Dutiful daughter had never been a role with which she was comfortable, but life was exhausting outside it. She couldn't wait for the day when she could escape. Her cousin wanted to go back to China. Fei Yen didn't know where she wanted to go, just someplace where there was peace. She would really like to live in a world where she wasn't seen as "less."

The priest stumbled forward, hawking and spitting as he got close. "You decide to marry up, Fei?"

His lack of cleanliness was an affront. More so than his abbreviation of her name. She bowed slightly. The priest looked over at the thief. “Are you sure about this one? He’s more likely to kill you than help you.”

Could no one stop harping on that? “My father made the choice.”

“Jian’s a strange one, but you’re a good daughter to do what he says.”

She wasn’t, but she tried. Sometimes. Bowing, she kept her voice. “It is my duty.”

The thief still watched her. She felt his gaze like that of a burn on her skin. He didn’t have the look of a thief. There was pride in his stance and an arrogance in the lift of his chin that one didn’t expect to see in a criminal.

“Are you sure he’s guilty?”

“As guilty as sin, Miss Fei,” the padre responded.

She still couldn’t believe it. The thief cocked an eyebrow in response to her searching look. There was something about the man that led her to believe he wasn’t what he seemed. Then again, neither was she.

“Are you sure your pappy won’t reconsider this one?”

Not looking up, she nodded. It was humiliating, standing there in front of men who knew she was purchasing a husband. And not even one of decent character or her race, but just the next available. Because they thought her father wanted it, and they thought she was an obedient daughter. When nothing could be further from the truth. It was her secret shame.

The prisoner’s eyes narrowed. For a thief he had quite an attitude.

"Sure you don't want to wait a bit, Miss Fei? There's bound to be a white man along shortly."

A white man who would feel superior to her because of the color of his skin. A white man whom all would see as superior to her because of her mixed heritage.

She kept her voice soft. "I cannot go against my father's wishes."

"Ain't natural, him pandering you out," Herbert muttered. Herbert was older, decent, a worn-out miner bent from too many hours panning for gold, and she'd often wondered what kept him among these men of no honor.

"Don't be talking a daughter out of her duty," the padre snapped.

She wished the priest's concern was for her well-being, but she knew it was from fear of losing her father's skill with explosives and what that would do to the income of the men who bought him his liquor.

"Don't see why the man can't just hire help like others," Herbert muttered.

"He's Chinese," Barney interjected. "They've got strange notions."

As long as they believed that, it would work for her.

"Well, what'll it be, woman? Either he'll do or he won't," the sheriff snapped. "If we're not going to have a hanging, then I want to get back to drinking."

Her stomach clenched. She had to make this decision. Years of discipline maintained her poise as she found her courage. "If you would please to ask him?"

"Don't know why we have to go through this," the sheriff muttered. "When a man's facing death, he's not going to quibble about taking vows he can abandon as easily as he makes them."

"I would feel better." She needed some illusion that this plan would work.

"You got a choice, injun." The sheriff jerked his thumb in her direction. "Die now or marry up with this little woman and start a new life."

"Why doesn't she ask me herself?" The thief's voice was smooth and deep and soothed her like fine tea on a cold day. It was very hard not to look up.

"It's forbidden for her to ask you herself, you ignorant ass," the sheriff shot back.

For once Fei was grateful for the rudeness of the men in this rough town. It saved her from having to respond or explain.

"So what's your answer?"

The horse shifted, tightening the rope, and, for a moment, the thief couldn't speak. Barney backed the horse up a step and when the thief found his voice, his arrogance was not diminished. "I want her to ask me."

The sheriff drove the butt of his rifle into the thief's stomach. He grunted and jerked in his restraints. The horse balked and danced out from under the tree limb. Smiling, Barney released the reins. With a slow slide, the thief reached the end of the rope.

Fei watched in horror as the thief's legs clung to the horse while the rope tightened on his neck. For four heartbeats, he was stretched out straight, suspended between the tree and the horse. His already dark skin took on a darker hue. His feet kicked as the pony stepped out from under him. The men laughed.

"I guess he made his choice, then."

"Looks like we're having our hanging, after all."

"No." They couldn't do this. "Cut him down."

Nobody paid any attention to her and she realized she'd spoken in her native Chinese. Not that they would have paid attention to her if it were English. Their macabre game had begun. Fei Yen darted through the men, grabbed the thief's calves and pushed up. With no result. The man was too heavy. Harsh laughter accompanied her efforts.

"No point in wasting your effort, girl. That boy's hanging. Fate's come to a decision."

No, it had not! It couldn't. The long American skirts tangled around her legs as she tried to jump and reach the rope. It was far above her. She controlled her breathing. Think. She needed to think. The man gasped and gurgled and kicked. His foot caught her in the side. She went down, amidst more laughter.

The men were getting the show they wanted. But what about what she wanted? Did it not matter? She'd worked too hard. Too much was at stake for their drunken play to interfere with her plans.

She pushed up onto her hands. Two feet from her position, a knife stuck out of a boot. Grabbing it, she ran back, climbing up the man's body like a tree, ignoring the abrupt cessation of noise as her weight was added to the noose.

"Son of a bitch, would you look at that?"

Ignoring the men, she sawed at the rope, using every bit of strength she had. With a snap, it let go, throwing them to the ground. But it wasn't enough. The noose around the man's neck was still tight. Still cutting off his air.

She didn't know what he did when he wasn't stealing horses, but no one deserved to die like that, staring at the sky while they starved for air. No one.

"Damn, that's one woman that's hungry for a man."

She ignored the growing threat around her and focused on the man. He started to struggle and buck, fighting for air. "Stay still."

His gaze snapped to hers. Wild. Defiant.

She put the knife against his neck. "It is not your jugular I wish to cut."

With a discipline that shocked her, he went still. Biting her lip, she wiggled the knife between his neck and the rope. "Maternal grandmother," she prayed, "let this work."

Blood welled as the knife slid like butter through a pinch of skin.

And please do not let me cut an artery.

As hard as she could, she pulled the blade toward her. The thief didn't move. The rope didn't give. His color took on an alarming blue hue. Maybe his neck was broken. What did she know? She jerked the knife upward and the rope separated under the sharp blade. The uncontrolled movement cut her breast. She cried out. The men around her swarmed in. She didn't fool herself that it was out of concern. They were like vultures, these men. Brandishing the knife, she ordered, "Stay back."

They laughed, but at least they stopped. The thief just lay there, not kicking, not moving. She thought he'd slid too slowly off the horse to break his neck, but he was certainly injured. She stood there, brandishing the knife, blood running down her chest, her voice far from the well-modulated tones her father insisted she always use as was proper for a woman of her station. "Do not come closer."

"You think you scare us, little girl?"

Shaking from head to toe, the knife clutched in front of her, bloody blade thrust out, she stepped down hard in the middle of the thief's broad chest to get his attention. He sucked in a wheezing breath and coughed.

"We must leave," she informed him.

His gaze met hers. There was no denying that he was a handsome man. It was an odd moment to notice such a thing, but with danger all about, her senses seemed sharper. She wasn't surprised that he didn't immediately answer. He rolled to his side displaying his hands and the thin rope binding them. A quick, harsh slash removed the bond. Pressing his hand up to his throat, he checked the blood. "You rescuing me or killing me?"

His voice was rough, masculine with a pleasant rasp. A shiver went down her spine.

"I have yet to decide." The men pressed in. This time she shivered for a different reason.

"Get away from him, Fei."

"No." She couldn't back down. Couldn't go forward.

The thief looked around. “Make up your mind.”

“I have. You are not listening.”

One cock of his eyebrow and she was suddenly reminded that dragons had long memories and couldn’t always be trusted.

“You don’t need a man as bad as that, Fei,” Barney said. “I’ll be glad to take care of your needs.”

“Hell, if we’re getting in line, I’ve got first dibs. I’ve had my eyes on this sweet thing for months,” Damon said, licking his lips.

Fear leaped inside her. This was not good. The thief just watched her, waiting. For what?

I want her to ask me.

For her to make a choice, she realized. The circle around her got tighter. Dragon or vultures? There was not much of a decision to make. Barney stepped in. The sheriff laughed. Herbert swore and turned away. The padre spat. Damon reached out.

“Marry me,” she gasped.

“I thought you’d never ask.”

With a speed that left her blinking, the thief was on his feet, the knife she’d been holding now in his hand, redder now with Damon’s blood. Before her Damon was screaming and holding his hand. Barney was on the ground, clutching at his face from the thief’s kick, and everyone was backing up while he just stood there, the slightest smile on his lips.

Dragon.

The sheriff slid his hand down toward his guns.

“I wouldn’t.” It was a warning given with lethal softness. The sheriff didn't complete the reach for his gun, but his bluster continued. "What do you think you're doing, injun?"

The thief snagged her hand. With disconcerting ease, he tugged her into his side. When she looked up, it was to find him looking down. She couldn't read his expression, couldn't read his eyes and didn't know what he was trying to tell her as he squeezed her waist.

"By the looks of things, getting married."

CHAPTER TWO

HIS NEW WIFE WASN'T MUCH of a talker. She'd been silent ever since their "wedding." Shadow wasn't sure the procedure they'd gone through was actually legal—hell, he wasn't even sure the drunken fool who'd married them was really a preacher—but whereas other women would have been completely concerned with the legality of the ceremony, his wife was more concerned that he get his ass in the wagon so they could head out. But not before asking, in that sweetly melodic voice of hers, that his feet be tied as well as his hands. The sheriff and his men had been more than happy to oblige and had even done her one better. They'd found shackles for his ankles. With a soft "thank you," his wife had dropped the key into the lace-trimmed pocket above her breast.

Of all the things that pissed him off about the last day, it was her drawing his attention to her breasts that he resented the most. He wasn't a marrying man. All he had to offer a woman was the pain and violence of his own upbringing and no decent woman deserved that. Hell, no woman deserved that, but his little wife had tucked that key into the pocket, and suddenly he was thinking in terms of rights and possibilities. Like how those small, pert breasts would look all creamy and white against his darker skin. How the nipples would feel, centered in his palm as he plumped them for his mouth. How she'd moan and whisper his name.

Shadow pulled himself up short. With what? Love? Who did he think he was kidding? Tracker might have found love with his Ari, but there were differences between him and his twin brother. Differences that Ari had seen. Differences Tracker refused to acknowledge, but, safe to say, the parts of his brother that Ari had found to love didn't exist in him. Inside him there was only darkness. If there wasn't, murdering the man who'd tried to kill his sister-in-law and her daughter would have given him pause rather than satisfaction. He was a killer, plain and simple. Despite all those years he'd been a Texas Ranger, now, with a price on his head, he was on the correct side of the law. An outlaw.

We'll get this settled, Shadow.

Tracker's promise the last time they'd met up had slipped past Shadow's guard, lingering in that weak place he'd never been able to kill off. The part of him that wanted to be worthy of softer things. Tracker had a way of saying things that made a man believe. Back that with the fact he was tenacious and loyal and his promises had weight. Shadow knew Tracker would never stop fighting and believing in him. Fighting even when Shadow stopped. He'd been Shadow's conscience all his life. His barometer for what was good, because for Shadow sometimes the lines blurred, as if all those beatings during his years growing up had broken something in him that had hung tough in his brother. When necessary, Tracker would kill without batting an eye, but he found it a lot less necessary than Shadow did. Maybe it was patience or some latent belief in good triumphing over evil, but whatever it was, Shadow lacked it. And he'd long since stopped searching for it.

Just stay out of trouble until we do.

Shadow leaned back against the backrest and smiled at Caine's warning. Caine might be as tough as nails and the leader of Hell's Eight, but he couldn't control everything, least of all the wildness inside Shadow that needed to lash out. Metal clanked against metal as Shadow shifted his feet. He wondered what Caine would think of this situation. A smile tugged his lips as he imagined the other man's curse.

The woman jumped at the sound. *Fei,* they'd called her. She eyed the shackles and licked her lips before releasing a slight sigh of relief and turning back to the road. Shadow didn't echo her sigh of relief. It took a whole lot of trouble to send a woman to the hangman's noose looking for a husband. And he wasn't feeling charitable.

"You know leaving isn't going to be the end of it?"

She nodded and snapped the reins against the old workhorse's back. It irked him that she didn't even look at him.

"You don't seem overly concerned."

"I have you."

He did like the sound of her voice, so soft and melodic. It made him think of a delicate flower swaying in the breeze, likely to be crushed by the most careless of steps. It was an interesting image, considering this was a woman who had climbed up his body as he was strangling for breath to cut the rope and free him. Those were not the actions of a delicate flower. Those were the actions of a fighter. And damn it! The contrast intrigued him.

"What makes you so sure? As soon as I get the shackles off I could be planning on robbing you blind and then heading out."

"You won't."

He cocked an eyebrow at her. He'd done a lot of things in his life as Hell's Eight. Hell's Eight weren't too picky about how they got the job done, but once they'd become Texas Rangers they'd usually stayed on the right side of the law. Keeping the women of Hell's Eight safe had cost him his badge and put him squarely in outlaw territory, but he hadn't found the adjustment too strenuous. Hell's Eight or outlaw, he was still only going to do what he decided needed doing. It just wasn't dressed up fancy now.

"You sound awfully sure."

She nodded again. "You are too arrogant to be a petty thief."

That might have been a shot right along with being a justification. The corner of his mouth twitched in the first glimmer of a smile. It had been a long time since he'd smiled. "Arrogant people don't steal?"

"Not those that carry your arrogance."

Interesting theory. People generally formed quick opinions of him when they met him, usually something dark. She apparently saw in him some sort of honor. "Well, arrogant or not, those men back there are likely going to head to the saloon to keep drinking. And the more they drink the more they're going to start thinking about the one that got away." He gave her a pointed look. "That would be you."

This time, she did look at him. A sidelong glance. "And you."

"I'm used to it."

"And you think I am not?"

He'd seen more than his fair share of women used to men coming after them when he'd been searching for Ari. Shattered shells of whatever they'd been before. He had no doubt that this woman was not accustomed to being any stranger's plaything. There was an innocence about her that had yet to be broken. "No."

"Oh."

That *"Oh"* was very small. It annoyed him that she kept the fighter in her hidden. "Are you deferring to me as your husband, or do you really not have an opinion?"

"I do not consider you my husband."

That was said with a scathing calm. He cocked an eyebrow at her. "What if I consider you my wife, and tonight my wedding night? What are you going to do, then?"

There wasn't a heartbeat between his question and her response. "Evade your advances until such time as I can rectify the situation."

Shadow didn't think she was talking about a trip to an attorney. He shifted on the seat. The rough wood picked at his clothing. The woman picked at his curiosity. She was small, with delicate bones and the slender build common to Asian women. But it was clear that she wasn't pure Chinese. Her skin was too fair. And her features were more those of a white woman with a touch of exotic in the slant to her eyes and the height of her cheekbones. Her eyes were beautiful, though. Large and dark green with amber flecks that reflected the brilliance of the setting sun. There was nothing about her that would imply a threat, but the hairs on the back of his neck rose.

"Interesting plan. Too bad you don't have the muscle to back it."

Was that the slightest bit of tension in her hands? She gave the reins another flick. The horse continued to plod on at its slow, even pace.

"Muscle is not required."

"Why not?"

She clearly didn't want to tell him. "Because there are other ways than force."

He wasn't in the mood to humor her. "Such as?"

She blew out a breath and shot him a glare. "I saved your life."

"What makes you think that makes a pig's snort of difference as to how I'm going to treat you?"

She shook her head. "You have arrogance."

"So you said before."

"Arrogance needs a sense of honor to keep it happy."

"You think I'm honorable?"

Her fingers tightened on the reins. It was the only indication that his skepticism gave birth to any uncertainty in her.

"Yes."

He rattled the chains on his shackles, just to rattle her nerves. He had the satisfaction of seeing her jump. "So, you're banking your life and virtue on my arrogance and some illusion of honor?"

She shook her head and set her jaw. "You talk too much."

And she didn't want to answer his question. "Never been accused of that before."

Another sidelong glance out of those pretty eyes. "This I find hard to believe."

"You calling me a liar?"

The pitch of his voice turned her head around. She swallowed, once, twice. At least she had the sense to know when to be cautious. In the fading light, he noticed the dark stain on her dress. In the next second, he saw the tear above it. A slit similar to many he'd put in men's clothing over the years. All inclination to tease left. Leaning forward, he grabbed the reins and pulled the horse up. As Fei snatched them back, he grabbed her arm, turning her toward him. "How badly are you hurt?"

She looked down, her dark lashes fanning her cheek, not meeting his gaze. "It is nothing."

The hell it wasn't. "That's a knife wound."

"The blade slipped as I freed you."

He remembered the jerk as she'd sawed at the rope around his neck. He reached for the buttons on her dress. She slapped his hands. He persisted.

"Don't get your feathers ruffled. I'm just going to check your wound."

"This is not necessary."

The dress tore as she twisted away. "Stop."

"Unless you want to end up naked, I suggest you sit still."

She continued slapping at his hands. He continued ignoring her protests, keeping her in place with his grip on her dress. She glared at him as the fifth button came undone and he could see the blood on her camisole.

"This isn't fair."

Life rarely was. "Next time, I'd suggest making sure your husband's hands are tied behind his back, not in front."

Her mouth worked. He waited for the inevitable retort. It died under a facade of calm. He shook his head. Damn, a man had to admire a woman with that much control, even as he had to wonder how she'd developed it.

"You keep swallowing bile like that," he said as he continued to unfasten buttons, "and you're going to find an early grave."

She looked back down the road they'd traveled. "I do not think bile will be what sends me there."

His promise to himself to not give a shit about anything that didn't concern him faded under that worried glance. He told himself it was because the woman had saved his life. "You're in bigger trouble than you let those yahoos think, aren't you?"

She tugged at his hands. "At the moment, yes."

There was an edge of panic in that calm statement. He looked into her eyes. As calm as her expression was her eyes flared with the emotions she was trying to hide. He paused. He'd never terrified a woman before. That he was doing it now didn't sit well with him. He might be going to hell for a lot of things, but he wasn't his father. He wasn't going for preying on those weaker.

"You can relax, Fei. I'm not a man for hurting the weak."

She jerked upright. "I am not weak!"

That's what got her dander up? "Compared to me you are. And that's a truth you'd best be accepting before that pride of yours gets you in trouble."

Her fingers tightened on his wrist, her short nails dug into his skin. Fear? Anger? "You will let me go after you look?"

"Providing it's not bad, yes."

"Then look and be done with it."

Anger. And pretty close to the surface. The woman had a temper. "Thank you. I thought I would." As Shadow hooked his finger under the camisole, Fei subsided against the seat, spine straight, chin up, her dignity drawn around her like a shield. Shadow didn't care. She could trot out as much dignity as she wanted. He was checking that wound. The fabric was stiff around the edges and stuck to the wound with drying blood. She stiffened as he gently pulled.

He paused, glancing up in time to catch her expression in a moment of vulnerability. "I'll be careful."

Her fingers tightened on his wrist. "You do not need to be anything."

Further investigation revealed a two-inch cut on her breastbone. A couple inches lower, a little deeper and the wound could have been fatal. He touched his finger to the softness of her skin. So creamy and pale. So perfect except for the mark of his entry into her life. A reminder that for him nothing changed.

"You're going to need a stitch or two."

She leaned away. Shadow let her. "We do not have time for this. As you said, they will come."

Shadow eased the camisole back up, over the wound. There was an awful lot of fear in her voice. He might bring hell to those he loved, but he could also bring it to anyone who threatened those under his protection. And as his wife.

"Let them."

"They'll kill you."

"Unlikely." He caught her chin between his fingers and examined her face. There was a faint discoloration on her cheekbone. At least he had a way to repay her for the sacrifice. "But in the meantime, you're my wife, under my protection and your care comes first."

"You speak like a fool."

"And here I thought I was speaking like a husband."

She jerked away. "It was a mistake to choose you."

He touched the faded bruise on her cheek. Someone

would pay for that. He smiled into her defiance. "No, honey. I think this time you finally chose right."

FEI'S HOUSE WAS SET OFF the road a fair piece. At some point, someone had tried to give it a bit of boundary with a white picket fence, but that was now falling down. Faded red curtains graced the windows. The place was a nice size, unusual for a railroad worker's compensation. Usually the best a worker could hope for was a crowded, tattered tent. Fei's father must have some worth, after all.

The house smelled of exotic spices—lemon and something Shadow couldn't quite put his finger on. The interior was spotless. Everything in the house was neatly hung in its place. It appeared there were two separate bedrooms, a parlor and a kitchen. Fei led him to the kitchen and then waved him to a chair at the table.

"Please sit. I will get water."

"Take off the shackles and I'll fetch water for you."

Her gaze started at his feet and traveled up to his knees and then just kept on climbing until it reached his face.

"Is Shadow your real name?"

"The only part that's pronounceable."

He hadn't gone by that name for over a year. He wasn't sure why he'd used it at the ceremony. There was a price on his head. A hell of a price. Things like that tended to happen when you killed a man under the protection of the U.S. Army right in front of them. It didn't matter that the killing was necessary or that the man was a cold-blooded murderer gunning for women and children. The army had a reputation and Shadow had sullied it. His brother and Hell's Eight were working to get him a pardon, but the governor wasn't feeling real friendly. The man Shadow had killed had been wealthy and connected, so right now Shadow was wanted dead or alive. And from the way people were taking shots at him, he had a feeling someone was offering a second bounty if he was brought in dead. That being the case, it was pure foolishness to have declared himself Shadow Ochoa during the wedding ceremony. But when it had come to identifying himself, he'd wanted Fei Yen to know to whom she belonged. Which was more foolishness. The marriage wasn't going to last. As soon as his wife got what she wanted out of him, she'd be gone. And he'd be ready to go. He'd stay because he owed her. A life for a life. But when it was over, it would be time for him to move on. Without Hell's Eight as an anchor, he preferred to keep moving.

With a brisk bow, Fei reclaimed his attention. Picking up a large bowl and a towel, she headed for the back door. "I will fetch water."

"Be easier if you took off the shackles and let me do the heavy lifting."

She glanced over her shoulder. "The shackles stay on."

The door slammed shut behind her as she left him in the kitchen with a nice selection of well-honed knives in the block at the end of the table. Shadow set his hat on the table and ran his fingers through his hair. Fei clearly thought, with his legs shackled, he didn't pose much of a threat. Smiling, Shadow picked up a butcher knife and sawed at his bonds until his hands were free. Grabbing a small paring knife, he started working the locks on the shackles. The first was a breeze. The second was a bit more stubborn.

The kitchen door creaked. Fei's small, black-booted feet came into view. Out of the corner of his eye, he saw her skirt swish abruptly as she stopped. Water sloshed over the side of the bowl and splashed on the floor.

"What did you do?"

Motioning to the heavy shackles as if they were nothing, he explained, "These things chafe."

No response. The mechanism gave. He eased the shackle open. He glanced up. She still stood there staring at him with something akin to horror.

"I won't hurt you, Fei."

She straightened and her chin lifted. "I am not afraid. I am annoyed. My knives—you have ruined them."

"I'll sharpen them back up. Any more complaints?"

He stood. She flinched. This close, it was hard to miss the why. Her head only came up to his breastbone. Her waist was so tiny he could probably span it with his hands. Hell, no wonder she was frozen. There wasn't enough of her to stand up to a gnat, let alone a grown man. He jerked his chin toward the kitchen table. "Sit."

She touched the towel draped over her shoulder. "Your neck—"

"Is only bruised," he finished for her. "You're the one who's cut."

He took the bowl from her hands, ignoring the wariness of her expression. On his best days, he intimidated, but he hadn't had a bath in two days, and being stretched by a rope probably hadn't put any shine to his appearance. He motioned to the table again, albeit this time with a bit less force. It was as close to gentle as he was getting.

"Sit down."

Fei stayed put. "I do not require your help."

"That wasn't the impression I got."

She motioned to her injury. "With this."

He motioned to the chair. "I'm particular about things being done right."

"So am I, which is why I shall care for it myself."

The angle of that chin was just more proof that her sweet, submissive air was just a good fake.

She looked at the shackles heaped on the floor by the table. It wasn't hard to tell which way her mind was working. Shadow set the bowl on the table. "You weren't any safer when I was wearing them, you know. You just thought you were."

She eyed them again. "I liked the thought."

She sounded as if she intended to hold a grudge about it. The thought made him smile. Shit. Twice in one afternoon. That had to be a record. "That wound is going to need stitches."

"I have a…" She motioned with her hands, pantomiming smoothing something over her skin as she said a word in Chinese.

"You mean salve?"

"Yes. This I have." With a cut of her hand she finished, "You no worry."

He made note of the grammar slip. It would be helpful to know when the woman was riding the edge. "You wouldn't be saying that just so I won't be seeing your br—" He bit off the word and substituted, "Anything inappropriate, would you?"

"My wound can be treated without exposure. This is not one of my worries."

It took a second to identify the emotion that took him then. Desire. The woman wasn't his usual type, but there was something about her. He'd dismissed her as a bored wife come to a hanging for the dark thrill when he'd first seen her hiding in the shadows. Mousy had been his first thought, but then she'd come flying across the distance, grabbed a knife, scaled his body as if it was a welcoming oak tree, and well, hell, he'd changed his mind. The woman had the ferocity of a badger under all that quiet. She was beginning to intrigue him.

Taking the towel, she dipped it in the bowl and wrung it out before holding it out. "You should keep the cloth wet and around your neck. The coolness will help with the bruising."

He took the cloth. The damp material was cold. "If the worst I get out of a hanging is a bit of bruising, I got off light."

"You were very lucky."

He shook his head, wincing as the tight muscles protested. "Any luck I had, you made."

"I would disagree."

Wrapping the towel around his neck, he gave her a smile, hoping to put her nerves at ease. The cool cloth did feel good. And hopefully it would lessen the swelling that was adding a harsh rasp to his drawl. He swallowed to ease the constriction. "I've noticed that you've got a habit of being contrary."

Her gaze flashed to his. He took the look like a punch in the gut. So much was revealed there. Fear. Determination. Uncertainty. She didn't know what to make of him. Didn't know what to do, but she was clearly mixed up in something where she felt she was out of options.

"Just how desperate are you?"

Again a flash of those beautiful, exotic eyes, but this time impatience was the predominant emotion. "I married a man about to be hanged," she snapped. "That would make me very desperate."

She had a point. Cold water dripped down his chest. He flipped the towel end over his shoulder, stopping the flow. "That you did, but that doesn't tell me why."

Her mouth worked as she debated her response. Such a pretty mouth. A lush bow of pink temptation that made him think of hot nights and satiated mornings. Hell, maybe he'd just been too long without a woman and that's why he reacted to this woman so strongly. Ducking the law and bounty hunters didn't allow for much fun in a man's life. As soon as he had the thought, Shadow dismissed it. He'd had plenty of whores who had let him know he was welcome. It wasn't the opportunity that was lacking but the compromise in him. He at least liked the illusion of mutual pleasure in his encounters. A straight cash exchange for a woman parting her legs just wasn't worth the effort it took to scrounge up an available one. The few women he used to visit had gotten married, so he'd ended up just doing without. Which was another oddity in his recent behavior. He'd never been a man who'd done without.

But in this instance, he wasn't going to go without. At least when it came to information. If he was to protect Fei, he needed to know what he was up against. He removed the towel from around his stiff neck and dipped it back in the bowl. "Let me know when you're done debating how much truth to mix with your lies."

Surprise chased across her face and then her expression took on that serenity that he was beginning to suspect was her shield.

"You think I would lie?"

He wrung out the towel. "Yeah, I do, but let me save you the effort. I need to know everything you're facing, if what you're wanting is my protection."

"Some of it is private."

Wrapping the towel back around his neck, he countered, "If it involves my life and your safety, it can stay private, but private between us."

While she debated that, he looked around the kitchen.

The bright colors screamed a love of life. The order spoke of a need for control. The strange pots and spoons spoke of a different culture. He looked at her again. The Chinese kept to themselves. Out of self-preservation and because it was their way. How much scope did "private" cover for her?

"You did marry up with me for protection, didn't you?" The last thing he needed was to be involved with a woman who just wanted to piss off Papa.

An expression he couldn't decipher crossed her face and then she nodded. Entirely too serenely. The lady was hiding something, giving him what he assumed was true too quickly for it to be everything. At this point, he had a choice. He could browbeat her and hope to get what he wanted or he could wait for a better time. Since any good hunter knew it was better to lie in wait than to chase, he opted for waiting. He was a very good hunter.

His stomach rumbled.

"You got anything for us to eat?"

"Nothing prepared. And there is not time to cook."

He cocked an eyebrow and waited, forcing her to talk, out of some perverse desire to hear her voice. She licked her lips. They glistened in the failing light. Shadow couldn't look away, waiting for them to shape around syllables so he could watch their play. So he could enjoy, he realized. He forced his gaze up, not liking the need that ruled him. Fei's lashes lowered, shielding her eyes. Her hands were folded in front of her. He wanted to reach down and break their grip, break her serenity. He wanted her to notice him, he realized.

"We can make time for a meal."

She was shaking her head before he finished the sentence. "You were correct earlier. Damon and the sheriff, when they get together and drink, they are like…" She wiggled her fingers around her head and made a buzzing sound.

"Bees?"

She shook her head. "Meaner."

"Hornets."

"Ah, yes. Hornets." She nodded. A tendril of blue-black hair slid out from behind her ear. "Like these hornets, if one gets excited so does the other. Around and around they fly, getting louder, madder, until they attack whatever it is that annoys them."

"And you annoyed them?" He caught her chin with the edge of his finger, bringing her gaze up.

"Yes."

"Did they give you this bruise?"

"No."

She was telling the truth. Shadow looked around the small house. There were no shutters on the windows. No bars on the door. No barriers to anyone who wanted to get in. A woman here alone would be an easy target. "Tell me, why haven't they done anything about it?"

"They are afraid of my father."

"Fear rarely keeps a drunk man from doing something stupid."

"Jian Tseng has a temper and he is *very* good with explosives."

"Has a habit of blowing things up, does he?"

"When he is displeased, or doing his job, there is none better."

There was a whole lot of unsaid in that sentence.

"A man who can make big holes in rocks exactly where they're supposed to be is valuable to the railroad. The bosses wouldn't take kindly to anything happening to him."

"No, they would not, but I think if the sheriff and Damon could find a way to kill my father without losing their bonuses, they would."

For every day a crew beat a deadline, they received a cash bonus. Shadow hazarded a guess. "Your pa's been making them a lot of money."

Fei eased her chin free, took a step back and resumed her demure stance. Modesty, fear or deception?

"Yes."

"And that's been keeping you safe."

It wasn't a question and she didn't treat it like one. She smoothed a nonexistent wrinkle in her skirt. "Yes."

Deception. Interesting. "Where *is* your father?"

"It is not a daughter's place to question where her father goes."

"You strike me as the questioning type."

There was the barest hesitation before she answered. "Perhaps, and perhaps my father is not the answering type."

She had a point, but Shadow still couldn't shake the feeling he wasn't getting the whole story.

"Is that old plug the only horse you have here?"

"Yes."

Damn. "Do you have a place in mind where you want to go?"

She looked up. "Yes."

"How far is it?"

She raised one finger.

"Would that be one minute, one hour or one day?"

"One day."

That was a far piece for a woman to travel alone. "On that horse?"

"Yes."

It'd take half the time with better mounts. Shadow grabbed his hat off the hook by the back door.

"Where do you go?" she asked.

"To steal better horses."

She reached out and then just as quickly jerked her hand back. "You were just hanged for that."

"Must be the lesson didn't take."

She just stared at him. "I don't understand you."

The bodice of her dress gaped open. He straightened it. She didn't even breathe as he closed the lapel. "You said you didn't think I was a thief. Maybe you ought to build up from that."

Her serenity cracked and she frowned at him. "I do not think that would be wise."

Nope, probably not, considering how much he wanted to kiss her right then.

"Sure?" He settled his hat on his head. "It would help soothe your nerves."

"Maybe I don't need help, after all."

"Honey, you need a hell of a lot of help. It's just a matter of how much and where. While I'm gone, it'd help if you'd resign yourself to reality."

She took the towel from his neck with a bravado denied by the slight tremor in her hands. "It is best *you* resign *your*self. You are not my father and not a real husband. Your say is limited."

The dismissal slipped under his guard, goading his anger. He adjusted his hat on his head. "Real enough that if I wanted to toss you on that bed and prove it no one would say a word in dispute."

"I would."

"Honey, if I decided to have my way, your words would be nothing more than pretty little squeaks."

The fire left her expression to be replaced by a cold certainty. "You would be wise not to dismiss me, thief."

"You'd be wiser to learn when not to buck the current."

"I have warned you."

So she had. "I heard you." With a wave of his hand he indicated the wound.

"Get some medicine on your wound. And after that make supper from something we can eat as we ride."

She glanced out the window. "It is dangerous to ride at night."

In one breath she threatened him, the most feared man in the territory, and in the next she was worried about a ride in the dark? The woman was a bundle of contradictions. "Going to be a Comanche moon tonight. We'll see well enough. Besides, you've got me to keep you safe."

"You just threatened me."

"No, I just told the truth. You were the one doing the threatening."

Folding her arms across her chest, she asked, "You think I should trust you?" She snapped her fingers. "Just like that?"

He smiled, lightly drew his fingers down her cheek and gave her another truth. "What other choice do you have?"

CHAPTER THREE

What other choice do you have?

Three hours later, riding beside the silent Shadow, Fei touched the wound on her chest, feeling nothing but the bandage and discomfort beneath. The bandage Shadow had insisted on checking when he'd arrived back from wherever he'd gone, bringing back horses, guns and gear with him. There had been nothing sexual in his touch when he'd checked it, but that hadn't stopped a quiver of awareness from going through her. Awareness she didn't need. She'd put away such feelings many years ago when she'd realized what marriage would mean for one of her mixed heritage. She did not want to be married to a man who would tell her what to do, who would take other wives and expect her to be grateful for the help. She especially didn't want the position of second or third wife, which was the best she could hope for among her father's culture since her blood was not pure. Worse yet, she might be relegated to concubine status. A woman of the moment with no real place.

No, she did not like her choices, so any foolishness she had felt in regard to falling in love, she had squashed. Whenever her heart skipped a beat in the presence of a young man, she reminded herself where those feelings would lead her—ruin. And not the kind her father feared could come at the hands of a man, but the kind of ruin that came from burying herself in a grave while she still took breath. She was twenty-three now. No longer a foolish girl. No longer a dreamer. So why did just looking at this man give her such pleasure?

"Did I sprout a wart on my chin?"

Even his voice gave her pleasure—deep and low, with a resonance that slid along her nerves like a caress. Harsher now for the trauma of the rope, but still so pleasurable. Fei ducked her head and feigned meekness, locking her gaze on the part in her mare's mane. "I apologize for my rudeness."

"You only need to be apologizing if you don't find my looks to your taste."

The statement jerked her eyes back to him. He had to be joking with her. There were very few women who would find him not to their taste. The darkness of his skin might be distasteful to many, but the danger he wore around him as easily as other men wore their shirts would easily overcome that. The sexuality he radiated would hold them. No, there would be very few women who would not find this man attractive. "You are old enough to know your worth."

The corner of his mouth creased. Amusement or annoyance? "Calling me old?"

"No." Even if she thought it, she wouldn't call him that. Not now, at least. There had to be an end to his patience and she did not want to find it before her duty was done.

The crease spread to a smile. "You, Fei Ochoa, do not give a man much to hold on to."

The sound of her new name startled her. That was who she was now. Not Fei Yen Tseng, but Fei Ochoa. She was an American now, no longer Chinese. American women were not meek. She dropped the pretense she no longer needed to carry. With a snap of the reins she said, "That is more than likely because I do not wish to be held."

He cut her a glance. "Everyone wants to be held."

"I was not speaking literally."

"Neither was I."

Fei sighed. And now she had a curiosity about him. When had he wanted to be held? And by whom? She did not need a curiosity about this man. He was already like dim sum to her.

She ducked under a tree limb. A leaf twirled wildly past her face. Such a little thing, but so relevant. Like the leaf, her life was spinning out of her control and she was running in circles, trying to catch up. The leaf landed on the toe of her ankle-high boot, clung for a minute, finding balance before being blown away. She looked over to find Shadow watching her, his gaze measured. Was this her moment of balance before the final tumble?

"Fei?"

She shook her head. "I am sorry. It has not been a good day."

"You look like you're chewing some tough meat."

"I do not understand."

"You look upset."

"Again, I am sorry. There are many aspects of being American I have not learned."

"You've been studying hard?"

"Yes."

His eyebrow cocked. Her stomach clenched and her heart missed a beat. He was a very attractive man.

"That was one tired yes."

"It is not as easy as I had thought."

He moved his horse closer. "I can help, you know."

Her knee bumped his thigh. Through her tunic and pants, she could feel the hard muscles. She'd never felt a man's leg against hers. It was not something she ever expected to feel. *"Xei-xei."*

"Now, that's a pretty word."

"It means thank you."

"Say it again."

She obliged, and when she was done, he repeated it to her. His drawl added an exotic lilt to the familiar sound.

"That right?"

She smiled, looked down and nodded, inordinately pleased that he'd tried to speak her language.

"Good."

There was absolutely no reason for her breath to catch in her throat or for her breasts to tingle under his gaze, but they did. She licked her dry lips and tried to pretend that she wasn't suddenly vitally aware of him.

It would probably help if she could pull her attention away from his hands. Those strong hands had surprisingly elegant fingers. Hands that probably knew exactly how to touch a woman to bring to her that perfect moment of pleasure she'd overheard her father's concubines discussing—

"Honey, you keep looking at me like that and we aren't going to make it to this place of yours before morning."

He'd caught her staring at him, worse yet, he had correctly interpreted her interest. But it wasn't really interest. Just weakness in her defenses. She was not a woman fated for a man. Her destiny lay elsewhere.

"I am not looking at you in any certain way."

He smiled. A genuine smile that took his expression from austere to charming. "Is that so?"

His fingers brushed her cheek. She blinked as the emotion inside her shifted to something more dangerous. And much more exciting. It was wrong to feel anything for this man. Shadow was an outlaw. A horse thief. A man without principle who made his way in this wild land through violence. He was everything her father would not want for her. Everything that was wrong for her, yet there was so much about him that was acceptable to her. At least on that instinctive level that would not be quiet. Bringing her hand up to her cheek, she rested her fingertips against his. Was this what her mother had experienced when she'd fallen in love with a man from China? This overwhelming push in a direction she knew she should not go?

The attraction her mother had felt for her father had to have been powerful for her to leave her family and suffer the insults and degradation of a society that had no place for Chinese ways and those who chose to embrace them. But her mother had embraced her father's culture even when she'd not been welcomed into it. She'd learned the language, learned the customs and she'd raised her daughter with the same beliefs. Fei shook her head. She wished her mother had lived long enough for her to ask for the answers to questions she still had. Questions about why and how. She wished her mother were here so her father would be here, but she wasn't, and he wasn't, and as surely as her mother was locked in her grave, her father was locked in the anguish of her death. Grief had stolen his will and his love and the man she'd left in the cellar at home was just an empty shell of the man her mother must have loved. She wished she could remember that man.

"I think I liked it better when you were staring at me like I was dipped in honey."

This time Fei didn't mind the interruption of her thoughts. Sad thoughts had no place in her new life. She placed her hand back in her lap. The heat of Shadow's skin lingered in the tips of her fingers. Curling them, she held the sensation to her, trying to hold the connection to him. To her mother. To her plan. "And how do you think I stare at you now?"

"Like I'm a rather disgusting bug you poked with a stick."

She couldn't restrain a slight smile. Shadow had

a way with words that painted images in her mind. "Maybe I'm hoping you'll run away."

His expression sobered. "Are you?"

She studied the guns he'd acquired, sitting so easily on his hips, the knives tucked so casually into the knee-high tops of his moccasins as if they belonged there, the rifle resting so casually across his lap. She remembered the way he'd fought the hanging party even when bound.

This time, you finally chose right.

Maybe she had. "No, I do not hope you'll run away."

"Good to know I have my uses."

"Everyone needs a purpose."

"And what is yours?"

To save her family's reputation. To save her cousin. To find a way for herself. "To fulfill my destiny."

"That's a tall order."

"It is the same for everyone."

"You think I have a destiny?"

"You do not?"

"Honey, I think my brother's and my birth was greeted with nothing but a curse."

"You are a twin?"

"Yes."

"Such good fortune upon your family."

Shadow pulled his horse up short. "My mother was an Indian whore. My father was a Mexican soldier from a family that didn't see their union, or anything that came of it, as a blessing."

Her horse carried on a couple more steps. Fei turned

in the saddle so she could meet his gaze. There was no emotion in his expression, no emotion in his eyes, but Fei understood the type of anger that came from that kind of pain.

"My mother was white, my father Chinese, of a good family. I know what it is like to have the ancestors frown upon you. It is a curse that doesn't leave and taints the fortunes of all around."

Shadow urged his horse closer. "Damn it, Fei. I'm sorry."

The horse whickered. He seemed such a nice horse, with soft brown eyes. How did he feel being ripped from his life? Leaning over, she patted his neck. "But it is not an excuse to do what you will."

"Are you about to lecture me?"

"Where did you get the guns?"

"I told you."

"This horse is well cared for. He was happy in his home. You can see it in his eyes."

"You're upset because you think I stole a horse from its happy home?"

"It is not fair to him."

"Maybe I'm his destiny."

"And maybe not."

"Haven't you ever done anything you weren't proud of simply because you had no other choice?"

She had. Like leaving her father alone in the room beneath the barn. The room was a sanctuary. It had a well and they kept it stocked with food. Originally, the door only locked from the inside, but she'd been forced to add the bar to the outside. She'd debated bolting the door behind her, but she feared too much that, if something happened to her, her father would never be able to get out. So she'd bound him to the room with lies, telling him the emperor's troops had located them and they were scouring the area for their hiding place. Hopefully that would keep him in that room and she wouldn't return to find all her plans broken around her.

"Fei?"

She glanced up to find Shadow studying her with those too-seeing eyes. "Yes?"

"I really can take care of whatever your problem is."

She was gambling on that very thing, and for that to happen, she had to trust him, but it was hard to trust a man who made his own rules, lived his own way, a man she couldn't read. Yet he was following her lead without question. She had to know why.

"Why are you doing this?"

"What?"

She motioned with her hands, at a loss for the phrase. She finally settled on, "Doing as I say."

"You saved my life. That gets you a certain level of cooperation on my part."

A certain level. That implied an end. "For how long?"

"As long as it takes."

"You are not curious as to my need? What if I want you to kill someone?"

"Then I'll kill them."

The shock went through her like a bolt of lightning. "Because I ask?"

He shrugged. "I owe you."

He would kill someone for no more reason than that she wanted it. Fei didn't know whether to be grateful or horrified. She'd prayed to her American ancestors for help. This is who they had sent? A man who made promises to kill as easily as other people promised to pick up the post.

"Xei-xei." Her thanks came out breathless and timid. Everything she didn't want to be. Shadow stopped her with a hand on her horse's reins. His eyes were little more than dark shadows beneath the brim of his hat.

"Honey, I'm damn good with a gun and even better with a knife, but I can't fight enemies I can't see. You need to tell me where the threat is."

Yes, she did. For better or worse, her destiny was tangled with his. The time for secrets had passed. She took a breath and held it, controlling the panic. Just this much could ruin everything. "I do not know the threat, but I know it will come to be."

"Explain."

"I have found gold."

"Gold?"

This was not the first time she'd encountered skepticism. When she'd first brought a trace to the assayer in town, just to see if it truly was gold, he had not been excited. But she had been, because she knew how much more there was and her first instinct had been to run home and bring back the nugget, but as she'd left his office and felt the gazes of the men who always hung around outside, she had realized her mistake. Any one of the hard-eyed men would have taken her gold from her. So instead of hurrying home, she'd lowered her eyes and slumped her shoulders. No one had followed her home. And no one had followed her since, but she couldn't continue to hide. She needed the gold. She needed help. Shadow was what she had. An outlaw. A thief. A man who said he would kill for her.

"Yes."

Shadow let go of the reins and sat up. "How much? A sprinkle in the pan or enough to build a mansion?"

Reaching into her pocket, she wrapped her fingers around the heavy nugget. Since the day she'd found it in her father's secret claim, her life had changed. Revealing it now would make it change again. For good or for bad, there was no telling.

"Fei?"

She eyed the breadth of Shadow's shoulders. By all her ancestors, there was nothing to keep this man from killing her and taking the nugget.

"I am afraid."

The truth hung there between them.

"Why?"

"I cannot stop you."

"No, you can't." He moved his horse closer. "But you can trust me."

"Swear on your ancestors that you will not hurt me."

"I'll do you one better."

She waited. His fingers skimmed up her arm, grazing the black silk of her tunic, skimming the sensitive skin of her neck before cupping her cheek in his palm. She was vividly aware of how easily he could hurt her. A tightening of his fingers, a twist of his wrist and her worries would be over. Her cousin's face flashed in her mind—angry, resentful and determined. She'd told Lin to wait, not to do anything impulsive. She'd told her to trust in her and their plan. If she died now, her cousin would be alone with no plan and only her reckless nature to sustain her. That couldn't happen.

Shadow's thumb stroked over her lips. Fei should be scared, but she wasn't. She couldn't look away. Not as his fingers caressed her cheek. Not as eyes narrowed and his gaze dropped to her mouth. Not as his grip tightened ever so slightly. And certainly not as he said, "Fei Ochoa, I make you this promise. As your husband, I *will* protect you."

As her husband. If she accepted his promise, she was accepting the marriage. It would not be honorable to deny it. She swallowed, searching his face for any sign of deception. There was none. He was giving her what she wanted. In exchange for what?

"Why should I believe what you say?"

"You're my wife. Your troubles are mine."

"Why?"

"Because I want it that way."

Could he truly be a man of honor?

"You are a horse thief."

"Only if you consider taking back what's yours as stealing."

"These are your horses?"

She expected him to smile. He didn't. If anything, his expression got harder. "What's mine stays mine."

It was a warning. She would do well to pay heed, but in that moment, she could see the man behind the calm. He was intense. He was angry. And…he could be trusted.

She took the nugget from her pocket. Catching his free hand in hers, she placed the gold in his palm, holding his gaze as she wrapped his fingers around it.

"I accept your promise."

THE STONE WEIGHED HEAVILY in Shadow's palm. He'd held enough gold to recognize what that weight meant. Son of a bitch, if there was more, she really had struck it rich. And she was right. There was no telling where her enemies would come from. But they would be coming.

"You no longer want to promise?"

There was no censure in Fei's question. Just an acceptance that rubbed Shadow the wrong way. He'd been fighting for others all his life. First for his mother, then his brother and then Hell's Eight. But now he had a wife, something of his own to fight for, and she wanted to deny him his right? Hell, no.

"I promise you this, too. As long as I live, no one will hurt you."

She shook her head. "That is too much. We only agreed on protection, not your life."

He gave her back the nugget. "Maybe that's what you thought."

She blinked and shoved it back. "Then I cannot accept your promise, after all."

He didn't take it. "I'm not giving you a choice."

Her lip quivered. She backed the little mare away. "You promise too much."

His horse followed instinctively, until the ledge was at her back and there was nowhere to run.

"You ask too little."

The mare was calm, but Fei was ready to come out of her skin. Shadow reached out, needing to remove that fear from her eyes, the quiver from her lip.

"What are you afraid of, Fei?"

She shook her head. "I cannot have your life on my conscience, too. I cannot."

His fingers slid around the back of her neck. His thumb pressed against her lip, stopping the trembling. "Too?"

Her eyes widened and her pupils flared. "Please."

He remembered that moment when she'd grabbed the knife from Hubert's boot and come for him, risking all to save his life. She hadn't been afraid then. She'd been full of fire, light and purpose. His exotic, avenging angel.

Tears welled in her eyes. This close, he could see the dark circles beneath, the unnatural pallor of her skin. The woman was exhausted and at the end of her rope.

"I do not want your life," she whispered.

"Just my protection."

She nodded.

"They go hand in hand."

"No."

He debated dragging her off the horse and into his arms. He badly wanted to hold her. To take that burden she wouldn't show him from her shoulders. That fear from her eyes. It was his nature to help the weak. He wanted to help her. Son of a bitch, when had he decided he wanted *her?* And what the hell good would that do? He was an outlaw with a price on his head. He hadn't been joking when he had said his days were numbered.

Reining in his desire, he let her put distance between them. "How much more gold is there?"

"Enough."

"For what?"

"A new beginning."

Starting fresh he could understand.

"And when you get this new beginning, what do you plan on doing with me?"

"You may have the claim."

"You're going to let me have all that gold? No questions asked?"

"I am Chinese, I cannot own anything here. And even if I could, I do not have the skills to fight those who would take it from me."

"I have enough skill for both of us."

She was shaking her head before he finished. "My destiny begins with the gold, it does not lie with it."

Interesting philosophy, he thought.

"You are a man who could do much with the power gold would give you," she continued.

He tipped back his hat. "I'll take that as a compliment."

"It was meant as nothing more than the truth."

He believed that. Fei went to great lengths to try to keep him at a distance. It was beginning to irk him. "Thank you."

"You are welcome."

So polite. So proper, when just a few minutes ago she'd been as aware of him as he was of her. He might not be her "forever man" as Tracker was to Ari, but he sure as shit wasn't that forgettable.

With a sharp motion, he sent her ahead. The silence stretched out to uncomfortable. Watching Fei's posture, Shadow noted the tension in her hands and the stiffness of her back. She was upset. The moon was high in the sky, bathing everything in white light. It caught on the silk of Fei's tunic. The hairs on the back of his neck said no one was following, but they were leaving a trail, so that could change at any time. He figured they were heading toward the foothills to the west. More specifically, Flat Top Mountain. He wasn't that familiar with the terrain, otherwise he'd stash Fei and go back and lay out some diversions. Once they got to the claim and he got her settled, he'd do just that, but for now he was just going to have to take a chance that no one would pick up their trail. Just another thing to irk him.

"What is it you want from this life, Mr. Ochoa?"

Mister? "To go home."

"Where is this home?"

"In the hills of Texas. With Hell's Eight." He didn't

mind her knowing that. He'd be drawing a map for her, so she could go there if anything happened to him. He'd sent a telegram to Tracker, using their special code when he'd been stealing back his gear. Breaking into the telegraph office and sending the telegram had been a risk, but it couldn't be helped. Fei needed protection. The message would be relayed from telegraph office to telegraph office in a preplanned pattern until one of Hell's Eight picked it up.

"Why did you leave?"

"A little disagreement between me and the army."

"You are a deserter?" She sounded shocked.

"Would it matter if I was?"

She turned and looked at him, eyes narrowed. Then shook her head. "You are not a deserter."

"No, I'm a murderer."

She threw up a hand. "Why you always wish for me to think bad of you?"

Because it was safer than the alternative. "Do you know your English slips when you're upset?"

"Do you know you get evasive when you worry I see too much?"

She saw too damn much. "Maybe we should just shut up and ride, then."

"And do you always get to pretend to be mean when you wish to end a talk?"

"Honey, there's nothing pretend about my mean."

She made a noise that sounded like *pfft.*

"What'd you say?"

"I scoff at your mean."

She was too far ahead to catch his muttered "Son of a bitch."

She slowed her horse and let him catch up. "And I ask why you tell me you are a murderer."

Leaning over, he gave the mare a light slap on the rump. The mare scooted forward. Fei grabbed for the saddle horn and shot him a dirty look.

He smiled back.

Settling into the saddle, she straightened her tunic and informed him, "If you do not ride up here with me, I will be forced to shout."

The brush was sparse enough that they could ride abreast. "So?"

"Ahead is an area popular with the Indians for stop-overs."

"You travel alone through Indian country?"

"It is necessary."

He swore again and kneed his horse forward. The slight smile on her lips at the victory irked him further.

"Do you always get your way?"

"I believe in persistence."

"And I believe you need your butt paddled."

"You are my husband. I cannot stop you."

"It would go a lot further to settling my anger if you sounded the least bit scared."

The smile grew. "You have promised that you would never hurt me. A paddling would hurt."

"I'd enjoy it."

She cocked her head to the side and studied him with

that way of hers before declaring decisively, "No, you would not."

There was no way she could know that any more than there was any reason for her to believe his promise. "What makes you so sure?"

"I just know. Just as I know that, if you murdered someone, there was cause."

"Not enough for the army."

Pfft. "I have had encounters with this army. Not all who are in charge are men of balance."

"Interesting way of putting it."

"I do not know all the words, all the time."

Neither did he. Especially when someone who had no reason to believe in anything had absolute faith in him. It made him uncomfortable. "I'm not a saint, Fei."

She pulled her horse to a stop. "No, you are a dragon. And for the moment, mine."

Mine. The claim settled far too comfortably on his ears.

"Be careful what you claim, little girl."

"Be careful how you judge," she retorted. "I have not been a girl for many years."

Son of a bitch, she challenged him. How he wanted to accept that challenge. "Just how many years?"

"I have seen twenty-three birthdays."

"So old."

"How old are you?"

"Coming up on thirty-one."

She nodded. "I see. Very old."

"Not that old." Urging his horse closer, he put an

end to the game with a simple maneuver. Her eyes widened, and her breath caught as he hooked his fingers behind her neck. Fear? Interest? Her attention dropped to his mouth as he leaned in. Her tongue came out and smoothed over her lower lip, leaving it moistly inviting.

Shit. Interest. He paused an inch from her mouth. So close her breath blended with his.

"Tell me to go to hell," he whispered.

"Tell me you desire this."

What he desired was her. Unreasonably. Wildly. Completely.

His lips touched hers. "Temptress."

"Dragon," she whispered into his mouth.

"I'm not a damn lizard."

She opened her mouth to protest, or explain. He didn't give a shit which. He just wanted her. And he took her the only way he'd allow himself. With a kiss he wanted to be soft, but came out hard. She gasped as he thrust his tongue into her mouth, struggled a second as he tasted her sweetness, and then, sighing softly, she wrapped her arms around his neck and pulled him closer. Christ, she didn't know how to kiss.

Then her tongue moved shyly against his and he found he didn't care about that, either, because no one had ever given him more pleasure than this woman, in this moment. Weaving his fingers into the thick bun at the base of her neck, he allowed himself the illusion that this wasn't impossible, that the women he held could love him. He pretended this was actually their wedding night and she was really his wife and this was the beginning. He pretended there was a future.

"Like this," he whispered, showing her how to use her lips and tongue to give pleasure, starting out lightly and gradually building the passion, taking her with him before letting her take over. And she did, with an enthusiasm that was all the more exciting for the lack of artifice. The woman enjoyed kissing him. Too much.

"Fei."

She laughed deep in her throat when he would have pulled away, and caught his lower lip between her teeth. His cock surged. His control slipped.

"You like that, yes?"

"Too damn much." *Shit.* He needed to slow down. She was, in all likelihood, a virgin. He didn't mess with virgins.

She's my wife.

She is the woman who saved your life, he corrected his baser nature. He owed her better than an animalistic rutting on the back of a horse. Easing away, he nibbled at her lower lip, kissed her cheek, the corner of her mouth, before stroking his thumb across her passion-swollen mouth. "Fei."

She lifted her lids. Dreamy-eyed, she stared at him, lips soft, expression full of wonder. An image that would haunt his dreams for years to come. Innocence, passion and trust, all bundled together in his deepest desire.

"What do we do now?"

He wanted to rip the silk from her body and take her

breast in his hand, then his mouth. He wanted to hear her gasp with the pleasure, feel her shock as he taught her how good a man could make her feel. He wanted to be her first, last, only. The need to possess shocked him, adding a bit of stability to his rocky control. Pressing lightly, he pulled her lower lip down that smallest bit, tempting himself with the moist heat beyond. She sighed and shifted in the saddle. The woman was going to be hell on fire in bed.

With someone else.

Understanding that didn't mean he couldn't enjoy what he had a little longer. Pressure from his knee urged Night closer to temptation. He'd always been a man to take advantage of the moment. No sense changing now.

With a growl of frustration, he laid out the truth. "I'm going to kiss you again, and then we're going to get your goddamn gold."

CHAPTER FOUR

"Is this it?" Shadow asked as they arrived at the edge of a stream that curved around the foot of a steep embankment at the foot of a small mountain. Fei shook her head and dismounted, stretching her back as the mare whickered and jerked her head toward the water. Stumbling, Fei went a step with her as the mare lowered her head to the stream. Fei couldn't blame her. She could use a drink, too. From the humidity in the air, the day was going to be a scorcher.

Shadow's horse echoed the nicker. She glanced over. Shadow was watching her, but this time there was nothing dispassionate about his expression. He was watching her the way a man watched a woman he desired. Something feminine and vulnerable inside unfurled with the knowledge. Smiling, she widened her stance and stretched again, arching her back a little more than necessary, letting the sun's early heat flow over her along with his gaze.

"You're playing with fire, Fei."

She was, and it felt good. "Maybe I have been cold too long."

"Maybe, or maybe you're—"

Reaching back, she undid the bun at the back of her neck and shook out her hair, wanting to moan with relief as the heavy weight spilled down her back. Shadow froze midway off the horse, his eyes locked on her. She didn't care. She was hot, she was exhausted and he was too complacent about everything that had happened between them for her peace of mind.

Lifting her hair off her neck, she demanded, "Maybe I'm what?"

"Going to get burned." The warning rumbled from deep in his chest. Without further ado, he got the rest of the way down and calmly led his horse over to the stream.

She hated him right then. For his calm, his proximity, but mostly for shaking up the beliefs she'd built around herself. It'd been six hours since Shadow had kissed her. Six hours in which she should have forgotten the sensation of his mouth on hers, but the imprint of his kiss was as vivid now as it had been when he'd first touched his lips to hers last night. She touched her lips without thinking. His hand caught her wrist. His gaze met hers. In their depths was all the heat she could have wished and more danger than any woman should desire. The step she took toward him was involuntary. His response was not. With a shake of his head, he killed off that kernel of hope she couldn't control. The one that looked at impossible and thought, *Maybe.*

"Don't even think about it."

"I'm not."

It was a lie. He knew it was a lie. She could see it in

his expression. Narrowing her eyes against the mid-morning sun, she dared him to challenge her on it. He cocked his eyebrow at her, but he had the common sense to keep his mouth shut, which was good. Pretending to misunderstand his look, she motioned to the rocky embankment. "We need to go up."

And that was another part of her problem. Her legs were stiff from riding the horse and the steep climb, which she normally did with little difficulty, felt insurmountable after two nights without sleep. Taking a bracing breath, she took the first step. He took her arm.

"What?"

"I thought you might like a little help."

"Xei-xei." Tugging on the mare's reins, she started up the hill. At least this part was easier than when she rode her old plow horse, Grandfather. He had a hard time with the climb. More often than not, the process involved her hauling him up by his bridle and sheer force of will. The little mare, however, nimbly climbed the slope. Sometimes a bit too fast. Fei jumped to the side as the mare lunged up some loose shale.

Shadow switched his grip to her waist. "Careful there."

She shoved at his arm, noting he didn't need to hold his horse's reins. His horse followed meekly on his own. Of course. That just irritated her more.

"Let go."

"Just watching out for my finances."

She shook her head. "You are a liar. You were watching out for me."

"And that's a crime?"

She didn't know. Yes. No. Maybe. It'd be easier to decide if she weren't so aware of him. "Just tell the truth of what you do."

"The truth isn't always pretty."

"Neither is a lie."

"Fair enough." Steering her up the embankment, he said, "We need to get you up to this claim so I can get on our back trail and erase it."

He released her arm. She turned. Standing above him on the embankment, they were almost eye level. It was surprising how much more confidence the illusion of height gave. "You can do that?"

"Probably not good enough that a professional tracker wouldn't be able to find us, but likely good enough that the sheriff and his cronies will be fooled. Or, at the very least, slowed down enough that you can get that gold you want."

He had the thickest lashes for a man, and the most beautiful eyes. So deep and dark, but oh, so haunted. Her dragon had demons. How bad did a dragon have to be scarred inside for demons to take root? "Thank you."

"You're welcome."

She couldn't help but watch his mouth as he formed the words. That was beautiful, too. Wide and full, but completely masculine. It spoke of a man of confidence. Of power. Of passions. Not a horse thief. The taste of him lingered in her mouth, in her senses. Tearing her gaze away, she glanced upward, to the heavens.

When I prayed to you, my American ancestors, I did not pray for a husband.

No answer came from the heavens. No answer came from her head, and the one from her heart she couldn't hear. She may not have wanted a husband, but she had one now. Not the figurehead she'd envisioned, but a man of heart. She didn't know what to do about that. He wasn't what she'd expected. Not at all. Clucking to the mare, she started up the hill. He fell into step beside her. She studied him from the corner of her eye, watching his long legs eat up the ground, one step for her two. The muscles bunched and contracted under his clothes. She remembered how they'd felt beneath her palm during that kiss. Hard and powerful. She remembered how she'd dug in her nails but there'd been no give. She remembered how she'd needed to get closer, but when she had, closer hadn't been close enough. And there was the danger of this man. He made her want.

She shook her head. She couldn't afford this distraction right now. They'd had their kiss, their taste, and it had been wild. But wild wasn't who she was, and she owed him yet again because he'd seen that and been strong enough for both of them. Taking his hand in hers, feeling very daring as he cocked an eyebrow at her, she gave it a squeeze. It was not something a Chinese woman would do, but it was something she'd seen many American women do. At least with family. And right now, Shadow was the closest thing to family she had.

"What was that for?"

"A thank-you for your strength."

Lifting her hand, he helped her over a rough spot. "We're not talking about my muscles, are we?"

She shook her head. "No. As nice as they are, I am not. It is not that I do not see the passion between us. And it is not that I wish to insult you, but if we were to make this marriage real, there is the risk of a child."

"Understood."

"I cannot have a child with you."

"I said I understood."

"So what happened before..."

"The kiss?"

She couldn't help her blush. "Yes. That cannot happen again."

He turned her, forcing her, with a finger under her chin, to look up. Her knees went weak immediately.

"Even though it felt good?"

"I have already confessed to the passion between us."

"I find I like hearing that you enjoyed it."

His eyes had the slightest crinkle at the corner. He could be joking with her. Or he could be serious. "I cannot indulge you in this."

"In what?"

"In this passion. I would get pregnant for certain."

He blinked, and his dark eyes went darker before the set of his lips softened and within her an equal softening took place. "I just bet you would."

He could at least sound unhappy about it. She took a step back. He shook his head and adjusted his hat.

With an easy flex of muscle that she envied, he popped her over a rut in the path.

Her hands were shaking and her breath was coming in unsteady rasps. As soon as he took his hands away, she straightened her shirt, taking a minute to control her reactions. She was tempted to see if he was having the same reaction, but she didn't dare because if he was, she might just be tempted to test his strength again.

He came up beside her. "Are you all right?"

There was no hope of disguising her reactions. "I do not understand how this is between us."

"Weren't expecting to be attracted to an Indian?"

This time, when she stumbled, his hand wasn't there to catch her.

She spun around so fast, the mare jerked back. She didn't like his tone. "I did not expect to feel this for any man, Chinese, white or Indian. It is not part of my plan."

"You never planned on feeling desire?"

She seemed to have shocked him. "I have been very careful about avoiding it."

"Why?"

"My husband would not be of my choice. To allow such feelings would only lead to disappointment."

"Son of a bitch."

Beyond the curse, he didn't seem to have anything else to say. They walked in silence for a couple of minutes. Finally, she had to ask, "Do you feel the passion, too?"

"You know the answer to that."

"Do you dislike this because I am Chinese?"

"Not a damn bit. And you know it."

She gave him his own words back. "Maybe *I* just like to hear it."

The sharp sting on her rear sent her skipping over the next rough patch. She spun about. "You hit me."

"I spanked that sassy butt of yours."

She rubbed the spot. "You promised not to hurt me."

The corners of his mouth twitched in a smile. "So I did. Are you going to tell me that hurt?"

She wanted to. The look he shot her was knowing.

"If it hurt at all, I'm betting it hurt good."

She dropped her hand from the spot, unable to look away. He was right. The little sting was settling into a disconcerting heat.

"As a matter of fact, I'm willing to bet that, if I threatened to do it again, you'd back into my hand."

She tossed her head. "You are crude."

"Maybe." He tipped his hat as he took the reins from her hand and resumed the climb. "That doesn't mean I'm not right."

She followed. "I would not like being spanked." Even to her own ears the statement sounded weak.

"In general, maybe not, but under the right circumstances, I bet I could make you scream in delight."

"You like to spank women?"

"The right woman."

She had to know. "What would make a right woman?"

"You sure you want to hear this? It might be crude."

With everything inside her she wanted to hear. "A woman should know the man she marries."

"The right woman would be a woman who could trust herself to the pleasure I could give her."

She was intrigued. She was horrified. And worst of all, she wanted to see if she was one of the women he could make burn. What was wrong with her?

"No woman likes to be beaten," she muttered as he and the mare cleared the ridge.

Turning, he held out his hand. She took it, only realizing it was a mistake when his fingers closed around hers in a viselike grip. He pulled her up the last few feet. Here the ground was level. Leather creaked as his horse came over the edge with a lurch.

Shadow walked over to the mare. Without warning, he hefted Fei over his shoulder. Grabbing his gunbelt, she squealed. "What are you doing?"

He sat down on a fallen tree, lowering her across his lap. Her hair fell over her face, blocking out the sun, heightening the sense of intimacy. "Satisfying your curiosity."

She kicked and squirmed. "I am not curious!"

He laughed and rested his forearm in the middle of her back. "Liar. Not only are you curious, I bet you're still feeling the heat from that little slap."

"I am not."

His hands moved over the smooth silk of her pants, raising goose bumps along her thighs. She shivered and froze.

"Sure?"

She braced her hands against the ground and pushed back. "I am positive."

That earned her a slap that stung just as sinfully as the first. Excitement skittered along her nerve endings. Her senses flared open. Dread. Anticipation. Pleasure.

"You're already feeling it."

"What?"

"The anticipation, mixed with excitement."

"I'm not." No amount of denial could contain her shiver as he trailed the backs of his fingers down her thigh.

"No?"

"No."

His arm in the middle of her back pinned her to his thighs. Against her stomach, she could feel the prod of his shaft. Against her rear the weight of his hand. She couldn't escape, couldn't do anything except lie there as his fingers cupped her right buttock. Hot and heavy, they burned through her pants like a brand. He didn't move. The tension rose within her, responding to that provocative heat, gathering in her core, weakening her resolve. She wanted nothing more than to disprove his claims, but when Shadow's fingers spread across her rear, teasing the crease, anticipation flared right along with it, gathering the heat into an ache between her thighs. She squirmed and bucked, driving his fingers deeper, the feeling higher. She wanted his hands on her rear, smoothing over her skin.

"Let me go."

"Not yet."

Now. It had to be now. Before she embarrassed herself. "Please."

But he didn't have any mercy for her, just more passion, more desire. Another tantalizing spank, just a little bit harder than the last, a little bit lower. Followed by another and another. She wished it hurt, she needed it to hurt, but each spank was carefully measured to give only the sweetest pleasure. It felt so good.

"Dear heaven."

"This isn't heaven, honey. Just the first step on the path."

The first step. She shook her head, digging her fingers into his thighs, throwing herself sideways, but he was too strong, too in control. And she wanted more. More of that pleasure/pain that pierced her with the sharp thrust of desire. She was so close to something sweet. She could feel it. "I can't..."

"Yes, you can."

The promise poured over her in a rough caress as hot as the emotion within her. She wanted to know where this could take her, where all this feeling went. And the only man who could tell her was Shadow. Her husband.

"Please!"

"You pleading for me to let you up, or for me to continue?"

A sensible woman would've demanded the former, but the wild woman inside her, the one she had not known existed before today, wanted her to continue.

The one who was still in control told the truth. "I don't know."

"Yes, you do. Spread your legs"

She did, helpless to do anything else. Soft as a feather, his hand slid between her thighs, cupping her intimately, pressing high between her legs, finding a sensitive spot, stroking and rubbing with ever-increasing pressure, until with a speed that shocked, the tension exploded, tearing through her in hard pulses of ecstasy. It was too much. Too much. She reached out, needing something, someone. A sob broke past her control.

There was nothing and then there was Shadow, turning her gently, lifting her into his lap, cradling her through the last few tremors. Shadow's lips brushed her temple. Her cheek. The balm of tenderness in the wake of fire was more than she could stand. And yet everything she needed.

"Are you all right?" he asked in that drawling rasp.

She didn't think she'd ever be all right again. She didn't recognize the woman she'd been in his arms. Didn't recognize the woman who wanted nothing more than to be back in them. She wasn't weak or needy, but he'd made her feel ecstatically both. The only answer she could give him was a shake of her head. Brushing her hair off her face, he wiped away the first tear.

"I'm sorry, honey. I didn't mean to go that far."

The most emotion she'd ever felt and he hadn't meant it? Another tear followed the first. She hated him and she hated herself. His thumb lingered on the corner of her mouth. "You'd burn me up if I let you."

She'd been without shame. Her father was right. She was fit only to be a concubine, but not because of her blood. Because of the lewdness of her nature. Lowering her gaze, she apologized.

"Honey, I'm not complaining. A man wants a wife who burns for him. And who can set the same fire loose in him."

"But that's not me, for you?"

His touch was gentle, but his truth was harsh. "No." He set her on her feet. The distance between them yawned like a chasm. "So stop playing with fire and remember how close you are to your new start."

Yes, she had to remember. She didn't understand how she could have forgotten. Maybe it was because there was so much she had to remember that she wanted something that could make her forget. Or maybe it was just him. Licking her lips, she wrapped her arms around her chest, flinching at the pressure against her sensitive nipples. How did he do this to her? "I will."

Walking over to the horses, Shadow took a canteen off Night's saddle. Uncorking the top, he held it out to her. On shaky legs, she walked over and took it.

"You'll thank me someday."

Maybe, maybe not, but today she was not in the mood to be patronized. "I'm not a child who needs to be told what is right and what is wrong."

"No, you're a grown woman, and that's the problem."

She gave him back the canteen. "There will be no problem."

"I'm not right for you, Fei."

The pronouncement hit her like a blow. She took a step back and held up her hand, keeping him from coming any closer. He stood there, backlit by the sun, a broad-shouldered, lean-hipped fantasy that could never be hers, shining light on her foolishness.

"You're a decent woman, Fei, and I owe you."

"And you pay your debts." He was just paying his debts. Somewhere, she found the strength to pretend it didn't matter. Picking up the mare's reins she led her toward the clearing on the right.

"Yes." Taking his hat off, he ran his fingers through his hair. "It can't be more than that."

She didn't look back. "I understand."

From behind, she heard him mutter, "The hell you do."

THE WOMAN DIDN'T HAVE a lick of self-preservation. Shadow followed Fei across the clearing, admiring the swing of her hips as she strode silently along. His fingers curled into his palm, cradling the sensation of her firm little ass. He'd never wanted anything more than he'd wanted to give her the experience she was so curious about. To bury himself in that hot little body and pleasure them both until she came for him and he for her. He'd almost lost his head and given in to the primitive need to take her, make her his, but then she'd cried. And the enormity of what he was doing had crashed in on him.

You've got the stink of the devil about you, boy.

His father's words echoed out of the past. Shadow shook his head and smiled the smile that absorbed the coldness he felt inside. If rumor was to be believed, he didn't just have the devil in him now, he *was* the devil. The shadow of death, passing over the land. But he didn't want to be the death of Fei. Fei was innocence and passion bonded together with a disconcerting honesty. She made him smile. She made him burn. She made him want to be better for her. And he didn't like it.

There was no point in him trying to be better than he was. He was a wanted man with a hefty price on his head. The only thing he could bring Fei was death. He didn't want to have to watch her die. Worse, he didn't want her to die because of him. And as they were out in the territory, it was more likely than not. But he'd give a hell of a lot for one night in her arms. Fei was a woman who knew how to love. The closest he'd ever felt to belonging was during that kiss earlier, when she'd held him as if she'd die if he let her go. But he had to let her go.

She stopped before a thick copse of bushes growing up against an old rock slide. Looking over her shoulder, she sized him up. "It'll be a tight fit."

"How tight?"

"Tight enough that I should have brought some goose grease in case you get stuck."

Goose grease stank to high heaven. "I won't get stuck."

Scooting back against the side of the rock slide she slid around behind a boulder that was half hidden by the brush. Son of a bitch, was it a cave? "Don't tell me this gold is in a cave."

"Quite a big one, once you get through the opening."

Perfect. Shadow took off his hat. The damn cave was probably only big from her perspective, but he had a lot more height and twice her breadth. As soon as he got to the opening, he saw that she was right. He was going to lose a layer of skin squeezing in. *Shit.* He hated close spaces that made a man feel as if the walls were falling in.

"You coming?"

"Not in any way that I could've been enjoying," he muttered, angling his body in.

"What?"

"Yeah, I'm coming."

The cave widened three feet from the opening and was much bigger than he'd anticipated. At some point someone had hollowed out a larger area, bracing the sides with timbers. Three tunnels angled out from what he could see of the larger room. From somewhere beyond the darkness, he could hear rushing water. Rather than dank, the air was fresh. More than one opening, then? The thought of an escape route helped with the closed-in feeling.

Fei stood in the center of the big chamber, braiding her hair. Against the wall, he saw dark outlines of leather sacks and leather bags. No doubt supplies and bedding. It made sense that she'd stock the cave. It took time to dig gold. Hell, he looked around at the shoring. It'd taken time to do this.

The scratch of sulfur against rock broke the silence. Glass rattled against metal as she lit a lantern. The dim interior took on a golden glow. Picking up the lantern, she held it high and turned back toward him.

"This is my claim."

Even with the lantern shedding light to the corners, there was nothing to inspire the pride in her voice.

"It's well hidden." The flat, gray rock absorbed the light. No flecks of gold shimmered and glowed. Darkening timbers vertically lined the walls and blended with the dirt around. "How did you find it?"

"I followed my father. He built it."

He studied an unsupported opening. "Did he finish it?"

"No."

Wonderful. His skin crawled with unease. "Then why did you come here?"

"I needed a place to hide."

"From what?"

She shrugged. "Many things."

He let the subject go for the time being.

"You found the gold here?"

She shook her head and pointed to an opening at the far end. "Farther back, by the waterfall."

"Show me."

Hefting the lantern, she led the way. Shadows wavered with the flickering flame. The walls seemed to waver with them. Shadow hated caves. The sound of the waterfall got louder, amplifying as the cavern grew in expanse. He was a little disappointed to see it was only about ten feet high. The stream curved away from the falls, widening until there was only a narrow shelf to the right side. Fei stopped at the shelf.

"Here."

This time, when she lifted the lantern, he was impressed. Below the shallow surface, gold nuggets glimmered amidst the common rock. It was a king's ransom, conveniently lying just below the surface, ready to be plucked. A fortune for which men would hunt and kill. And Fei sat on it all.

He picked up a nugget. It had the heft of gold. "You had it assayed?"

"Yes. It's gold."

"Did anyone see you bring it in?"

"Yes, but the rock I brought in was small and I pretended disappointment."

The hairs on the back of his neck stood on end. But the assayer knew the truth. And men had killed for less than the hope of more. With Fei's father gone so much, Fei would be an easy target. Son of a bitch. Sooner or later they would come for her. The hilt of Shadow's knife slid into his grip with the easy welcome of a trusted friend. And when they showed, he'd be waiting.

But he didn't want Fei anywhere around, which meant the sooner he got on erasing their back trail, the better.

Catching Fei's chin in his other hand, Shadow brought her gaze to his.

"Stay here and stay out of trouble."

CHAPTER FIVE

FEI WAS OUT OF THE CAVE and into trouble within three hours. Not because she wanted to be but because Culbart's ranch was only an hour from the claim. And Culbart had Lin. With Shadow expecting to be gone for several hours, she had time to check on her cousin and get back before he returned. Very carefully, she sneaked around the back of Culbart's barn. Inside, a horse whinnied. From the bunkhouse on the far side came the sound of men's voices.

Stay here and stay out of trouble.

She could do neither. Her cousin was being held hostage here. Bartered away by her father in a moment of madness two weeks ago. She'd only had time to slip Lin some supplies during her last visit before Culbart had returned home. Those supplies would be running out. She hoped Lin had followed the instructions. She hoped she was all right. She hoped she remembered their signal. Reaching into her pocket, she fingered the small vial. Without the elixir, Lin's virtue was lost.

At the back right corner of the barn was an apple tree beneath which was a stack of wood and a broken ax. Hugging the shadows, holding her breath as if that alone could contain all noise, Fei crept toward the pile. By the time she reached the ax, her skin was crawling in dread. At any moment she expected to hear a warning shout, to feel a hand descend upon her shoulder. Releasing her breath slowly, she carefully turned the ax blade to the right. Hopefully, Lin would see the signal and manage to make it out to the barn. But that was only if Lin was watching for her, and the chances of that happening in the next few minutes were slim, which meant Fei had to find a hiding place. She'd only been to the ranch once, so she only knew of one place. Hopefully, it would be available today.

Counting down the barn-siding boards, she tested the tenth one. During the busy spring and summer months the Culbarts didn't waste effort on repairs, for which she was grateful. She pulled it back and slipped inside, reaching back to grab her pack before gently letting the board ease back into place. The ancestors were still smiling upon her. The horse stall was empty. Huddling in the darkest corner, she piled the hay up around her. Mice scurried out of the corner. She swallowed back a scream and forced herself to stay because, quite simply, there was no other place to hide. Too many men came in and out of the equipment room. Too many men crept into the hayloft for napping and other things.

Picking a piece of straw out of her hair, Fei breathed slowly, controlling the urge to search for another hiding place. She hated the sneaking. She hated her father for putting her in such a position. She hated the man who thought her cousin was something to be bought or sold.

But mostly, she hated her inability to do anything about it right now.

She had tried talking to Culbart. He'd laughed her off the ranch. The only other way to bring Lin home was to buy her freedom. The only way to do that was to get the gold. A lot of it. Soon she would have that, but in the meantime Lin had to be protected. Clutching the elixir like a talisman, Fei settled in to wait.

The minutes passed slowly. People came and went. Every time the door opened, every time she heard a voice, she imagined somebody was going to discover her in the tiny stall and she'd be caught.

Stay here and stay out of trouble.

She wished she could've done that. She wished she could have trusted Shadow with this, but she couldn't risk him storming onto the Culbart ranch and getting her cousin killed. Lin was all she had left.

Minutes stretched to hours. Night fell. The temperature dropped and a chill nipped at her skin. Slumping down deeper into the hay, Fei tried not to think of everything that might possibly be crawling in it. She worried about the little mare, Jewel, that Shadow had given her. She hoped nobody found her. She worried that Shadow had returned.

Moonlight crept through the slats, illuminating the dark interior, lifting a bit of her fear. The door creaked. She heard footsteps so light that they were almost inaudible. Someone crept down the alley between the stalls. Hay rustled as the footsteps came closer. The door to the stall scraped open. Fei stopped breathing altogether

"Fei?" Lin whispered.

Kneeling, Fei pushed the straw off her shoulders. "I'm here."

Lin rushed to her side, dropped down and wrapped her arms around her.

"You came."

"I told you I would. What's wrong?" Fei asked when Lin started to sob.

Lin cried harder and shook her head.

"Tell me."

"I need to leave now."

"We can't. I don't have the gold yet."

"You don't understand. He doesn't care about that anymore. He blames me."

"For what?"

Lin wiped at her face. Even streaked with tears, Lin was beautiful with classically proportioned features, stunning large deep, brown slanted eyes and a perfectly pale complexion that always made Fei jealous. "Because he's not a man."

"Did he find out you were dosing him with the elixir?"

She shook her head vehemently. "He would kill me if he knew that."

"Then why does he—"

Lin cut her off. "He says I'm a bad omen." She waved her hands. "Bad luck. He says he will give me to the men."

"He wouldn't do that."

Lin shook her head again. “He would. He is a crazy man. You have to take me with you this time.”

“I can’t.” They had no place to go and no money to get there. “We have to stay with the plan. If I take you now, Culbart will just ride to town. Father isn’t protected. *We* aren’t protected.” Shadow flashed into her mind, but she dismissed him. Against Culbart one man was the same as none. “We have nothing. If we go now, we will die.”

Lin grabbed Fei’s arms, her eyes wild. “I don’t care. I will not survive such a rape and he will not be stalled any longer.”

Fei closed her eyes and tried to think. She believed Lin, but she also knew her own words to be true. “We just need a little longer,” she whispered, feeling the weight of obligations she wasn’t equipped to deal with. They needed more time.

A shout came from the house.

Lin froze and whispered, “Oh, my God, they know I’m gone.”

Fei’s heart dropped to her stomach.

“You’re sure he won’t be delayed any longer?”

“Yes.”

There was no choice, then. There was only one thing to do. “Did you bring your things?” she asked.

“There’s nothing here I want.”

Fei could understand that. “We need to move fast. Take off those petticoats. You must run.”

Lin looked at her and without a word unbuttoned the

skirt and stepped out of everything except her pantaloons. "I can run."

It was a measure of how terrified her shy, modest cousin was that she could stand there almost naked without a qualm.

"Good."

"Let's go, then."

They made their way to the loose board and Fei lifted it. She motioned her cousin ahead. Lin stepped out and immediately pressed her back against the side of the barn. Fei followed, doing the same. A quick check revealed no Culbart men in sight. Another positive sign?

The moon was just peaking, flooding the open areas with light. Not a cloud to provide cover. There was no hope for it. They would have to rely on speed. "Stick to the shadows on the other side of the fence, but run straight toward the tree line. Don't stop, no matter what. Even if they shoot, keep running."

Lin bit her lip and nodded.

"When you get to the trees, look for two fallen side by side. There's a narrow path to the right. Step carefully there, stay on the path, but when it widens to a meadow, run as fast as you can straight down the middle then through the woods on the other side. There's another meadow. You'll find a brown horse there. Her name is Jewel. Wait for me with her."

"What will you be doing?"

Hopefully, everything right. Fei reached into her

pack and pulled out two sticks of dynamite. "Slowing them down."

Lin gasped and cringed. "Fei!"

"It's the only way."

"Do you know how to use that?"

"Father taught me."

Lin sidled away, her gaze locked on the explosives. "How well?"

"Good enough that I can slow them down. Now, are you ready?"

Lin nodded.

"If anyone comes who's not me, get on that horse and ride."

"Home?"

"No." Culbart's men would look for her there first. "You can never go there again. Just go east or west."

"What will I tell your father?"

Her father. Fei wanted to scream as she realized what her death would mean for her father. Would he be trapped by his fears in that cellar forever? Would he be freed by a moment of lucidity? Closing her eyes she took a breath. Either way, she would not risk Lin. If Fei died she could not send Lin back to the man who might just hand her over to Culbart again.

Ancestors, give me strength.

She took a breath and whispered, "If I do not come back, tell your father to come for his brother. He is in the cellar beneath the barn."

"Fei! In the cellar?"

Fei opened her eyes, facing the censure in Lin's. "You know he is not well."

"But to put him in a hole in the ground..."

Guilt clawed at her stomach. She felt the dragon's breath on the back of her neck. "I could not risk him getting out, others seeing how he is." She shook her head. "I had no choice... I could not leave you where you were, could not leave that wrong undone."

Lin caught her arm and squeezed. In her eyes Fei saw understanding blend with the shock. "I did not mean to sound ungrateful, but you must understand, I cannot leave *you*."

Fei forced a smile past her fear. "If anyone gets to you, then leaving me no longer matters. I will already be with our ancestors."

"No, Fei..."

Fei checked the length of the fuses. "It's just a possibility. And not a big one. Father taught me well, but this dynamite is a little old."

Old dynamite was unstable.

"Then leave it and come with me," Lin ordered.

She shook her head just as another shout came from the house. Giving Lin a push, she hissed, "Run!"

BY THE TIME SHADOW FOUND the little mare, his heart was in his throat and he was as pissed as all get out. He'd told the damn woman to stay in the cave and not get into trouble, but from the looks of things, she was already in over her head. The mare whickered as he approached. He patted her neck.

"Easy, girl."

She wuffled his pockets, looking for carrots. "When I find your mistress, she's going to get a spanking, but not the kind she was hoping for."

He didn't want to think what trouble Fei could be in. He didn't know what could have driven her out of the safety of the cave and into the wilderness, but it couldn't be good.

The mare tried to follow. "You stay here just a little longer."

Through the trees, he could see lights. That had to be where Fei had gone. If she'd been a welcome guest, she wouldn't have left the mare out here. Which meant there was trouble and she'd walked right into it. Son of a bitch. She didn't even have a gun.

Shadow cut through the woods, moving quickly toward the lights. Twenty feet in, there was a commotion. Someone was coming fast. Ducking back, he blended into the shadow of a pine tree. Pulling his knife from its sheath, he waited. The person came closer. Small and female. Shadow grabbed her as she came even, putting his hand over her mouth to stifle her scream. "I told you to stay put."

The woman screamed again and clawed at his hand. It wasn't Fei. Taking his hand just far enough off her mouth that she could speak, he demanded, "Who the hell are you?"

The woman babbled on in Chinese, which did him no good. She was half-naked, terrified and she was coming from where Fei must be. It could only mean one thing. Fei was in trouble.

"Where's Fei?"

She froze. Eyes wide, she looked at him. Putting his lips against her ear, he growled, "Goddamn it, where is she?"

The terror didn't leave her face, but he recognize the expression that settled over it. He'd seen it on Fei's often enough. Pure stubbornness. "You two have got to be related."

She blinked. "You know Fei?"

"I'm the one who gave her the horse." She stared at him blankly. Had Fei not spoken of him at all? "I'm her husband."

As if he'd poked her with a stick, she jerked away. Another spate of Chinese.

"You're wasting time. I don't speak Chinese."

"Fei no married."

"As of two days ago she is."

"She no say."

He took a shot in the dark. "Was there time?"

She licked her lips. Even in the dim light, he could see she was a pretty woman with a round face, large brown eyes, a dainty bow of a mouth and a lissome figure. And she wasn't saying a word.

"I promise you, I'm not going to hurt her."

"You lie."

"You're right. I'm going to spank her ass for putting herself in danger. I told her to stay put and stay out of trouble and—"

"She came for me," the woman interrupted.

"I'm gathering that."

"I could not stay any longer."

Taking in her state of undress, it didn't take a genius to figure out why. "Where is Fei?"

She pointed back the way she'd come.

"She slow them down."

"How?"

"I don't know. She said I wait here. That the dynamite was old but she would be all right."

He grabbed her arms. "Are you telling me Fei is out there facing armed men with dynamite?"

Cringing, she stared at him with big eyes. Gritting his teeth, he fought for patience. Scaring the woman wasn't going to get what he wanted.

"Yes."

"Son of a bitch."

"She said she was going to slow them down," she repeated.

Like Fei, Lin's grammar slipped with her agitation. "I heard you the first time."

A shot rang out.

She grabbed his arm. "You have to help her."

Shoving the woman toward the mare, he ordered, "Stay with the horse. If anyone you don't know comes, hide."

"But—"

He didn't hear the rest. Pulling his revolver, he took off running. More gunshots followed the first two, then shouting. A woman screamed. He couldn't run fast enough.

Fei!

He vaulted over a fallen tree, and bounded off a rock. Every second dragged like an hour. He was going to kill her for putting him through this.

Another volley of shots and then another man's shout, this time pitched higher with victory.

Run, Fei. Goddamn it, run!

The silence was worse than the chaos. Silence left too much to his imagination. Suddenly, an explosion vibrated the ground under his feet. It was quickly followed by another and then another. The shouts turned to screams. Shadow pushed harder. He was so focused on getting to the chaos he almost ran Fei over as he burst out of the woods. She was crouched down behind a boulder, sticks of dynamite in her hand.

In a split second he took in the scene. She'd set the trap with great precision. Mounds of exploded earth fanned the edges of the meadow, pinning all within. "Goddamn, honey, that's impressive."

She didn't respond, just kept staring straight ahead.

"Ah, hell."

She was in shock, staring at the dismembered bodies as if she couldn't comprehend how it had happened.

He knelt beside her and took the sticks from her hand before setting them carefully on the ground.

"Fei, it's time to go." She didn't move. He could hear more men coming. Caution would slow them down, but not for long.

Shaking her arm, he hauled her up against him. “Fei!”

She blinked. “Shadow?”

“Who else?”

Staring at the carnage behind him, she whispered, “I didn’t have a choice.”

She was looking for absolution. “No, you didn’t.”

“I had to stop them. They wanted Lin.”

Lin must be the woman he’d found in the trees. “You did exactly what you had to do, honey. Don’t be apologizing for it. But there are more. We’ve got to run.”

She reached for her pack. “Just let me—”

“Leave it.”

“No, I can’t. I have to do this.”

He’d thought she was talking about the pack, but reaching into her pocket, she pulled out a strip of cloth. She draped it over a branch. It was silk from the sheen but of a different design than she wore.

Grabbing her arm with one hand, his revolver in the other, he hauled her along. “You can explain that later.”

He shoved her down the path. “Any more traps along the way I should know about?”

“I was going to do one farther down, but there wasn’t time.”

“Good.”

“Wait.” She turned back. “I need to find Lin.”

He propelled her forward. “She’s waiting with your mare.”

“She’s with Jewel?”

Because she seemed to do better when distracted, he asked, "You named the horse Jewel?"

"Yes."

She stumbled and he picked her up, half carrying her along as the sound of pursuit grew. They were close. Too close. Setting Fei down, he pushed her ahead of him.

"Go."

She planted her feet. "I can't leave you."

"Yes, you can. This is what I do best."

"This is not the best of anyone."

He shoved her. "Go."

She turned, clutching the pack, lip clenched between her teeth. "I can't."

"Lin needs you."

That did the trick. She turned and ran. He turned and blended back into the shadows. Surprise was going to be his only advantage. From the sound of it, there were three, maybe four, men coming. He stayed tucked in the shadows until they passed, then came up behind the last one. Shadow didn't waste time. Covering the man's mouth with his hand, he slit his throat. Blood sprayed as he lowered him silently to the ground before dropping back to the shadows. One down, three to go.

The men were moving fast, faster than Fei.

"She went off to the right," the point man called.

The hell she did. He'd told her to go straight to the horses. He followed more cautiously. One of the men went to the right. Two steps later, the ground blew up in his face.

Goddamn it, Fei.

She was bad with orders, but hell on wheels when it came to dynamite. If that explosion had gone off a second on either side of when it had, it wouldn't have been nearly as effective. Two down. Two to go. As the men milled about in indecision, he circled around behind them. It was time to end this.

He drop-kicked the man on the left, landing just behind the other, rolling to his feet as he'd done in many other battles many times before. Snatching the knife from his mouth as he landed. Throwing it with deadly accuracy. Blood sprayed in a high arc as the second man dropped to the ground, clutching his throat. The man he'd kicked rolled to his feet. He looked at his partner and then at Shadow before dropping into a fighting stance. With a crook of his fingers, he invited Shadow in. Shadow smiled. A good fight was a good fight, no matter where a man found it.

"I'm going to take care of you, injun, and then I'm going to take care of that pretty girl you're running with." Ice-cold rage settled over Shadow. "You won't touch my wife. Ever."

"Wife? You put your hands on a white woman? That's a hanging offense."

"So is rape." Soft, sweet Fei, who should have been racing up the trail, made her contribution to the conversation, holding two sticks of dynamite in her hand.

"Fei, don't be blowing us both up."

"Then run."

He wasn't running. He was in the middle of a fight

and Fei being there gave the other man the advantage, because Shadow had to watch both of them.

Fei took a step in as the man circled, looking for that moment of distraction that would allow him to get a blow in. She waved the dynamite like a sword.

"Get the hell back, woman."

"We need to run."

"You need to do as I told you."

The man landed a blow to his midsection. Shadow countered with one to his jaw. The man blinked and stumbled before shaking his head. If Shadow had managed a direct hit, he likely would have gone down.

"We have not time for this."

"It's not like I'm having a drink here."

Jumping back, he evaded the other man's next lunge.

"Kill him."

"Bloodthirsty little thing, isn't she?" the stranger grunted.

The man feinted in. He was quick, but not quick enough. He also favored his right side where Shadow had kicked him. Shadow brought his elbow down on the back of the man's neck. He fell but rolled to his feet.

"She's just got an eye for what's not worth saving."

A sulfur scratched across rock. Fei stood there, a lit sulfur in one hand, dynamite in the other.

"Don't do it, Fei."

The other man swore and stopped short. "That's dynamite."

"Yup."

Now the odds were even. The other man was as worried about Fei as he. Just for different reasons.

Fei touched the match to the fuse. It immediately began the familiar sizzle.

"Hell!"

Fei brandished the stick. "Get away from him."

"You letting a woman fight your battles?"

Shadow eyed the sputtering fuse. It didn't look nearly long enough. "Apparently, I'm not getting a choice."

"Tell her to put it down."

Shadow obliged. "Put it down, Fei."

"I said, get away from him."

Shadow shrugged and met the other man's gaze. "She doesn't want to."

The man backed up, one step, two, but not far enough for Shadow to be safe from the blast if Fei tossed the dynamite. "No wonder her family let her marry up with you. She's fucking crazy."

The fuse was getting dangerously low. "They don't know yet."

"In that case, give her back."

Shit, he hated dynamite. It was unpredictable, unstable and rarely gave the results one hoped for. "I might just do that."

He could see from the wildness in Fei's eyes that she was operating on nerves and fear. "We don't need the dynamite."

"He will hurt you."

The hell he would. "We're just having a discussion."

He glanced pointedly at the other man.

"You might be having a discussion, but I'm—"

Shadow jerked his chin in the direction of the dynamite. The man raised both hands and stepped back.

"Two dollars a week ain't enough for this shit."

Shadow turned back to Fei. "See, he was just about to leave."

"I don't trust him."

"You don't have to. Just trust me."

"It's not safe."

It was safer than that dynamite. She'd told Lin it was unstable and she was holding it in her hand as if she had all day. Son of a bitch.

"What do you have against this guy, honey?"

"He hurt my cousin."

The man shook his head and took yet another step back. "I didn't have anything to do with that."

"You lie!"

"I just signed on today."

It might be true, or it might be a lie. Either way, it didn't matter. That fuse was going to take the choice away from all of them. "Honey, do you remember me telling you all you had to do is ask?"

She nodded.

"Ask me now."

"I can't."

The man took another step back.

With a shake of his head, Shadow drew him back with a soft warning, "Don't."

Immediately realizing his mistake in putting distance between them, the man stepped back into the safe area. Shadow was waiting. With a sharp uppercut to his chin, Shadow sent him flying backward. He hit the ground with a thump. He didn't get up.

"It's about time," Fei snapped. Gone was the irrational, panicked woman. In her place was the Fei he was used to seeing. Calm and composed. As cool as a cucumber, Fei plucked the fuse from the dynamite and dropped it on the ground.

It took Shadow a moment to comprehend. "You were bluffing?"

"I bluff much better than I kill." She shrugged. "Is he dead?"

"He's out cold."

"I would prefer him dead."

Very carefully, Shadow took the dynamite from her hand. Shit, this stuff made him nervous. Always had. The fuse sputtered on the ground. He ground it under his moccasin while sliding his knife back into his sheath. "He's going to have a hell of a headache when he gets up *and* be out of a job."

"It's not enough."

"Yeah, well, don't be about blowing us both up just to get even."

"I won't."

She was glaring at the man, rage darkening her eyes, tightening her lips. She wanted revenge. Shadow understood that, understood the rage that demanded retribution against any and all. Hell's Eight had been formed under such rage. When the Mexican army had devastated their village leaving eight boys orphaned, they could have just given up and died. Instead, they'd banded together, scrabbled to stay alive and sworn revenge against the men who'd killed their families.

Not that Tracker's and his family was anything to mourn, but Caine's family had been. The Allens' house had been the Ochoas' sanctuary. There, he and Tracker had always been able to get their bruises treated, their bellies filled and, even though it had made them uncomfortable, they'd gotten a few hugs. The Allens had been the embodiment of every fairy tale Shadow had ever heard. A loving family who hugged, not hit, who laughed, not raged. Who'd open their doors to two boys who'd only had them slammed in their faces. And those people had been viciously murdered.

As Shadow had dug their graves, he'd felt the first touch of what purpose could do to rage. As he'd tossed the first shovelful of dirt on the mutilated bodies, he'd made a vow. The ones responsible would die. That vow had been picked up by each and every one of Hell's Eight. And it had been kept.

Eventually, they'd hunted down and killed all those who had murdered their families. And in the process, they'd developed skills and a hell of a reputation. When the last man had been killed, Shadow had waited for the satisfaction to fill the hole where the rage had lived so long. It hadn't come. There'd just been rage with no purpose. So when the Texas Rangers had offered him a job, he'd accepted, as had all of Hell's Eight. Not because he'd wanted to uphold the laws of Texas—he had no use for any laws except those he made himself—but because rage without purpose could eat a man alive.

Hiking his sleeve over the heel of his hand, he wiped a smudge of dirt off Fei's cheek. He didn't want that empty rage consuming Fei from the inside out. For her, he wanted a future filled with light and love. A home like the Allens' with a man who saw her as the best part of his day. For that to happen, this needed to be settled.

He palmed his knife. "Do you want me to kill him?"

She blinked. "I don't know."

"Make up your mind, but make it now. Don't carry it around like a cancer in your gut."

She bit her lip. "It's not the same, killing him now."

"As killing in the heat of the moment to defend yourself? No, it's not, but in the end, killing is killing."

She touched her hand to her throat. "You would really kill him for me?"

"Ask and find out."

"What kind of man are you?"

Picking up her pack, he emptied out the last few sticks of dynamite onto the ground. "The kind you need right now."

CHAPTER SIX

THEY WERE MAKING GOOD TIME, all things considered. It was doubtful Lin had ever been on a horse before, so anything faster than a walk was likely to pitch her to the ground. He didn't know, however, how much longer they could go on. The horses were tired. *They* were tired. He looked over his shoulder to see how Lin was faring.

"We need to stop," Fei said.

Shadow held her a little tighter, remembering those moments when he'd heard the gunshots and her screams. "No, we don't. Culbart is going to want revenge for what you did."

"I only took revenge for what he did."

"That's the way it goes. Someone starts something and then someone feels the need to get even. And then that revenge begs its own retaliation."

"He bought my cousin as if she were a bag of flour."

"Fei!"

Shadow felt sorry for Lin, who appeared as if she wanted to sink into the ground.

"When I tried to explain the mistake, he would not

release her. He laughed and said I would have to pay twice as much to get her back."

Enough for a new beginning.

"That's why you wanted the gold."

"Yes. To buy her freedom and to leave."

"Who sold her in the first place?"

It was Fei's turn to look ashamed. "My family has lost much face over this."

"That a fancy way of saying your father?"

"Yes."

"So Culbart thinks he made a deal, fair and square?"

"No one has right to buy another."

"I agree, but that doesn't change the man's belief that you just stole something from him."

"I will go to the claim and get his gold."

"I think the opportunity to make a deal is pretty much dead and gone."

"He will want the money."

"By the time you get that gold cashed out, you're going to have every yahoo in the territory on your tail."

"For this, I have you."

Shit. "For a plan that stupid, you're going to need the whole U.S. Army."

"The army that doesn't like you?"

Shadow nodded. "That would be the one."

"Then there is no choice. We go to the claim."

"Only if you want to kiss your gold goodbye. You won't be able to go back there until things calm down. Likely for a few months. The claim is too close to the Culbart ranch. There's no place to hide the horses. No way to hide your presence there. And unless you've got a supply of jerky there, there's no way to cook without the smell carrying."

Lin gasped. "You think they hunt us?"

"I'd bet my horse on it."

She exchanged a glance with Fei. "We must go home."

"That's the first place they'll look for you."

"Uncle is there alone," Lin countered.

"Is this the uncle that sold you to Culbart?"

"Yes."

"I'm having a hard time working up to concern."

"He is ill."

"So?"

Fei made a motion with her hands. "In his head. He does not always know where he is, what he does."

He didn't care how crazy he got, Shadow couldn't see himself selling his niece. "No."

Fei's chin came up. "He is my father. I have a daughter's duty."

He noticed she wasn't making a claim of love. "And I'm your husband, which means I have a few duties of my own."

"And that duty extends to my family."

"It does?"

"If you claim the role you must claim it all."

"All or nothing?"

"Yes."

He turned Night south, toward her house. "I'll keep that in mind."

THERE WAS NOTHING LEFT of the small house and barn except smoking ruins.

"No, no. Oh, no!"

Fei slipped from the saddle and ran to the barn, dropping to her knees in front of the collapsed beams. Lin followed more slowly. Shadow urged Night over, taking in the scene. Smoke hung in the air in an acrid cloud, along with the odor of charred flesh. Animal or human, it was hard to tell. A lot of anger went behind this much destruction. Lin didn't look the type to instill such passion in a man, but some men could be funny when it came to their possessions. Shadow swung down from the saddle, dropping Night's reins to the ground, effectively tying him.

Suddenly Fei jumped to her feet and lunged toward the ruins. He barely caught her before she burned herself on the smoking timbers. Her shoulders were delicate, fragile beneath his hands.

"My father!"

The stench of charred flesh took on a more sinister connotation. Shit, had her father been in there?

"There's nothing to know, honey. If your father was in there… There's nothing left."

"He was in the barn."

Lin covered her mouth with her hands and shuddered.

"How do you know?"

"I locked him in."

Way too slender to take on that kind of guilt.

"Why?"

"He lost his mind, but not his skill. He would believe strange things. Do strange things. I couldn't trust him."

"Not to blow something up?"

She nodded.

"Oh, Fei, it was you," Lin whispered.

Fei nodded.

"All this time?"

Another nod. "We needed the money."

Shadow looked between the two girls. "What are you two talking about?"

There was another of those looks between the cousins that gave him the uneasies. Turning Fei so she faced him, he asked, "What did you do?"

"I pretended to be my father. I did his work."

He couldn't believe what he was hearing. "For the railroad?"

"Yes."

Now the cloth she'd left behind on the bush made sense. She'd wanted people to assume her father had been there.

Handling explosives for the railroad was one of the most dangerous of jobs. And not only because of the materials used, but because the railroad regarded Chinese workers as disposable so didn't waste much time and money on safety. "How did you pull it off?"

"To the whites, we all look alike," Lin snapped.

"You don't look like a man," he retorted. No matter what, he couldn't imagine thinking Fei a man.

"If I stoop my shoulders, dirty my face and wear the

large hat my father favored, I do. No one gets too close to the explosives."

That he could believe.

"And Uncle was…" Lin made a motion with her hands, searching for the word.

"Eccentric," Fei finished for her. "Always, he made his wishes known through me."

"His English was bad," Lin explained.

Fei continued as if her cousin hadn't interrupted. "When he insisted no one be within a hundred yards on blasting day, no one questioned him."

"You had it all figured out."

Fei stared at the rubble, silent tears running down her face. The shiver that went through her snaked its way up his own spine. "No. I did not know how to restore Jian Tseng's mind. I did not know how long I could fool the railroad. I did not know how to control him when he went from the father I knew to the man I didn't."

Shadow touched the fading bruise on her cheek. "He's the one who hit you?"

"Yes."

"So you started locking him in the barn."

She shook her head. "He was in the storm cellar below."

Lin took a step forward. "Maybe he survived."

Shadow felt like a heel, killing off their hope. "If the heat didn't get him, the smoke did."

Fei moaned and wept. He didn't know what to do to ease her pain. She pulled away. She stood beside him, her arms wrapped around her waist, so isolated that she might as well be halfway across the world. He'd kept the rage out of her life, but how did he protect her from the guilt?

"At least he's at peace." It was a poor offering. Shadow was surprised when Fei nodded.

Lin brushed off her hands. "He must be buried properly."

Fei nodded again.

Shadow had to be the bad guy once more. "It's going to take days for that rubble to cool down."

"We will wait."

"If Culbart doesn't have someone watching this place, he's a fool." He looked at Lin. "Did the man strike you as a fool?"

She shook her head. "He is mean and cunning, like a snake."

The cousins had a thing about reptiles. First he was a dragon and now Culbart was a snake. From the little Shadow had heard when he came into town, Culbart had a reputation as a hard-ass and for being ruthless when it came to protecting his property lines, but he had never heard anything particularly bad rumored about him. But a woman might see him differently.

"Then we can't hang around for a funeral."

"My father's soul will not rest without a proper burial," Fei argued.

"Then say a few words to settle him down."

Both women gave him a dirty look. He didn't care. The old man was dead. The women were alive and it was his job to keep them that way. Gentling his tone, he pointed out, “There’s nothing you can do here.”

“I can grieve,” Fei told him.

“You can do that a hundred miles away just as easily.”

“A hundred miles?”

It was actually more like two hundred miles to Hell’s Eight. “There’s nothing left for you here.”

Fei waved her hand wide. “What is there for me out there?”

Safety. “Maybe a future.”

She shook her head. “I will not do this.”

“I’m not giving you a choice. All or nothing, remember? Now, mount up.”

NEITHER WOMAN SAID A WORD during the rest of the ride. Not that Shadow was much of a talker, but there was silence, and then there was *silence.* This silence rubbed like a burr stuck in a boot. After about six hours of that, his mood was as foul as a bucket of soured milk.

“We’re stopping here for the night.”

Lin exchanged a glance with Fei. These two had secrets. At the moment, Shadow didn’t care. There was nothing they were hiding that would change his plans.

He dismounted. Reaching up, he helped Fei down. She didn’t acknowledge his help. Lin didn’t wait for assistance. Just slid off the horse. Once her feet hit the ground, she leaned against the horse, clinging to the saddle as unobtrusively as possible. She was going to be sore tomorrow.

"What is here?"

"Enough bramble to provide cover, and from the sounds of things, a stream for water." He pointed to the deer path that cut through the thicket. "And a place to camp for the night. Any objections?"

Both women shook their heads. Taking Night's reins, he led him through the thicket. About thirty feet in, there was a small clearing. Another twenty feet beyond that was a stream.

"You two get the bedrolls settled out while I get the horses taken care of."

Lin stared at him blankly.

"Fei, you'll be sleeping with me."

"Why can I not share with Lin?"

"Consider it part of that 'all or nothing' thing."

He had the satisfaction of seeing the fire come into Fei's eyes. She opened her mouth to argue. Lin stepped forward, interceding. "What is a bedroll?"

"It looks like a roll of blankets tied to the back of the mare's saddle."

"Her name is Jewel." The soft whisper reached him across the space.

"You told me that before. When you were running around with dynamite in your hand."

It wasn't a good memory.

"Fei," Lin interjected. "A wise woman does not provoke her husband."

"This one does."

"Fei!"

Fei turned, a bit of fire entering her stance. “Why not? He can do nothing. He has promised not to hurt me.”

“Maybe not,” Shadow interrupted, “but right now your life is in my hands and my temper is on the edge, so you shouldn’t be pushing, because if you push hard enough, I might break my word.”

Fei didn’t bat an eyelash. Either she had tremendous faith in his willpower or the day had taken its toll to the point that she didn’t care anymore.

“You won’t break your word.”

Untying his bedroll, he tossed it to Fei. “What makes you so sure?”

She caught it easily.

Lin grabbed the other bedroll, and clutching it in front of her, stood beside her cousin. “Yes,” she asked. “What makes you so sure?”

“Because his word is the one thing that has always been his.”

Lin studied him, obviously looking for what Fei saw. And just as obviously not finding it.

“But that doesn’t mean I have to do as he says.”

Shadow shook his head. The woman didn’t know the meaning of quit. “Until you find a way to end this marriage, you do.”

“We do not know if the marriage is legal.”

“We don’t know that it’s not.”

“We don’t have to act like it is.”

He smiled. “All or nothing, honey.”

“Then I choose n—”

Lin grabbed Fei’s hand. “No more.” Before Fei could

form a protest, Lin ordered, "Do not provoke this man more."

He could get to liking Lin. He tipped his hat. "Thank you."

"You're welcome."

"There is nothing to thank her for," Fei snapped.

"Why, because she's right?" he asked, holding her gaze. "Are you trying to provoke me? Or tempt me?" His pulse picked up the pace at the possibility. "Is that what this anger is about? Because you didn't have to risk your life, your cousin's life and my life to make that happen. You could just—"

"How dare you say this to me!"

He folded his arms across his chest. Serene, sweet or pissed off, the woman fired his blood. "Honey, I dare a hell of a lot, or haven't you figured that out by now?"

"My cousin is standing right here."

"Yes, she is. And looking appalled, too."

Fei turned to Lin. "Why are you appalled?"

Lin looked as if she'd rather be anywhere but there. "He is your husband. Your behavior is unseemly."

"It would be, if he were my husband."

Lin looked down and smoothed a fold in the bedroll. "He came after you when he didn't have to. He fought for us when he didn't have to. You say he is not your husband? Then you tell me what man other than a husband does this? And what other than a wife would he do this for? Your lack of respect shames me."

Fei stood as if stricken. Her lids lowered and she adopted that properly submissive stance Shadow hated.

"I am not the one who declared him not to be my husband."

The truth hung between them. Shit. *Had* he been the one to say it first?

Fei licked her lips. "I am sorry." She bowed deeply. "Lin is right. Respect is lacking from my speech."

He'd rather have her spitting at him. "I'm not the type who needs a display of false respect to feel good."

"The respect is not false."

"Why do I hear a but?"

Her chin came up. "You give too many orders."

"Why is that a problem? It's not as if you follow them."

Her eyes narrowed and a bite entered her soft voice. "Because you do not say please."

"You've been pecking at me because I don't say please?"

"It is annoying."

"So is dying."

Lin grabbed the other bedroll, tugging hard enough that Fei stumbled. "I do not understand either of you."

Cocking an eyebrow at her, he said, "I wasn't aware you needed to."

Lin nodded. "You are right. This I do not need to understand. This is between you two." She yanked the bedroll free. "Please, talk." She shooed Fei away with a quick motion of her hand. "Elsewhere."

Fei looked a little lost. "Perhaps I don't want to talk."

Shadow held out his hand, feeling a bit sorry for her. "Would you rather fight?"

"Maybe."

"Too bad." Half walking, half dragging, he brought her to the horses. Grabbing her hand, he placed the mare's reins in it. She left them there, not closing her fingers around the leather strips. She looked as though he was going to bolt. Picking up Night's reins, he left the option open. For about a second.

"You jump on her and ride away, and I'll run you down."

She opened her mouth. He put his hand over it, stilling the protest. Her eyes went wide and her breath caught in her throat. She was afraid of him. Despite all her big talk, she actually feared him. Son of a bitch.

"Not because I want to hurt you," he explained, his voice sounding harsh even to his own ears, "and not because I can't stand anyone telling me no, but because the memory of how close you came to dying today is too fresh in my mind." The look of fear changed to surprise. "It makes me crazy to think of you dying."

Her lips moved. He had no idea what she said. Wasn't sure he wanted to know. If it was a fight she wanted, he'd give it to her, but it wasn't likely to end well. When she challenged him as she did, he wanted nothing more than to lay her down on the ground and fuck her, just to prove that she was no different than the rest. Just to prove to himself that he didn't need her. Just to prove to himself that he could still walk away.

Tears gathered in her eyes. Her slender fingers wrapped around his wrist and squeezed ever so gently, as if he were some wild beast that needed taming. Or soothing, he realized. A tear spilled over, trailed down her cheek, caught on the edge of his hand and spread out, binding them together. And he knew what was a lie. He could never walk away. Removing his hand from her mouth, he motioned toward the stream.

"Don't say anything. Just walk."

She did, silently, head down, a half pace behind him. That pissed him off, too. Reaching back, he grabbed her hand and tugged her up beside him.

"Just because I'm mad at you doesn't mean I think you're less than you ever were. You're not my fucking slave."

Another flash of those green-brown eyes. The tears were thicker now, gathering in her lashes. He didn't want to care that she was hurt. He didn't want to care that she was afraid. Another tear trembled. He set his jaw. It rolled down her cheek. He made himself watch. It dripped off her chin and he swore. If they weren't only three steps from the creek, he would have taken her in his arms, but it would be cruel to leave the horses just steps from water. So he held on to his control, but as soon as the horses got to the water, he dropped all pretense. His hands closed over her arms and she stiffened as if braced for a blow.

"No, honey. Don't."

She stood still, not braced, not welcoming.

He pulled her into his chest. "Ah, hell, Fei. You scared the shit out of me."

The tension left her muscles. Her hands came up his back.

The next tear dampened his shirt. "I am sorry. I do not know anymore why I do what I do."

Neither did he. He took chances that made no sense, got careless when he should be vigilant, and drank when he needed to be sober.

"Sometimes you just need to spit in the devil's eye."

"But it is not the devil's eyes into which I spit."

Long tendrils of hair were escaping from her braid. He pushed one back, tucking it behind her ear. "I think I'll survive. I guess it's hard to trust a man you meet at the end of a hangman's noose."

Rubbing her cheek against his shirt, she admitted, "It is hard to trust anyone."

He knew how that felt, too. "You have to start somewhere."

"You think I should start with you?"

"What better place than your husband?"

"We are married, aren't we?"

"Yes."

She sighed. "It does not make sense to fight each other, then, does it?"

"Not when there are so many others willing to take a shot."

She made a sound between a laugh and a snort.

"Was that a giggle?"

She quickly covered her mouth with her hand. "Yes."

"Then don't cover it up."

"It is rude to expose one's teeth."

Pulling her hand from her mouth, he shook his head. "I like your teeth."

He'd like them even better skimming over his body.

"The front one is crooked."

"I didn't notice."

"Because I haven't let you see."

He rubbed his finger over her lower lip, tempted to pull it down and see the offending tooth. "I'll start paying attention."

"It is not *that* crooked."

He smiled. "You want me to take your word for it?"

"For this, you would have to trust me."

His smile faded as the truth rolled over him. He did trust her. Kissing the back of her hand, he agreed. "I guess I would."

She didn't say anything. She didn't have to. They were both going to have to trust.

"Are you all right? You didn't get hurt today?"

"I do not have a scratch."

And that was a miracle in itself. "I don't want to see another stick of dynamite in your hand again."

"We have discussed this."

"I didn't like the answer."

"That doesn't mean it will change."

The few rays of the setting sun that penetrated the trees caught on the smooth surface of her thick braid. The black color gleamed almost blue.

"Want to bet?"

"No."

He loosened the braid one curve at a time, one breath at a time, letting the simple ritual drain some of the tension out of him.

"You're a beautiful woman, Fei."

"Thank you."

"I want you."

She touched the small scar on his jaw. "I know."

"It doesn't change the fact that nothing good can come of this." He fluffed the rest of her hair free.

"So you say."

"It's the truth."

Her hands came around his waist and squeezed in a tentative hug. "Shadow?"

"Yes."

"I want something from you."

He should have expected it. "What?"

She looked up and the sadness in her eyes about broke his heart. "I have lost my mother, my father and my culture. Soon I may lose my life."

"I won't let that happen."

"I'm hunted." She shrugged. "It could happen."

"No."

She continued as if he hadn't spoken. "Because of this, I do not want you to fight this passion between us tonight."

"Your cousin is sleeping right over there."

"I think she is nursing her anger. She is not happy with us."

"For such a meek woman, she has a way of getting her point across. But that doesn't change the fact that she's just thirty feet away."

"You will have to make sure I do not make noise."

He wanted to make her scream. "What's she going to say when you fetch our bedroll?"

"I will tell her that I wish to be with my husband. She will understand."

He wished he did. "Why, Fei?"

"Because I want something for me. I want something that is mine, not forced upon me. Something that I have not compromised to accept. What I feel with you, I have never felt with another. I do not know if I will live long enough to feel it again, but I want to know where it goes, if only just for tonight. I am your wife, so it is not wrong. Can you give me that? Can you pretend for tonight that I am your wife for real?"

He touched the corner of her mouth with his thumb. She wanted him as he was. Not what he represented, but him. He'd give her the whole damn world in that moment. "I can give you tonight."

"Without the anger?"

"Without the anger."

"You will think I'm special?"

"You are special."

She shook her head. "I know I am not. I have not the attitude of the proper wife or the purity of blood to give to your children."

"My kids aren't going to need pure blood. They're just going to need a lot of attitude to carry them through."

"We are only pretending for tonight."

"Tonight could have consequences."

"What?"

"You could get pregnant."

"There are ways to prevent this."

How the hell did she know that? "What makes you think I'm going to use them?"

She slid her hands up his back, across his chest and over his shoulders, sending sparks of pleasure flickering over his skin. Her smile was shy and sweet. She did have a slightly crooked tooth and it was as erotic as hell.

Her hands linked behind his neck. "I will trust you."

CHAPTER SEVEN

FEI WANTED EVERY WOMAN'S DREAM—a wedding night to remember. One in which she was cherished. Loved. And she'd picked him to give it to her. A man who didn't have the slightest idea what that felt like.

Skimming his fingers down her neck, Shadow backed her up against Night's side. Her breath caught in her throat with a sexy little catch as he stepped between her thighs. "That's a tall order."

"I am sorry if I offended."

"I'm not offended, but I don't think you know what you're asking, and from whom."

"I am asking my husband to show me the pleasures of the marriage bed."

"You're asking a man who has never been loved to show you love."

Her gaze slid from his. "I know you don't love me."

"And that's my point. A woman's first time should be with the man she loves."

"In my culture, my virginity will be given to whomever my family decides will be a suitable match. It is doubtful I'd even see him before the ceremony."

He'd heard of such things. "You won't have a choice?"

Smiling slightly, she unbuttoned the top two buttons of her high-necked, silk tunic, spreading the material and exposing the hollow of her throat. Desire rippled along his nerve endings, bringing them to attention. "Not unless I make one for myself."

He nudged aside the smooth material. "Undo another button."

The order came out harsher than he had intended. She didn't flinch and didn't look away. When his fingers slipped beneath the material to caress the nape of her neck, her lips parted on a breathy moan. "I like that."

"So do I."

"There's fire in you, Fei."

Arching her neck, she gave him better access. "Only for you."

Only for him. It was a fantasy. One with infinite allure. He'd never had a woman who'd known no one but him, burned for no one but him. Never wanted one. Until now. "Good."

The press of his fingers tilted her head back. The whisper of his name drew his head down.

"Shadow."

He didn't kiss her right away. Just teased them both with the potential of contact. Her breath got shorter. Her lips softer. He loved her mouth. Wrapping his fingers in her hair, he angled her head back.

"Such a pretty mouth, honey. Open it for me."

She did, a soft moue of anticipation.

"So hungry."

"For you," she whispered.

"What do you want?"

"Your kiss."

"How? Hard or soft? With my lips only, or do you want more?"

"More." Fei definitely wanted more. Clinging to Shadow's shirt, she slumped back against Night's side. She wanted all of that.

"Greedy woman."

"Yes." She shifted against him, her hip grazing his erection, her breasts teasing his chest. She wanted to experience everything she could this night. To know it all. "I am greedy for all you can show me."

"No holding back?"

This time it was she who brought his gaze to hers with her palm against his cheek. "Not a thing."

The effect on him was like lightning. His muscles snapped taut, his eyes narrowed, his nostrils flared. She cupped both his cheeks in her palms and kissed him softly. Her dragon. A dragon who spread fire with his touch, not his breath. But a dragon nonetheless. The only one who could make her burn.

Arching against him, she whispered, "Kiss me, Shadow."

"How?" It was her turn to shiver as the low drawl rumbled over her passion with all the possibilities.

"Like you cannot wait another minute to have me."

"I can't."

"Then let me see it. Feel it."

"You do not know what you're asking."

"I know."

She was asking for him. Lifting her hips, she found the hard ridge of his erection. It was a simple shift of her hips to nestle him against her intimately. His breath hissed in, but he still didn't move. She'd reached the end of her experience. She didn't know how else to tempt him.

His head came up. He looked down the length of his nose at her. A challenge. "Show me how you want me."

"I do not know how." She twisted against him. "You will have to teach me."

His shaft jerked against her, sending a piercing ache deep into her core. Oh, he liked the thought of that. Her flesh swelled and ached, demanding more. Of him.

His fingers fisted in her hair. "Run your tongue over your lips."

She did, feeling foolish.

"No," he murmured, his voice as much a caress as his touch. So deep and rich, like rare chocolate. A feast for her senses.

"Not like that." He pressed gently with his thumb. "Do it slow and easy. Tease me. Let me see how hot and wet they're going to be." He slid his thumb inside. "Make me imagine how good they're going to feel wrapped around my cock."

She did, going him one better, tilting her head forward and taking his thumb to the first joint. She was a virgin, but she'd seen the picture books her father thought he'd hid.

"Shit."

"Like that?" she asked around his thumb.

"Hell, yes." With a tug, she was away from the horse and up into his arms. His hands cupped her rear, palming it lightly, sending tingles inward and outward. Tingles that flared to sparks as he lifted her up into his kiss. "Exactly like that," he growled into her mouth.

She laughed and wrapped her hands around his neck, pulling him closer, opening wider. "Kiss me, Shadow. Make me forget about tomorrow."

He caught her lower lip in his teeth, biting gently, and she discovered the edge of pain had its own unique thrill.

"No tomorrow, honey. No yesterday."

"Just now," she breathed, pulling him in.

And now was hot and eager. Now was curiosity, passion and pleasure. Now made her burn. Now was wonder.

"Son of a bitch." He pulled back, letting her slide down his body, and rested his forehead against hers, air soughing in and out of his lungs in a harsh rasp. "You go to my head."

That wasn't where he went on her. "You go different places on me."

He blinked, and then as he understood, he laughed. His eyes dropped to the front of her tunic. Her gaze followed his. She instinctively wanted to fold her arms across her chest and hide the betraying peaks.

He caught her hands before she could bring them down. "No. That's too pretty a sight to hide."

Pretty. She held on to the thought as embarrassment threatened to take over. He thought she was pretty.

"I'm going to unbutton your tunic."

A faint pink tinged her cheeks. "All right." She wasn't going to look.

In case she didn't understand, he added, "I want to touch your breasts."

"I am embarrassed, not dumb." She was immediately sorry for the sarcasm. "I did not mean—"

"To snap," he finished for her.

"I want you to touch me."

"I know." Unbuttoning her tunic, he spread it wide. She wasn't wearing anything underneath. Cool air whispered across her skin. Her nipples drew up tighter. Her breathing got shallower. And way down deep, the ache got stronger.

His fingers traced the outline of her breast. Round and round in ever decreasing circles, in whisper-light touches, never touching the nipple. "You're just a little nervous."

He understood. Her knees went weak. As always, he caught her, steadying her. "Thank you."

He smiled, revealing even, white teeth and that softer side of his personality that he rarely showed. "Anytime."

She took a step back as he unbuttoned his shirt. He took one forward, spreading her tunic and his shirt so they were skin to skin. Heartbeat to heartbeat.

"Oh, my."

He shook his head. "Don't talk, don't think. Just feel how good we are together."

She took him at his word, literally, opening her hands against his back, rubbing them up and down.

Closing her eyes, she leaned her head against his chest, listening to his heartbeat.

"What do you feel?"

"Heat. You're very warm."

"You make me burn."

She smiled. "I like knowing that."

He chuckled. "I bet you do."

Her hands skimmed up his back and around to the front, creeping over his pectorals and up to his neck. She touched his lips.

"I can feel your smile."

"That's because I'm happy."

Her fingers explored his mouth, tracing the rim. "Such a nice smile."

"Thank you."

"What do you feel now?" Shadow asked, his voice a husky incentive to tell all.

"I can feel your breath. It's coming faster."

"And how does that feel against your skin?"

"Hot. Moist. Fast."

"That's because you're touching me. It's exciting. I like your hands on me." Pushing her hair out of her face, he asked, "Would you like to feel more?"

"Oh, please."

"Just a little now, honey. We're not alone." He leaned

down, bringing his mouth closer to hers, lifting her up. "Put your legs around my waist."

She locked her ankles behind his back, bringing her groin in contact with his. Her pants leg caught on his gun belt. He yanked it free. The tunic and pants she wore made it easy to tuck his…cock against her. The sensation that shot through her was mesmerizing. Paralyzing. Perfect.

"Can you feel how hot I am there? How hard?"

"Oh, yes." She nodded.

"That's for you. All for you."

She didn't want to fool herself. "Any woman would make you that way."

He shook his head and laughed. "Honey, I'm almost thirty-one years old. The time when just looking at a woman got me hot and excited was sixteen years ago."

"But you get hard looking at me?"

His breath hissed out between his teeth. "Every time."

"And you like it."

"Part of me likes it a hell of a lot."

Part. Only part. "And the other part?"

Better than the gift of his passion was the gift of his honesty. "I don't trust it. I don't like being out of control."

She felt the same way. As if this was beyond her control but good. So good. "Then you have to trust me, like I have to trust you."

"Maybe."

She shook her head and snuggled tighter against

his cock. The feeling was blissful. Commanding. She wanted more. "Not maybe. Yes."

Cupping her rear in his hands, he nudged her with his shaft, rocking her gently, his cock slid along the silk of her trousers, the heat and pressure caressing her with a slow steady pressure until the thick length caught at the top. And it was her turn to feel the lightning. Her lids lowered and her head fell back as she savored the lush feeling.

"Ohhh."

He took advantage of that little moan. "Kiss me again."

She did. Passionately. Wildly, nibbling at his lips before holding his mouth to hers and kissing him deeply.

His hand slid through her hair, pulling slightly. The pleasure/pain only added to her excitement. "Honey, tell me to take it easy."

"I don't want you easy."

"You don't know what you're asking."

"Then show me."

She opened her mouth the minute his touched hers. She wanted him, wanted this. He made it all so good.

Breaking off the kiss, he hugged her tightly. His groan vibrated against her neck. "How come every time you make me burn there's no place to go?"

"I do not know."

He let go of her hips. "Hold tight."

She wrapped her legs around his waist, not caring where he took her as long as he didn't break the kiss.

He turned, resting her back against Night's side. The horse sidestepped. He went with it. Night went farther. Shadow stumbled. Fei dropped her legs from around his waist.

"Oh, no, you don't."

"It is not working."

"I want you." It came out a growl. She shivered. Desire and lust blended into thought-stealing bliss.

"Goddamn, honey, I want to take this slow, but I don't know if I can. I want you too much."

"I do not fight you."

"You should. You should be kicking and screaming and telling me to mind my manners."

Her fingers went back to the buttons of his pants. "I want you the way you are."

"That man will hurt you."

"Not on purpose."

"Pain is pain."

She shrugged. "Then you will hurt me, but I want the real you, not the one you give other women. I want the you that you hide. The you that you are afraid of. I do not want secrets. I do not want pretense. When this is between us, I want it to be honest."

"You want a lot."

She shook her head and pressed her lips against his chest. "Just you." Touching her finger to the spot, she whispered, "I like that you do not have hair here."

He chuckled. Such a deep, pleasant sound. "Glad I could oblige."

Feeling daring, she touched her tongue to his chest.

He stiffened, but his hands drew her closer. He liked it. And she liked knowing she could give back the pleasure pouring through her.

"What are you doing?"

"Tasting you."

He shuddered. Ducking her head, she hid her smile. "You taste salty."

She pushed the shirt off his shoulders and stopped. And stared at the pattern of violence. So many scars marred the darkness of his skin. So much damage. So much pain.

"Oh."

"What's wrong?"

Her fingers traced a scar across his abdomen. "You have been hurt."

"Just an old wound. It doesn't pain me now."

Covering the scar with her hand, she whispered, "My warrior dragon."

He shook his head. "Just a man, honey."

"My man, tonight." She pushed at his pants. Her gift to herself.

"Yes." His finger under her chin forced her gaze away from his body.

His eyes were dark. Mysterious. Hot. "Have you ever done this before?"

So fast she couldn't hide the impact, shame washed through her. What was so exciting for her was boring him. "I am sorry. I have not the experience—"

His finger against her mouth cut off the apology.

"I wasn't criticizing, but there are some things a man needs to know."

He was worried about her. She kissed his finger and rocked on his manhood, following the surges of joy rather than the drag of worry. Tomorrow would come no matter what she did tonight. But tonight she wanted to enjoy being a woman. Shadow's woman. "I am a virgin, and you have too many clothes on."

There was only the slighted of hesitations, before he drawled, "Naked might be a little bit too much for you now."

It was very sweet he wanted to protect her. Her hair tumbled about her face as she shook her head. "I would like to see what I have touched."

"Who am I to argue with that?"

"Fei?" The call came from beyond the copse of bushes. Lin. She was looking for them.

Shadow let her slide down his big body. A shudder went through her at the stroke of all that muscle. An equally strong shudder went through him.

"I am sorry," Fei said quickly, stepping away.

Just as quickly he hauled her back with a hand behind her neck. His mouth met hers in a biting kiss that marked, claimed, owned. "Don't be sorry. Just be ready."

"For what?"

He set her away. "To finish what we started."

Fei laughed. "I will be." She felt desirable and womanly and powerful. Before she straightened, she stroked over hands over Shadow's stomach, dragging her short nails across the slabs of muscle. He moaned and his hips bucked.

Very powerful.

"Fei?" Lin called again.

With a twitch of her hips, she took a canteen off the saddle. "Coming."

"What are you doing?" Shadow asked.

"Getting ready."

His eyes narrowed. "Fei…"

Backing up, she said, "I will bring her water and tell her you wish to bathe and will be back shortly."

His expression was knowing as he looked at her face. She was immediately aware of her swollen lips, flushed cheeks and tangled hair.

"That's not going to fool anyone."

She smiled. "I do not need to fool her. I just need to let her know that we need privacy."

"I guess I can live with that."

FEI WAS BACK IN JUST a few minutes, carrying the bedroll. She looked surprisingly relaxed for a woman who was about to make love for the first time. And with her cousin just a few feet away. Shadow had met women who liked to be watched. He wouldn't have pegged Fei as one of them.

"What if your cousin comes down?"

She smiled. "She will not."

There was something in that smile… "What makes you so sure?"

"I made her tea."

"I don't understand."

"She has had a very full day. It would do her well to sleep."

"You…drugged her?"

Fei shrugged. "If I had not, she would have spent the night talking and I would not have had this time with you."

Son of a bitch. He didn't know whether to be flattered or appalled.

Fei laid the bedroll on the ground. Deciding to be flattered, Shadow picked it up. "Not there. It's too close to the stream. The damp will get to you."

"Then where?"

"Here." He took her to the side where he'd cut and laid down pine boughs.

"You made us a bed."

She smiled as if it were a four-poster. That smile did something…soft to his insides. "No reason for us not to be comfortable."

"And you took off your guns."

It didn't feel right not to. "Yes."

"But not your pants."

"No." No matter what she said, he wanted this to be a night she remembered with a smile.

Her smile was shy as she followed him. "Thank you."

He tossed the bedroll on the pine boughs. "Not feeling as brave as before?"

"It is not that I am not brave. When you touch me, I am very brave. When I am left to my own thoughts—"

she shrugged and glanced away "—I feel awkward and silly."

She was beautiful and everything he desired. There wasn't any other way he ever wanted her to see herself.

"Well, then, honey…" He opened his arms. "Come here and be brave."

The smile came again, stronger, surer. Shadow couldn't wait any longer. Pulling her to him, he kissed her. Slow and easy. Easy turned to passion, passion to fire. Fei moaned and opened her mouth to the thrust of his tongue, inviting him in with excited little moans that shot past his control to the seat of his desire. She tasted of mint and woman. Of hope and desire. Of innocence and sex. She tasted good.

She felt even better. Slim and supple, sleek like a cat. He cupped her breasts through the silk of her tunic. Small but plump, they swelled to his touch, enticing him to stroke and squeeze. She gasped and moaned, turning into his palm. He left his hand there a minute, letting her get used to the sensation. The nipple grew hard and prodded against his thumb. He gave it a flick, taking her gasp as his own, wishing he could see her response as well as feel it.

"Very nice."

"Do it again," she whispered.

He did, again and again. She twisted against him, trying to get more of that sensation. He gave it to her in a light pinch, holding it for a little bit longer the next time, giving her a little more pressure, a little more persuasion. He wanted that wild woman in her to come out. He wanted the same honesty from her that she wanted from him. When she moaned, he smiled. Her nails dug into the back of his neck, pulling him closer. Her mouth opened wider, inviting him deeper.

"God, Fei, I've got to have you."

"You've got me."

Yes, he did. In his arms, in his life, and now in his bed. He scooped her up. She had him too hot. If he came at her like this, he'd hurt her. He straightened and tilted his head back, sucking in long drafts of air. It carried the scent of her skin, the beauty of the night, the promise of her passion.

"Give me a minute, Fei."

She didn't even give him a second. Kissing her way down his chest, she sprinkled random little kisses that fractured his control. She had no idea what she was doing to him, couldn't know. Son of a bitch, he was on fire.

With fingers that shook, he spread the lapels of her tunic, forcing himself to be gentle. Her delicate breasts, tipped with those luscious nipples strained for attention. He skimmed the outside of her right breast, tracing the circumference, resting its weight in his palm, cupping it from underneath, plumping it up just that little bit as he leaned in.

"Oh, yes," she breathed above his head.

He smiled. There was a lot to be said for having an honest woman who wanted it all. He flicked the hard nub with his tongue, centering her attention before taking her into his mouth. She squirmed and wiggled.

He sucked and nibbled. When she arched, he took more, increasing the pressure, the suction, until she cried out and held him to her. Goddamn, she was sweet. He smacked her ass lightly, smiling as she writhed. His passionate wife. Kissing her nipple one last time, he whispered, "You're beautiful, Fei."

Switching positions, he lowered them both until she was cradled in his lap. Working his hand lower, between her legs, he cupped the heat of her pussy, coating his finger with her juices, searching with his middle finger until he found the well of her vagina.

Virgin.

He had to be careful. Go slowly. He pressed lightly.

She froze, barely breathing as he teased the tempting hollow.

"It's all right. This will feel just as good."

"Shadow?"

She was afraid. He didn't want her afraid. He wanted her wild again. He rubbed her clit with his thumb. Just a little. Very little, but enough that she felt it. When she was quivering and arching up, he pressed his finger in, taking her that first little bit. She shook under the shock. Her pussy flexed against his palm. She quivered under the next pass of his thumb. So delicate, so fine, so eager. Another circle of his thumb. Another press of his finger. A little deeper. A little faster. Her fingers dug into his forearm as she pushed up, every muscle, every sense, attuned, waiting for the next pass, the next press. He gave it to her in a firmer stroke.

"Come for me, Fei."

"I can't."

"Yes, you can."

He started over, light to hard, waiting until she started to squirm and arch up, showing him that she was ready for more, begging. And he gave it to her. Harder. Faster. Always being aware of her pleasure, her need. It was all about her tonight. Even if it killed him, it was going to be all about her. He could feel the hardness of her nipples poking into his chest. Hear her gasps of pleasure and anticipation. He could see the anticipatory flex of her muscles as she awaited what he would do next. She was ready. More than ready.

Sliding his fingers between her buttocks, he grazed the rosebud beneath. Just a little touch. Just enough to tease them both.

Jerking up, she gasped, "I do not think—"

"You don't need to think. Just feel." He swirled his finger back through her thick juices, finding her clit and pinching it lightly.

She slumped across his lap, in total surrender. His to do with as he willed. He eased his hand farther down.

"Spread your legs, honey."

It took her a second, but she did, exposing herself gradually. She wasn't sure of this, but she trusted him.

"I'm not going to hurt you. I'm just going to build this fire a little bit more."

Shaking her head, she gasped, "I do not think I can take any more."

She definitely needed more. He wanted her to come. "You can."

Her juices were creamy against his finger, her scent a light spice in the air. He found her clit easily. Hard and distended, it begged for his touch. He rubbed it gently, very gently, easing her back into the sensation, letting the pleasure build gradually, letting her make it happen for herself in the slow pulses of her hips, learning her rhythm as she learned it.

"Shadow…"

"It's all right. Don't fight it. Let me make you feel good." He added a bit more pressure. She cried out and shook, every muscle going stiff as the pleasure crested. "That's it, just like that. Come for me, Fei. Just for me."

He needed to feel it happen the first time. If not around his cock, then the next best thing. Keeping the pressure on her clit, he add a second finger. Going farther, taking more.

She came hard, his name on her lips, her fingers digging into his arm, her thighs clenched around his hand, holding him to her with everything she had. He milked her clit, milked her climax, his own pleasure threatening to erupt as she sighed his name one last time.

Turning her toward him, he lifted her up, cradling her against his chest, kissing her cheek, her chin, her nose, not wanting her alone in that moment, that first time.

"Mine." The claim whispered from his soul, oblivious to their pact, uncaring of the obstacles between them.

Fei clung to his neck, her tears wetting his chest,

her nails pressed into his nape as tiny quivers rippled under her skin. "Yes."

Shit, she shouldn't say things like that to him. He wasn't one of her civilized men. He thought in terms of possession. Of control. And everything in him wanted to keep her. Regardless of the consequences. Cupping her breast in his hand, Shadow kept kissing her softly until she finally relaxed against him.

Mine.

This time he was the only one who heard.

FIFTEEN MINUTES LATER, Fei started to cry. Big fat tears that were prefaced by a near-silent hiccup. When she started to inch away, Shadow almost let her, but as the space between them increased, the dissatisfaction inside him expanded, too. A whisper of a memory came to him then, of being young and hurt, of standing in the dark, afraid to cry for fear of another blow, afraid to remain silent in case this time was the one in which comfort would be offered. He hated those memories, hated to be reminded of how weak he'd been. But what he hated more was seeing Fei wrestle with the same uncertainty.

"Do you want me to try to wake Lin?"

Fei froze, her tunic in her hand. "No."

Another hiccup.

Shit.

"I will be all right."

He knew that lie. How easily people believed it. How easy it was to let people believe it.

I want the real you.

The hell with that. He'd rather give her the man she saw when she looked at him. Reaching out, he cupped her shoulder in his hand. She stiffened beneath his touch.

"Fei?"

She didn't turn.

He didn't know what to say. They sat for a minute, connected yet distant. Her next sob vibrated down his arm. *To hell with it.* With a tug, he tumbled her back to his side. Her hair snagged over his shoulder, tangling with his. She lay there gripping her tunic as he propped himself over her, staring past his shoulder, her composure as fragile as their connection.

He didn't know what to say any more now than he had a minute before. Drawing the backs of his fingers down her cheek, he wiped away the tears. "I'm sorry."

She took a quavery breath and closed her eyes. "It is not your fault."

"Maybe, maybe not, but I'm still sorry."

"For what are you sorry?"

She opened her eyes. The pain in their tear-drenched depths made him want to go out and kill something. Taking her hand in his, he worked her fingers free of the tunic and brought them to his shoulder. "For whatever's making you hurt."

"Damn you." Yanking her hand free of his, she thumped him on the chest, saying something in Chinese he'd bet his last dollar was a curse. "I was in control—"

Catching her fist in his, he tucked it against his chest while pulling her close. "That kind of control you don't need around me."

She sniffed and shook her head against his chest. "The bargain was just for this night."

She felt so small in his arms, so delicate. So right.

The next sob shook her from head to toe. Her palm opened against his chest. Pressed. His senses flared, absorbing the heat of her touch "Do not let me do this, Shadow."

"Do what?"

Her hands crept up around his neck, clung. "Be weak with you."

"You're not weak, Fei, you're just hurting."

"He was my father." Another sob, less contained, punctuated the sentence.

Brushing the hair away from her face, Shadow caught the next tear on the edge of his index finger. "And you loved him."

"Yes, even at the end."

He kissed her then. Softly, gently, the way he hadn't been able to earlier. "Then cry for him."

"It is not fair to you."

Cupping the back of her skull in his hand he pulled her closer, wanting to pull her so close nothing could ever touch her again. "Let me decide what's fair."

She shook her head. "You wanted passion."

"Maybe I lied."

Her nails dug into his neck and her entire body went still. "I lied, too."

Whatever she'd lied about it was tearing her up. "How?"

"I told my father the emperor had found him. That his soldiers were hunting him. If I had simply locked him in he might have tried to escape, but in his mind he was so afraid of the emperor's soldiers he stayed where I put him."

"Fei…"

"It is my fault."

"No." Fisting his hand in her hair, Shadow pulled her head back. "Look at me."

He had to wait, but she did. Finally. And the pain in her face was like a punch in the gut. So was the hope. She wanted pretty words to make it right. He didn't have anything except the brutal truth.

"Life isn't fair, Fei. Sometimes no matter how carefully you plan, no matter how hard you pray, shit just goes bad. You rage against that all you want, but you don't blame yourself. None of this was your fault."

She shook her head. "You cannot know—"

He cut her off. "I know and so do you. Underneath that guilt trying to eat you alive, you know it, too."

Her eyes searched his, seeing more than he wanted. "You know this guilt?" she whispered.

Shit, she saw too much. Brought up too many memories he didn't want to recall. He kept his answer short. "Yeah."

"How did you deal with it?"

He'd buried it so deep he couldn't feel it anymore. "The way that felt right."

Her cheek rubbed against his chest. "I want to cry and scream and rage."

He cupped her head in his hand and cradled her against him. "Then do it."

Her cheek slid against his chest as she looked up. "Where will you be?"

He brushed his lips across her hair. "Right here."

Holding her, and keeping her safe the way she needed. He might not be able to give her forever, but he could give her that.

CHAPTER EIGHT

DAWN BROKE THE SKY with little fanfare. Shadow watched through the leaves of the trees as the pale rays of pink and orange spread across the horizon. Beside him, Fei slept, her head pillowed on his shoulder. That in itself was a novelty. He'd never slept with a woman. When the pleasure was done, he was gone. He didn't like the trapped feeling that came with the morning after, but this time he didn't mind. He was looking forward to waking Fei and watching awareness steal the sleep from her eyes.

Carefully sliding a strand of hair off her face, he touched a finger to the creaminess of her complexion. Nothing marked the differences between them more than the differences in their skin. His skin was darker than hers, rougher than hers. Scarred, whereas hers was smooth. She was a princess, whereas he was the dragon she called him. A glorified lizard, ready to breathe fire. For her.

He wasn't going to leave her. Not yet, at least. Not until he got her safe. And there was only one place he knew where she'd be protected. He kissed the top of her head. "Fei, it's time to get up."

With a mewl of protest, she nestled closer. Her hand slid down to his groin. He'd been semihard all night, but he got harder as her soft palm cupped him.

A few feet away, Lin slept, just as oblivious as Fei to the potential danger all around. Only the innocent slept so deeply. Shadow tried to remember when he'd ever slept like that. He couldn't, but then again, he couldn't ever remember being innocent.

Fei rubbed her cheek against his chest. The hand on his cock measured his length from base to tip, his thickness in intermittent squeezes. His breath hissed out from between his teeth. When he looked down, Fei was watching him with an age-old question in her eyes, and a temptress's smile on her lips.

"Good morning."

"Morning." With an arch of his brow he indicated her hand. "Feeling brave this morning?"

"Maybe." She snuggled closer to him. The trust displayed in the gesture soothed his raw nerves. "You did not have pleasure last night."

"The hell I didn't. Watching you come was very pleasurable."

"That is not the same." She shifted her grip on his cock, encompassing as much as she could through his pants. "It is not a good wife who does not give pleasure to her husband. I very much desire to be a good wife."

Shit. A decent man would remove Fei's hand, give it a kiss and tell her it wasn't the time. He'd just finished establishing that he wasn't innocent and apparently he wasn't decent, either, because not only did he not remove her hand, but when she reached for the ties on his trousers, he beat her to them, ripping them open. There was a lot he couldn't have in this world, but her hand wasn't one of those things.

She hesitated. "Is there a certain way that pleases you more?"

"However you want."

She didn't touch him immediately. Instead, she ducked under the blanket.

"What are you doing?"

"I would see you."

A shiver went through him. She popped out from beneath the blanket.

"It is too dark," she informed him in a soft whisper.

He put his hand over hers. "Then you'll have to feel me."

She smiled and squeezed. "*That* I will enjoy."

The honesty of her desire shot through him like a lightning bolt. His cock jerked. She chuckled. "You like that."

"I like you."

For some reason it mattered to him that she know that it was different with her. That she was unique. He groaned under his breath as she fondled him. Even her touch was unique. She held him as if he were breakable. Caressed him as if he were fragile and milked him as if he were precious. Usually he preferred a rougher touch, but instead of telling her that, he lay still, biting back a moan, and savored the uniqueness of what she gave him. Everything was different with Fei. More intimate. More personal.

"Fei?"

At the whisper of her name, she glanced up. Her lips were parted and moist. Her hand soft and loving. He wanted those lips wrapped around his cock, to slide his length along that hot little tongue, to watch his shaft pump between her lips. Goddamn, he wanted her mouth.

Cupping her head in his hand he dragged her mouth to his, mating his lips to hers, kissing her passionately as she gripped him harder, pumped faster, catching the rhythm of his breathing, dragging his orgasm from him with long, firm strokes. He came in hard spurts, moaning under his breath as the pleasure stole his control.

"Oh, shit, honey."

"You liked?"

He stole the smile from her lips, taking it as his own, growling. She nipped his lip. "You know damn well that I did."

She took a handkerchief out of the pocket of her clothes and delicately wiped up the remnants of his passion. When she was done, she propped herself up against his chest and grinned down at him. "I am a good wife, then?"

"The best I ever had."

"How many have you had?"

"Just one."

"You are funny in the morning."

"Hmm." Closing his eyes he stretched and yawned. "Is that what you think?"

"Yes, and I think I am the reason."

He cracked a lid. "You look pretty damn pleased with yourself."

"I am." Leaning forward, she whispered in his ear, "Did you really wish that it was my mouth on you?"

Had he said that out loud? Pushing her hair out of her face, he checked her expression. No fear there, just, God help him, interest. "Yeah."

"Maybe we can try this next time."

"You've got nothing to prove to me, Fei."

Her face fell. "I disappoint?"

Shadow didn't let her pull away. "Not a goddamn bit."

"You prefer a woman with more..." Cupping her hand in front of her chest, she made her point.

How the hell had she gotten there? "I prefer you." He kissed her hard and fast. "And me." Another kiss. "Going at a speed we both can enjoy."

Her voice rose. "You do not think I would enjoy this?"

He cut a glance at her cousin through the bushes. She stirred but then settled down. "I hope so, but there's a lot of pleasure between here and there that I'd like to explore first."

"It is because I have not known a man?"

"Yes."

"You think I cannot enjoy you because of this?" He

wasn't going there. With a smack on her ass, he slid her to the side.

"I think you could burn me up, but as much as I'd like to find out how much, it's time to get up and get moving."

"To where?"

"To a place you'll be safe."

"Where is this?"

"Unless I come up with something better, home." He was going home. "To Hell's Eight."

"YOU SHOULD NOT PROVOKE HIM," Lin said a half hour later as they foraged for firewood.

Fei shrugged off the criticism. Lin didn't believe in questioning any man at all. "And what else would you have me do? Be the rug upon which he wipes his feet?"

"I think you should have respect for your husband."

The stick she grabbed was stuck. She gave it a yank. It broke in two. "Even if he doesn't intend to stay my husband?"

Lin grabbed a stick out of a thicket and added it to the stack in her left arm. "He is your husband *now.* He fights for you and—"

Fei cut her off. "You mentioned that before, but it doesn't make any difference to him. Fighting is what he does."

"I think it is foolish if you do not try to change his mind."

"He is not a man whose mind changes easily."

Lin didn't meet her gaze. A light flush tinted her cheekbones. "Then why did you lie with him?"

Try as she might, Fei couldn't control her blush. She'd wanted her night and now that she'd had it, she wanted more, not less. "I do not know if there is one answer."

"Do you worry that your father would not have approved?"

The last thought in her mind had been her father.

"The match my father would have approved would not have pleased me."

Lin nodded and shifted the stack in her arm. "I have often thought you would not be a good second wife."

Fei looked up. Lin's blush deepened. "My father spoke to you of his plans?"

"No, but the mix of your blood would mean no good family would consider you for first wife."

She said that so matter-of-factly. Just a fact of her father's culture. But she was not only of Chinese culture. Her mother's blood ran in her veins. And it was to her ancestors she prayed. She hadn't told Lin of that yet. Her cousin was very traditional. Fei didn't know if she would understand.

Lin shifted positions. The way she did when she had something she wanted to discuss.

"What is it?"

"I have not heard of your father's plans for you, but I have heard the uncles talk."

The uncles were her father's five brothers. "What have they said?"

"They do not think it is seemly that you live out here with only your father."

"That's why they sent you?"

"I am only the excuse for their visit."

"Oh."

The uncles and her father fought a lot. If they had come only for a visit her father would have been suspicious. But it was reasonable for them to escort Lin back to Barren Ridge and then on to San Francisco. No proper Chinese woman traveled unescorted. The uncles were very proper. It had been hard to keep her father's illness from them the last visit. The hostilities between them had made it easier. But now they would never allow Lin—or Fei—to stay. It simply wasn't done. It was another complication. "What else have they said?"

"They've started a search for an alliance for you."

Alliance, not marriage. Fei sat down on a log. "They think I will make a good concubine?"

"A woman of your lineage could be a concubine to a lord. There is much power in such a position."

"And what if I don't want to be a concubine?"

Lin sat beside her. "Then you should stay with the marriage you are in."

A few sticks fell off Fei's pile. She bent to pick them up. "He plans to repudiate me."

Lin stood and gasped. Not a stick dropped, even in the midst of her indignation. Lin was always graceful. "You would be shamed before all!"

"Yes, but that doesn't matter."

"You will only be fit to be the lowest of concubines."

If that. And it would be a worry if she planned on letting her uncles control her future. "I understand. But it is the price I must pay to leave here."

"It is too high."

No price was too high if she could have her freedom.

Lin sat down again. "I will intercede with the uncles. I will find you a place in our house."

"You intend to go back to San Francisco, then?"

"Of course. Our family is there. I will tell Uncle Chung that you saved my virtue. He will pay the debt owed with a place in our house."

Fei didn't know Uncle Chung very well. It might be that he was an honorable man, but it was also just as likely that an unmarried young woman in his home would find herself in the role of concubine anyway.

"I do not think so."

That shocked Lin into dropping the bundle of sticks and covering her mouth. "You would be a prostitute?"

No. Never. She carefully straightened the sticks in her pile. "I thought I would become an American."

"Leave your family?"

Lin made it sound as if becoming a prostitute would be preferable. But that was how it was in their world. Family was everything.

"With the exception of you, my family is dead."

"Your father's family in China would take you in."

Fei remembered the disapproving looks when she'd lived there. The cold shoulders. The less-than-choice rooms, the less-than-choice clothes, the always less-than-choice welcome for the mixed-blood daughter of a third son. "I would not be happy there."

"You cannot be alone."

Being alone scared her to death. It went against everything she'd been raised to believe. She'd always lived under someone else's rule and command. It was terrifying to live without that shield, but American women did it. Not frequently, but they did it. "It will not be easy."

"It is not done. I will not let you do this."

There was no way Lin could understand. She was full-blooded Chinese. Her father and mother still lived. She was pampered and adored and very comfortable in California. If Lin's family had known of Fei's father's illness, they never would have entrusted Lin's care to them. There would be much dishonor on her family name if one word of that came out. Fei highly doubted that Lin's family would welcome her into their embrace when they found out how her father had betrayed them. They would feel as she did. That she should have been able to stop it. But Lin did not have to be burdened by that. She'd been through enough this past week.

"You could stay with me."

Lin blinked. "I'm not like you, Fei. I do not crave independence."

Fei knew that. She just had to try, because there were parts of her world she liked. Mostly her friendship with Lin. But it was time to grow up and put childish needs behind her. Lin wanted to go home to San Francisco. Fei would make sure she got there safely. And then she'd make her own plans. "I know."

She headed back to the campsite.

"I knew this would happen, but I hate that our lives are taking different paths."

"It makes me sad, too, but first we are having an adventure." Lin dumped her sticks on the ground and smiled behind her hand. "It is very American to have an adventure. So..." Putting her hands on her hips, Lin surveyed the pile of sticks. "What do we do now that we have cleaned up the forest floor?"

Fei honestly didn't know. She was out of sulfurs and didn't know any other way to make a fire.

"Your new husband didn't leave you sulfurs along with that big knife before hunting for our breakfast?"

Fei tossed her sticks on the ground and glared at the knife, sitting on its sheath, propped against a tree. "No."

Lin smiled and started rebraiding her hair. "Well, I don't think the squirrels will be hiding any."

Fei borrowed an American expression. "Well, shoot."

"What orders did your American husband leave, other than building a fire?"

"What he always says. Stay out of trouble."

Lin sniffed her shirt. "Bathing could not be construed as trouble."

No, it couldn't. Fei sniffed her own hand. Bathing was definitely in order. It would be safe. After all, how much trouble could they get in by taking a bath?

THEY HAD TO GO A LITTLE WAYS downstream to find a place wide enough in the stream to actually bathe. It wasn't the fragrant bath that Fei took at home, but it felt good to get the dirt off her skin and she'd been able to find wild mint with which to scent the soap. She was just rinsing her hair when there was a rustle in the bushes. She thought it was a bird, and as the noise got louder, Shadow. But then she realized as goose bumps raised along her arms, Shadow would not sneak.

Very quietly she ordered, "Lin, get dressed."

She reached for her tunic. Lin did the same.

"What is it?"

"I do not know."

She'd left the knife on the far bank of the stream. Too far to get to quickly.

Stay out of trouble.

It was too late for the mental repeat of the warning. Trouble was here.

What came out of the bushes wasn't Shadow. It wasn't even human.

"Don't move, Lin." From her expression, the other woman couldn't move even if she wanted to.

"What is it?"

"A boar."

There was nothing more fierce. Nothing more unpredictable. And it was staring at them with beady, angry eyes. Fei inched slowly toward the far bank, where she'd left the knife. The boar grunted and pawed at the ground. His tail twitched.

"Fei, he sees you."

"I know."

"Do not move. If you do not move, maybe he'll go away."

The boar took a step forward and tossed its head. Fei inched a little bit farther. The boar squealed. Grabbing a rock, she threw it at the animal.

"Go away!" she screamed. The boar screamed right back, tossing his head again and flashing those deadly-looking tusks.

"Fei," Lin whispered. "Run!"

Mud flew as the boar charged. Jumping to her feet, Fei scrambled to the far bank, splashing through the narrow stream. Her feet slipped on the rocks. Behind her, she heard the boar splash into the water. She screamed for Shadow, wanting nothing more than to jump into his arms and let him handle this.

The knife was just feet away. So was the boar. With a lunge, she grabbed the knife and raised it above her head. The boar kept charging, its stout body moving like a cannonball.

The knife was nothing against such a creature.

"Climb a tree," Lin shouted, throwing a rock at the oblivious boar. Fei held tightly to the knife and bolted. She tripped in the mud. The boar stopped and snorted before lowering its head again. Desperate, Fei reached out. Her hand hit something hard. Grabbing it, she turned and braced into the ground. The boar charged. It was such a puny stick and it was such a big boar. She closed her eyes. The boar screamed. Something warm sprayed across her face. She opened her eyes.

The stick was buried in the boar's mouth. Every time he shook his head, blood sprayed. It was still alive and madder than ever. Every time it lowered its head the stick gouged into the ground. The pain should have stopped the animal, should've made it run away. But it didn't. It just kept trying to come at her.

The only thing that saved her was that stick.

"Hurry, Fei!" Lin screamed.

Yes, she had to hurry. Her legs felt like jelly. She worked her way backward, scrambling toward the knife. When she reached it, she grabbed it up in both hands and held it in front of her like a spear.

"Over here!" Lin called.

There was nowhere to go. No matter which way she tried to run the boar was there, ready to cut her off. So much blood. He had to be dying. She screamed for Shadow. The boar charged again, this time keeping it's head high. Fei couldn't look away from its beady, hate-filled eyes. Time slowed to a crawl. Every detail became magnified. She could see the course black hairs around its snout, the flecks of bloody foam frothing from the corners of its mouth. The brown stains on its tusks. Instinct said *run!* Logic said stand. In her heart, she knew she couldn't win either way.

"Fei, climb a tree!"

There were no trees close enough to climb. None big enough to hold her weight. But she had to try. It wasn't in her just to give up. Spinning on her heel, she sprinted toward the biggest one. If she was lucky, boars couldn't jump and maybe she'd be safe.

The boar squealed. Lin screamed. Fei didn't need either to know the animal was in pursuit. She could hear it behind her, tearing up the ground, gaining with every step. Beyond that she could hear Lin screaming encouragement to her and threats to the pig. It all crashed together in a squall of noise that blended with her heartbeat and the pounding of her feet as she ran. She made it to the tree. With the last of her strength she leaped for the lowest branch, which was two feet above her head, forgetting about the knife in her hand.

The blade nicked her hand. She couldn't get a grip. Her free hand slipped and she fell backward, landing on the boar. With a bloodcurdling squeal it tossed her in the air. She went flying. She hit a smaller tree and slid down. The force of the blow stole the air from her lungs, or maybe it was just terror. It did not matter. The boar was charging again. Random memories of her life flashed across her mind, her father's first lesson in befriending dynamite, her cousin's teasing, her mother's smile and laughter. Laughter. Her mother had been happy.

Fei wanted to be happy, too. She wasn't going to die without knowing what it was like to be happy. No pig was going to take that from her. She brought the knife down, aiming for the back of its neck. Just before she struck, the boar spun, catching the blow midmotion. The knife plunged into its eye, scraping on the eye socket as the momentum drove it forward. For a second, the pig stood frozen, hate and blood mixed together into terrifying threat. And then it dropped like a stone to the ground. No squeals, nothing but a silent fall.

Pinned between the tree and the boar, Fei held her breath, waiting for it to get up. It didn't move and neither did she.

"Is it dead?" Lin called.

Fei didn't know. She didn't want to check. Its mouth, just inches from her foot, was big enough to take it off with a snap.

"Fei? You have to check."

Yes, she had to check. Very cautiously, Fei tiptoed around the monstrous head. Blood seeped from the corners of its mouth and down over its snout from the knife wound to its eye. "I think it's dead."

"Check."

How was she supposed to do that? She nudged it with her toe. It didn't move.

"It's dead."

"Are you sure?"

She wasn't sure of anything. "I do not kill pigs every day, Lin, but it's not moving."

Lin climbed down out of her tree. "Maybe it's pretending."

Fei had heard boars were smart, but had never heard that they could hold their breath. "It's ribs aren't moving."

Lin came over, lifting her borrowed pants legs out of the water as she crossed the stream. She stopped a safe ten feet away. "It's very ugly."

Not as ugly as it had been when it was alive and charging her. "But good to eat."

"Do you know how to butcher a pig?"

"I have seen it done." Once. From a safe, clean distance.

Lin poked the carcass in the hindquarters. "You are going to need your knife."

Fei rubbed her hands down her pants. They came away wet. She looked. Bright red blood coated her palms. Her stomach churned.

"Oh, my fathers! Are you hurt, Fei?"

"No." She wiped her hands on the boar. "It's not my blood."

This close, the stench was overwhelming.

Lin knelt gracefully beside the carcass. "If you were a man, this would be a moment of which to be proud. Your first kill."

Fei knelt beside Lin, still gasping for breath. "If I were a man, I think I would not be wanting to vomit right now."

"You were very brave."

"I was almost too scared to even run."

Lin bumped shoulders with her. "But when you did, you ran like the wind."

Relief bubbled over in laughter. "While you cursed the boar's ancestors."

"I was trying to slow him down, but there was no need. If you hadn't stopped to poke him with the stick, he would've had to follow you all the way to San Francisco."

Fei took another breath into her tortured lungs. "We should thank the ancestors for sending such a clumsy boar."

"What are you going to tell Shadow?"

"That I have breakfast."

Lin reached for the knife. Fei's stomach heaved. "What are you doing?"

"You saved my life. The least I can do is cut the steaks."

"Do you know how to do this?"

Lynn covered her mouth and smiled. "No, but I think, if you can learn to kill a wild boar with your bare hands, then I can learn to butcher it."

Lin gingerly drew the knife from the pig's eye. Blood and brain matter welled. They both gagged. "When he asks where we got the steaks, what will we tell him?"

Fei glanced at the bloody knife and then her cousin. "The truth."

CHAPTER NINE

"YOU GOING TO TELL ME now how you killed that hog?" Shadow asked, hiking Fei up more securely in his lap, enjoying the warmth of her bottom against his groin.

Fei shook her head. "I already told you."

"You tripped."

"Yes."

"And he fell on your stick and then you fell on him and the knife just happened to stab him in the eye. Honey, I've been told enough whoppers in my life to recognize when I've been handed another."

Again, a little shrug that told him nothing. "It is the truth."

"And can you tell me how going hand to hand with a boar is staying out of trouble?"

"The boar picked the fight. I wanted a bath."

He was glad she couldn't see the smile on his face. She was fast on her way to unmanageable.

"You should not be so concerned with how I got it and just be glad that I did. The one rabbit you brought home would have left you with an empty belly."

"Uh-huh. You realize that's not going to get you out of trouble?"

"A full belly helps in all things."

"Not with death."

"I did not go looking for trouble."

"It just found you. Again."

She sighed. "Yes."

"This isn't your house or town, Fei. A lot of things can happen to you out here and all of the dangers aren't human."

"We are sorry," Lin said from behind. "We did not see the harm."

"Sorry isn't enough. If I tell you to stay put, you stay put."

Fei squeezed his hand. "I promise, next time I will stay put."

Shadow didn't want to know how scared she had to have been to make that promise.

"How long before we reach this town?"

"Changing the subject?" he asked with a cock of an eyebrow.

"Yes."

She did make him laugh with that honesty of hers. "We should be there by sundown."

"They are on the stage route?" Lin asked.

"Had enough of my hospitality?"

"It is not what I am used to."

He just bet. "But think of the stories you'll have to tell."

"There have been adventures."

"You don't sound excited."

"Fei is the one who loves the excitement."

Yes, she was.

"While you prefer the quiet of home?"

"I like order."

"Then you'll be happy to hear they also have a telegraph. We can contact your kin."

"Xei-xei."

"Where will we stay?" Fei asked.

Most hotels did not allow Chinese to rent rooms.

"I have a friend who runs a boardinghouse. We'll take rooms there."

"This friend will not mind that we are Chinese?"

"There isn't much that gets Ida in an uproar."

"She sounds like a very nice woman," Lin offered.

"You'll like her," Shadow informed them. "But before you do meet her, we need to go over a few things."

BY THE TIME THEY GOT TO TOWN, they were so well coached that Fei's heart was in her throat. She was used to hostile stares when she came into a new town. Chinese were rarely welcomed with open arms. But what she wasn't prepared for were the looks that Shadow got. He had timed their arrival for nighttime, when he'd be less likely to be recognized. It had made sense to Fei on the way in, but now that they were there, she didn't see where night was helping, because the streets were full of drunken men looking for a fight. The way they were eyeing Shadow, and her, suggested that maybe they'd found it.

Keeping her head down, she silently urged Night on.

"Keep up, Lin," Shadow ordered. Even his voice was

different here. No undercurrents of laughter colored the deep baritone. Here it was flat and hard and…deadly, she realized.

Lin clucked her tongue. The mare picked up her pace.

It was not a friendly town.

From the right side of the street a man called out, "What're you doing with a white woman, injun?"

Her heart sank. They couldn't tell from that distance that Fei was Chinese. That would bring more trouble. Shadow kept riding. "Don't look right or left, honey. Just ride."

She kept her gaze locked between the horse's ears.

"Lin, move that horse up here. Keep tight to me." Lin didn't hesitate. The boardinghouse was, fortunately, only four houses in, but word of their arrival was spreading up and down the street, stretching far beyond where they stopped. The house was a simple two-story building with a wide front porch, whitewashed walls and some of the most spectacular landscaping Fei had ever seen.

Shadow slid off the horse and held up his hands. She put hers on his shoulders.

She licked her lips, feeling the stares like a wall pressing in. "I did not know it would be like this."

"It's not like anything, honey."

"They do not like us."

"It's my homely face they're not happy to see."

He turned and helped Lin down.

"Ain't right, injun putting his hands on a white woman."

The front door of the boardinghouse opened. A big woman with iron-gray hair came to the door, tall and heavy, dressed in a dark blue dress. In her arms, she cradled an old-fashioned shotgun. Stepping out onto the porch, she snapped, "You out here harassing my boarders, Paul Davis?"

"I ain't harassing no one. Just making a stand for public decency. No injun's got call to being so familiar with a white woman. Especially in front of decent folk."

Fei turned around. "He is my husband."

The crowd went immediately from amused to hostile.

"Shit!"

Grabbing her arm, Shadow gave her a shove up the stairs. "Go stand with Ida and keep your mouth shut."

The old lady aimed her shotgun above her head into the crowd.

"Yes, get on up here, sweetie. No sense standing in the street."

"You can't be having those kinds of goings-on in your house, Ida," Paul Davis called out. "It's unnatural. No decent woman or man is going to stay there after such goings-on."

Fei cringed, turned and gasped. Ida just snorted. So much derision captured in one short sound. Fei was impressed.

"Hell, Paul Davis, I let you stay here just last month

with that spiteful wife of yours. If my business can survive that, I don't see how this is going to even cause a ripple."

The crowd laughed. Davis swore. Fei studied the woman named Ida. No wonder Shadow admired her. She was strong and unafraid, and commanded respect all by herself. This was the type of woman Fei wanted to be. This was the future she wanted for herself.

Davis spat. He was a skinny man with a big nose, wild beard and a bald head. "Never understood your fondness for that Indian, Ida."

Ida didn't miss a beat. "Well, I never understood your fondness for drink, so again, I would say we're even."

Fei watched as Shadow positioned himself between the steps and the crowd. Though he was standing, he gave the impression of being crouched and ready to fight. Her dragon. She looked longingly at her pack. A couple of sticks of dynamite would help the situation.

"Lin, get on up there with Fei."

Lin hurried to comply. Her gaze followed Fei's. "I thought Shadow took all your sticks," she whispered.

"He took the ones I had in the pack at Culbart's."

He hadn't thought to check her saddlebag after they'd left the burnt-out ruins of her home.

"She your wife, too?" another man asked.

Shadow straightened. The breeze whipped his hair about his broad shoulders as he stated, "She's under my protection."

Dragon.

A shiver of pride went through Fei.

"Coming into this town with two women you're carrying on with, it's not decent. We won't stand for it."

Shadow's hand dropped to his gun. "*You* won't?" he asked very calmly.

Davis backed up, looking around for support. Like rats deserting a sinking ship, people backed away until there was just Shadow and Davis caught within a semicircle of onlookers.

Ida shook her head and aimed the shotgun. "Paul Davis, you need to move along before I put a little lead in your ass."

"You're not scaring me away on this one, Ida."

"The man brought his wife and his wife's friend for a good night's sleep. It's no different than when you bring over your wife and your sister-in-law. Are you going to be telling me that you're sleeping with both of them?"

"That's scandalous talk!"

Ida just harrumphed and kept that shotgun pointed. "Well, you're creating a scandal here on my porch. If you don't want it thrown back at you, don't be throwing it at anybody else. Now, it's late, gentlemen, and my supper is waiting. So if you don't mind, move along."

"The sheriff isn't always going to be able to protect you, Ida."

"Then I guess I'll just have to protect myself, but for tonight you need to take your nonsense and your alcohol and just go."

"It ain't right."

"Right or not, do it." With a wave of the gun, she ordered, "Someone help him find his way."

A couple of men detached from the crowd and took Paul Davis's arms. Ida waited until they crossed the street before lowering her shotgun, taking Fei's hand and shaking it.

"Ida Bond."

"Fei Yen."

"You're Michael's wife?"

Fei blinked in confusion and then remembered Shadow was a wanted man. He must have assumed a new name. Bowing, she said, "Yes."

"Got a bit of Chinese in you, I see." There was no censure in the comment.

"My father."

"Ah." Ida did an awkward bow in return. "Forgive me if it's not as pretty as yours. My arthritis is acting up."

Fei liked Ida more and more. "I am honored by your consideration."

Ida turned to Lin. "And you're her...?"

Lin took Ida's hand before the woman could attempt to bow and shook it. "I am her cousin, Lin. You have a lovely home. I am honored that you share it with us."

The rest of the crowd dispersed. "It's my pleasure."

Ida called down the stairs, "You know where the barn is, Michael."

Lin cut Fei a questioning look. Fei shook her head. She didn't have time to explain now.

"Unless you moved it, it should be behind the house," Shadow called back.

Ida snorted. "When you get those horses settled, wash up and come in for dinner."

Shadow tipped his hat. "You got any cheese biscuits baking?"

"I might."

"Then I'll hurry."

"As if there was ever a doubt," Ida muttered before calling out, "Be sure to close that door behind you, Michael. We don't want any riffraff sneaking in."

"I swear to God," Ida said, ushering Fei and Lin into the house, "no matter how dire an event, a man never stops thinking of his stomach."

"*Do* you have cheese biscuits?" Lin asked.

Ida chuckled and closed the door behind them, setting the shotgun just inside the foyer. "We will by the time he gets done."

IDA'S HOUSE WAS VERY NEAT. The parlor had two horsehair sofas, a wingback chair and a small table. White lamps with pink flowers painted on the glass shades perched on lace doilies laid on well-polished side tables. On the wall opposite the door, a small fireplace sported a white wooden mantel. On the mantel was a bible. Everything was spotless. It was a room where people would come to relax and talk. It was perfect for a boardinghouse.

Ida motioned to the sofa. "Sit."

Fei was too nervous to sit. She wanted to be with

Shadow. To make sure he was all right. Crossing to the window, she pulled back the curtains.

Ida made mincemeat of her intentions with a slash of her hand. "You're not going to do the boy any good pacing at the windows."

Boy? She would call Shadow many things, but boy wasn't one of them. "I am worried."

Ida sat in one of the wingback chairs. "They won't bother him in my shed. If they're going to do anything, they'll jump him when you all leave town. So, for tonight, at least, you're safe."

For tonight. One night. They were going to be in town more than one night, yet they only had one of safety. A pang of longing for the sheltered upbringing she'd fled struck Fei.

"It is very different here."

Leaning forward, Ida patted her shoulder. "Don't you go worrying about anything. It's a good man you've got there. He'll have it figured out before you wake in the morning."

Lin took a seat on the sofa. Fei didn't see any choice but to join her.

"How did you two meet Michael?"

Again, Lin looked to her. Fei didn't have an answer. How much to tell? What was safe to say? Shadow was a wanted man. He was here under a false name. This woman thought she was his friend. But if Shadow hadn't told her the truth, was she? Ida shook her head at the long hesitation. "Not much of a liar, are you?"

"No."

Lin came to her defense. "There has not been much need to practice."

"Uh-huh. Well, I was going to leave you both here while I went into the kitchen and made some tea, but I think you best be coming with me. You're the jumpy sort. I never trust the jumpy sort."

Fei *was* feeling jumpy and tea did sound good. This time when Lin looked at her, she nodded.

The kitchen was in the back of the house. A large, square room, it had the same feminine, efficient decor as the parlor. Fei liked it immediately, the same way she'd liked Ida immediately.

Fei's mother had always said one could tell a lot about a person by the way they kept their kitchen and this one was neat, well stocked and everything was in its place. A bowl of orange flowers sat over on the cabinet, and some red roses stood in a tall vase in the center of the table. Lin walked over to the roses, touching the petals before inhaling the scent.

"I see you like my flowers."

"They are beautiful."

Ida nodded as she put fresh kindling under the front burner of the stove before filling the kettle from a bucket by the back door.

"I always said there's nothing like a nice display of flowers to brighten the darkest days."

Fei nodded. "I feel the same. My favorite flowers are orchids."

"Can't grow them here." Ida sighed. "But I tried."

"My favorites are roses," Lin said.

"I could have guessed that from the way you went straight for them."

Ida put the kettle on the stove.

"Are these from your garden?" Lin asked.

"Nope, those were a gift." She winked at Fei. "Got me an admirer or two."

Lin gasped and covered her laughter with her hand. Fei was so stunned, she forgot to cover her smile.

Ida laughed out loud. "I know, at your age, it's hard to think that someone my age would have a man interested in her, but life doesn't end at twenty and neither do any of the emotions we live with all our lives. To tell you the truth, inside I still feel twenty."

Fei would like to have that kind of spirit when she was old.

"You enjoy your life."

"Well, about the only choice a body has is to make the most of what they have or just curl up and die." Ida motioned to the right. "Lin, could you bring three cups from the cupboard there?"

"Of course."

Ida took a tin off the table. "Now, would you both like tea?"

"Oh, yes, please." Fei and Lin spoke in unison.

Ida laughed again.

"Been that kinda day, huh?"

"It has been very challenging," Lin said.

"That a polite way of saying Michael's dragged you hither and yon?"

"Yes, but at our request," Fei felt compelled to explain.

"No need to get to his defense. Just because I know him doesn't mean I don't like him. The opposite, as a matter of fact." She put a measure of tea in a perforated metal ball and dropped it in the kettle. "I don't have any boarders at the moment so supper is light, but I've got some ham and fresh bread to go with it if you'd like."

Fei's stomach answered for her, rumbling loudly.

Ida lined up the cups and saucers. "I guess that's a yes."

Fei was so flustered that she forgot her English. *"Xei-xei."*

"You hungry, too?" she asked Lin.

"Yes."

"Well, then, make yourself useful." She pointed to Lin. "There's bread over there. Why don't you get to slicing. And, Fei, you can grab some tomatoes and greens from the basket over there by the window while I get to fixing those biscuits Michael sets such store by."

Ida was like a commander, the way she barked out orders, but it was hard to take offense because there was no meanness in her manner. She was just a woman who liked order.

"Are not tomatoes poisonous?"

Ida shook her head. "Don't go telling me you believe that hoo-ha."

"Everyone knows this," Lin answered.

"Well, I'm someone, and I'm not dead." She poured

the tea carefully into the cups. "I happen to love the things. Can't get enough this time of year."

Fei hesitated, knife in hand. Lin shrugged. Fei sighed. She'd come this far.

"I got me some buttermilk dressing here for our greens. You ever have buttermilk dressing?"

Fei shook her head.

"It's heaven in your mouth."

Right now Fei would eat any kind of dressing, she was so hungry. She wasn't sure what to do with the tomatoes, though.

"Just cut them in wheels, honey." She did, making them as thin as possible. If she were forced to eat one, she'd prefer it thin. There would not be so much poison that way.

Twenty minutes later the back door opened and Shadow stepped in, taking off his hat and hanging it by the door with the aura of a man comfortable in his environment. His hair around his face was slightly damp from washing up. He looked handsome and desirable.

Ida's lined face dissolved into a smile. "Come here and give me a hug."

To Fei's surprise, Shadow smiled and did as he was told. She could only stare as he hugged the old woman back with every appearance of genuine affection.

"Don't go getting jealous there—" Ida said over her shoulder. "I've known him a lot longer than you."

"Are you jealous, Fei?" Shadow asked with a small smile as Ida stepped back.

The knife sliced through the tomato like it was

butter. It hit the wood cutting board with a loud smack. Jealous? She was not jealous just because he gave another what she would want for herself. “If you grin at me in such a way…*Michael,* I will leave your biscuits to burn.”

He came over with the slow easy grace that melted her bones. His hand cupped her cheek, before sliding around to the nape of her neck. Anticipation shivered down her spine. “You don’t like the way I smile?”

She set the knife on the cutting board. “I like the way you smile at me right now.”

His eyebrow cocked up. “And how is that?”

She studied the softness of his mouth, the relaxed crinkle at the corner of his eyes. The genuine warmth in his eyes. She leaned into his hand. “Like you mean it.”

The narrowing of his eyes was the only indication of his surprise. “I always mean it with you.”

Holding his gaze, she turned her head and kissed the inside of his wrist. “Good.”

Heat flared in his gaze. And answering heat gathered in her core. What was it about this man?

“There’s time enough for that later, you two,” Ida called, breaking into the moment. “Right now supper is waiting.”

Shadow didn’t let her go immediately. Fei didn’t want to go. When he touched her, there was a feeling that there was so much more to come. That *they* were so much more.

Ida heaped ham on the platter. “Lin and Fei, you

bring that stuff over to the table, you hear? Michael, you go sit down. We'll get you something to eat."

Ida grabbed a cup out of the cupboard and filled it from another pot. The smell of coffee wafted by as she set the cup on the table. "I know you don't want any tea," she told Shadow.

"Thank you." The smile Shadow gave Ida was different than the one he gave her, Fei realized. It was still warm but lacked…intimacy. Inside Fei that warmth built. His smile for her was special.

"It's for sure I've been missing your coffee," Shadow told Ida.

The older woman nodded brusquely. "Take a seat now. It's not fancy tonight, but it'll fill you up."

When everyone was seated and their plates full, Ida took a sip of her tea. "Now you can tell me, Michael, what foolishness you've got yourself involved with this time."

Shadow took a bite of salad. "Just a misunderstanding, Ida."

"I've known you long enough to know when you're lying to me. You got the look of trouble riding you and it has nothing to do with those yahoos outside. Does it have anything to do with these two?" The sweep of Ida's hand indicated Fei and Lin.

"Now, why would you think that?"

Fei kept her gaze on her plate.

"As much as I like you, Michael, you're a hard man. Hard to know and hard to love. There's no way you'd meet anything this sweet through ordinary means."

"And yet, I'm married to her."

"Which is why I'm asking you for the story."

Fei tensed, wondering what he would say.

"What can I say? I took one look at her face and fell into her arms."

It wasn't a lie. It also wasn't the truth.

Under the table, Lin took her hand and squeezed. Fei squeezed back. "So you two really are married?"

"For the moment."

"What does that mean? Either you're married, or you're not."

That was becoming Fei's opinion. This back-and-forth was wearing on her nerves. And she could not help but think that maybe the ancestors had known what they were doing when they had brought Shadow to her life. She took a bite of salad. Ida was right, the dressing did taste like heaven.

Taking a sip of his coffee, Shadow dashed her hopes with dismissive calm.

"I'm just getting Lin and Fei back to their people. They ran into some trouble a few days back."

"Where are your people?" Ida asked.

"San Francisco," Lin answered. Fei couldn't. Her breath had stopped coming after Shadow's words.

"It's a long way between here and there, especially for two girls alone."

"Lin has family a couple towns over. They'll escort them."

Ida speared some salad. "Do they *know* they'll be escorting her?"

"As soon as they get the telegram I'm sending, they will."

The food turned to ash in Fei's mouth. Now she knew. No matter how pleasurable their time together, Shadow didn't want her. Despite all her vows that it would never happen, she'd ended up a concubine anyway. But it least it had been on her terms. It wasn't as bracing a thought as it should have been.

"I'm sorry," Lin whispered beneath her breath.

Fei tucked her head, relying on her years of deportment training to hide her distress. *"Xei-xei,"* she whispered.

"Ah, so you've got a few days," Ida said.

"Yup."

Fei couldn't bring herself to eat.

"So, who are you hiding from?"

"What makes you think I'm hiding?"

"Please, Michael. It's a safe bet it was a long ride here and those horses didn't look lathered, which means you waited outside town for dark."

"I was coming in with two women. You know how people are. No sense getting them stirred up for no reason."

"But you've got someone stirred up."

Fei licked her lips. "That was my fault."

"Your fault?"

Ida said it as if Fei was incapable of causing trouble.

"I did not like where my cousin was staying. I insisted she leave. There were hard feelings."

"Must have been some fight to have you on the run."

"Let it go, Ida," Shadow ordered.

"Seems every time you ride in here, Michael, you're telling me to let something go. You'd think by now you'd learn it only makes me more curious."

Fei forced a piece of ham into her mouth.

Lin spoke up. "He is protecting my honor."

"Now, *that* I do believe."

"Fei stole me back from men who would do me harm."

"You were stolen."

Lin lowered her eyes and shook her head. Fei knew how embarrassed she was. For a woman of good family to be sold as little more than a slave was an immeasurable loss of face.

Fei swallowed the piece of ham. For a horrible moment she thought it would stick. "My father became ill. In his last days he did things that made no sense."

Ida looked between the three. "He sold your cousin, didn't he?"

"Yes."

"Lucky for you that you had family who cared enough to get you."

Lin nodded. "Yes." Her voice was a bare whisper.

"How long before your cousin fetched you back?" Ida asked.

"A week."

Ida reached over and patted Lin's hand. "Men can be beasts, honey, but the Lord made women so that we can endure. You're going to live a lot longer than any of those men who hurt you. You live well and make that your revenge."

"They did not…hurt me," Lin explained. Her slight hesitation gave her words significance.

Shadow's head came up and Lin looked away. Fei didn't know what to do.

"You were stolen away for a week and nobody touched you?" he asked.

Oh, dear. Dangerous territory. Beneath the table Fei kicked Lin's leg in warning. Shadow cocked an eyebrow at her. *Oh, rats. Wrong leg.*

"Fei helped me."

"How'd you do that?" Shadow asked.

"I did nothing." Trying to catch Lin's eye, she put just the slightest emphasis on "nothing."

"She gave me the elixir."

"What elixir?" Shadow asked, sitting up straighter.

"The special one that makes men not interested."

Ida started to chuckle.

Shadow frowned. "By not interested, you mean…?"

Ida's chuckle turned to all-out laughter as comprehension dawned.

"Are you telling me, girl, that you doused the boy with saltpeter?"

"The hell you did!"

Fei winced at Shadow's exclamation and licked her lips. "It was necessary."

"The hell it was!"

This time she did not wince. This time she met his gaze squarely. "It was very necessary."

The Reader Service - Here's how it works:

Accepting your 2 free books and 2 free mystery gifts (gifts valued at approximately $10.00) places you under no obligation to buy anything. You may keep the books and gifts and return the shipping statement marked "cancel." If you do not cancel, about a month later we'll send you 6 additional books and bill you just $5.19 each in the U.S. or $5.74 each in Canada. That's a savings of at least 17% off the cover price. It's quite a bargain! Shipping and handling is just 50¢ per book in the U.S. and 75¢ per book in Canada.* You may cancel at any time, but if you choose to continue, every month we'll send you 6 more books, which you may either purchase at the discount price or return to us and cancel your subscription.

*Terms and prices subject to change without notice. Prices do not include applicable taxes. Sales tax applicable in N.Y. Canadian residents will be charged applicable taxes. Offer not valid in Quebec. All orders subject to credit approval. Books received may not be as shown. Credit or debit balances in a customer's account(s) may be offset by any other outstanding balance owed by or to the customer. Please allow 4 to 6 weeks for delivery. Offer available while quantities last.

▼ If offer card is missing write to: The Reader Service, P.O. Box 1867, Buffalo, NY 14240-1867 or visit www.ReaderService.com ▼

BUSINESS REPLY MAIL
FIRST-CLASS MAIL PERMIT NO. 717 BUFFALO, NY
POSTAGE WILL BE PAID BY ADDRESSEE

THE READER SERVICE
PO BOX 1341
BUFFALO NY 14240-8571

NO POSTAGE
NECESSARY
IF MAILED
IN THE
UNITED STATES

"Don't mind the boy." Ida waved off Shadow's concern. "There isn't a man alive that can rest peaceably with a woman messing with that part of his anatomy."

She said that so easily, as if a man's anger was nothing.

"There isn't a man who should," Shadow snapped.

"Nor is there a man who should see it as his right to rape as he wills," Fei snapped back.

To her surprise, Shadow nodded. "True, but damn, woman, that's a harsh solution."

"I believe your solution to that crime has always been death," Ida interjected.

"Death's cleaner," Shadow muttered, shifting in his chair.

"I did not give enough to be permanent," Fei offered.

Ida laughed. "Well that's a blessing."

"Mr. Culbart wasn't happy," Lin interrupted quietly.

"Can't imagine he was," Shadow said dryly.

"Oh, my goodness." Ida laughed harder. "It was *Culbart* you doused with saltpeter? That man's as randy as a billy goat and right proud of it."

"He is not so proud anymore," Lin said with surprising vehemence.

"I can't imagine that he is! It does beg the question why he wants you back, though."

"I am hoping by now he has found a more willing woman."

"And one that doesn't make him into a limp noodle," Ida interjected.

Shadow nudged Fei's arm, getting her attention.

"You got any more of that elixir?" She nodded. He held out his hand. "I'll take it."

"It's in my pack."

Leaning back in his chair, he smiled a smile with no warmth, "I'll wait."

At that, Ida grabbed her sides and howled, gasping for breath, managing to get out between guffaws, "You've got him running scared, girl."

As Fei stood, she realized she didn't want Shadow running scared. She didn't want him running at all.

CHAPTER TEN

"HERE WE ARE. This is your room," Ida told Fei, handing her some candles, soap and towels.

Fei nodded. "Thank you." She hesitated in front of the door.

"Nervous?"

Fei nodded and touched her fingers to the glass knob. "We have not been married long."

"Well, I've known Michael a long time and have never known him to be anything but honorable."

That knowledge didn't extend to his real name, which begged the question just how much of Ida's opinion about the man could be trusted.

"When I met him, they were hanging him for stealing a horse."

Ida's eyebrows went up. "Michael steal? Michael's never had to steal a thing in his life. Horses, women, they all come to him. He was born on the wrong side of luck, but he's been pulling himself up ever since."

"I do not know what that means."

Ida patted her shoulder. "It means you have a good man and no reason to worry, but if you're wanting to sleep alone tonight you let me know and I'll put your husband elsewhere."

Fei would love to sleep alone tonight, not to worry about who she had to be or what was going to happen. But at the same time she had so few nights left with Shadow. Wasting them might be a large regret.

"He does not intend to stay married."

"I heard him." Ida smoothed her hair. "I also saw the way he looks at you."

"He desires me."

"And you desire him."

She blushed and nodded.

"More important, you like him." Ida patted her shoulder. "That's a better base than most marriages have."

"But he intends to send me away."

"He's doing what he thinks is best. That's what people who care about each other do."

"For him or for me?"

"If it was the best for him, he'd keep you locked in the bedroom and to heck with the consequences."

Ida was right. "I still do not like it."

"I don't imagine he does, either, but even if you never see him again, it wasn't because he didn't care. So that's something to hold on to. Now," Ida asked brusquely, "where do you want your husband?"

Where indeed? Did she want to hold her hurt or the man? "Here would be fine."

Ida smiled. "I'd want him with me, too. It's good to have memories, even the bittersweet ones."

"I hope so." Because by the time this was over, Fei was going to have a heap to remember. And maybe regret, but her choices were limited and the answers to the ones she could pose always pointed in one direction. Shadow. He was the choice she'd started with and the one she kept coming back to. Bidding Ida goodnight, she entered the room and shut the door behind her. Leaning back against it, she closed her eyes.

What are you telling me, ancestors?

There was no answer. Taking her pack, Fei dropped it on a chair by the bed. She wasn't sure what to do. Should she sit on the bed and wait? Stand by the door? And what was she waiting for? A husband who wanted to bed her? A stranger who wanted her to leave? Or a friend who rested somewhere in between? Whatever Shadow decided to be, when he came through that door, it didn't change who she was. And how she chose to respond to him was her business. No one else's. And she'd already decided she wanted to hold the man.

Placing the soap and towel on the bed stand, she poured a little water into the basin. Dipping her hand in, she let the cool water flow over her fingers, watching the ripples distort the image of her skin. If she believed what she was seeing, her hand was dissolving, insubstantial. But she wasn't afraid, because she knew what was real. Maybe that's all that mattered. Maybe it didn't matter what Shadow wanted. Maybe the difference lay in her perception of what others believed. If she was going to be her own woman and run her own life, then that meant she had to make her own decisions.

And be comfortable with the reactions they brought about.

She turned at the sound of a soft knock on the door. "Come in."

Shadow came in, saddlebags over his shoulder, hat in his hand. He didn't ask permission to close the door, just did it. She rather liked that decisiveness in him. He put the saddlebags down by the chair opposite the bed and hung his hat on a spindle on the back.

"Did you really dose Culbart?"

She nodded.

"Dangerous game you played there."

"It was the only thing I could think to do."

"Men who can't perform tend to get testy."

"Yes, but I was hoping he would not be so testy for a few more days, until I got the gold to buy Lin back."

He nodded. "But you ran out of time."

"Yes. His testiness was quicker than desired."

"How much did he want for your cousin?"

"One thousand dollars."

Shadow whistled through his teeth. "That's a lot of money."

"Are you implying my cousin isn't worth it?"

"No, I'm thinking he'd want to know where you came up with it if you got it, which would just borrow a whole lot of trouble."

"I don't think he thought I could. I think it was a joke to him."

"I'm thinking it might have been part joke, and part of it might have been curiosity. You didn't, by any chance, bring any gold into the assayer's office, did you?"

"As I said before, just a little."

"Ah."

"What does 'ah' mean?"

"'Ah' means you're damn lucky you didn't get the gold you wanted to buy your cousin back and you're damn lucky Culbart's patience ran out and you dragged her out of there, because if you'd gotten the money to buy her, he would have been after you for your claim."

"I didn't think of that."

"I'm not surprised. He had you over a barrel and he was pretty confident he could keep you there."

"Yes."

"How did your cousin end up with Culbart anyway? She's a decent girl, of good family. I can't believe your father selling her didn't raise some eyebrows."

"Culbart is a powerful man."

"Your father seemed to be, too, amidst the railroad, at least. If your father had said no, I doubt Culbart would have up and stolen her."

"The illness my father had made him think strangely. Act strangely. Become sly. I do not think anyone but my father and Culbart truly know what my father did. And only my father knew why."

"And you."

"No. I do not know the why." She would never know that now.

He unbuttoned his shirt and rolled up his sleeves. "Did your father know about your claim?"

"My father?"

"Yes, your father. Did you tell him about the claim?"

"I am his daughter."

"You just got done telling me he was ill and not thinking straight at the end of his life. A smart daughter would not be telling a man like that secrets." He soaped his hands, picked hers up and washed them gently, sliding his fingers over her palms, between them, massaging the muscles at the base of her thumb and in the center of her palm. It felt surprisingly good.

She didn't hear any censure in his voice. "It was my father who found the gold, but then forgot, but no, I did not remind my father of the claim."

"You were buying your way out from under him, too, weren't you?"

She nodded.

"Did he know?"

She shook her head. "He did not even suspect. Chinese daughters do not leave their homes unless they go with a husband."

"But you've decided to be American."

"Yes." It was hard to concentrate with him standing so close behind her, his hands on hers, the heat of his body wrapping around her like a hug. All she needed to do was step away. That was all. It was the one thing she couldn't do.

"Hard choices."

"Yes."

He handed her a towel, then picked up a washcloth and dipped it in the water. He rubbed soap into it.

"Turn around."

She did, but he didn't back up. His hips touched her groin, her breasts his chest, his finger under her chin lifted her face for the gentle wipe of the facecloth.

"What's your choice going to be tonight, Fei?"

"What do you mean?"

"I may not be as honorable a man as Ida let on. Not when it comes to you. It means the day after tomorrow, when Lin's relatives come for her, I am going to send you with them. Give you your fresh start. But tonight, tonight I'm feeling selfish. Tonight I want to know what it's like to make love to my wife in a bed."

He wasn't making sense. "What do you do, Shadow?"

"The hell if I know."

The cloth stroked over her cheek and down over her chin to her neck, hitting the barrier of her collar and then sliding sideways over the nape. It felt cool and wonderful. His hands felt cool and wonderful.

"I've always been on the outside looking in, Fei. Other people's lives. Other people's families. Other people's loves. I've got a price on my head and that's not going to change. Keeping you with me would just bury you with me, and that I won't do."

"But you want tonight."

"Yeah." The first three buttons of her shirt surrendered to his fingers without a whisper of a protest. "Bastard that I am, I want my wedding night."

"I do not know what the female equivalent of a bastard is."

He blinked, cocked his eyebrow at her, and the cloth paused at her collarbone.

"But I want my wedding night, too. I want to stay with you."

"I won't force you."

"I know."

"You've got people waiting for you."

He didn't understand the hierarchy in family. Didn't understand where her mixed blood put her. She didn't correct him.

"You can start over in San Francisco."

Yes, she could. She wasn't going to, but she could.

"I will be fine, Shadow. You do not have to worry about me."

"I seem to do it anyway."

He didn't look as though he liked it, either. She could tell. He hooked his fingers in the tiny buttons on the front of her shirt. She could feel his frustration build.

"If you rip this one, I do not have another."

"Then maybe you ought to do it."

He was giving her a choice again, she realized. If she would not undo the last buttons on the shirt, then it would all end. She would have had her taste of wild and still be pure. Her cousin's family could find her a match, and her future could go on in the way it had always been planned by all the people who had a say. Everyone except her.

She undid the next button and watched his pupils dilate, his nostrils flare. The next button wasn't so easy and, by the time she got to the fourth, her courage ran out. He touched the cool cloth to the pulse pounding in her throat and eased it down into the V she'd created.

She caught his wrist in her hand, wrapping her fingers around the heavy bone and lean muscle. "What's wrong?"

"I find I'm not prepared to seduce my husband on my wedding night."

He froze.

She fought the urge to lower her gaze. "I have that awkward feeling again. I do not know what will please you, if I will please you."

Kindness softened the hard edge. "Are we back to you worrying that these breasts are too little for my taste?"

"American women are much more—" With a gesture in front of her chest, she finished the sentence.

"You're an American now, you said so yourself."

"Declaring it did not make my bosom grow."

Shadow dropped his forehead to hers and chuckled. "Fei Yen? Has anyone ever told you you're an honest woman?"

"I do not believe those are the words that have been used."

"Well, I like your honesty and I like your breasts. They're not too small and your hips are not too wide and your mouth is not too lush."

She didn't know what to make of that litany. A list of her attributes. Was it a condemnation? Was it a compliment?

"Hell." Shadow sighed. "I'm not doing too well here, am I?"

"I don't know what you're doing."

"I'm trying to seduce you, but I'm not doing much of a job."

"Why did you not say so?"

Dropping the washcloth in the basin, he picked her up. "It's one of those things a man isn't supposed to have to say."

As he carried her to the bed, she asked, "You have seduced many women?"

"More than my fair share. Enough that you don't have to worry that I don't know what I'm doing between the sheets."

That wasn't what she wanted to hear. But she, too, found his honesty refreshing, so she didn't complain.

"How many is a fair share?"

"Enough."

"There have been so many you cannot put a number on it?"

"Fei, I don't remember a goddamn one of them right now."

He was telling her he could see only her and that was good. He laid her gently on the bed. His fingers went to work on the tie of her camisole. She glanced at the lamp. He shook his head.

"No. I want to see every inch of you."

"I am feeling shy."

"Then it'll be my job to get you past that, but I don't want to force you."

"You are not, but I find modesty makes me want to throw nos in your face as we go."

"Just modesty?"

She nodded.

"Not fear?"

Ah, so that was his concern. Cupping his cheek in her hand, she looked into his eyes.

"I do not fear you that way, Shadow Ochoa. I desire you. The only fear I have is that I will be clumsy in my desire and you will turn away."

His hand caught hers, his fingers twining between hers, before he tucked them behind her back, arching her into him.

"That will never happen."

She watched the passion flare in his eyes, making them darker still. When his gaze dropped to her mouth, her lips parted, and her tongue teased across the surface in a slow glide, tempting him like a harlot, wanting him like a wife. Never was a long time.

"Kiss me, Shadow."

He did. Hard and passionately. His tongue thrust into her mouth, claiming her completely, while his hands pulled her deeper into the kiss, pushing her further. Passion, so much passion, flowed over her, finding her inhibitions, drowning them.

"Yes."

Did he say it, or did she? Did it matter? In this they were in total agreement. Bringing her legs up, she wrapped them around his waist, binding him to her with everything she had.

"Be very sure, Fei," Shadow whispered, separating their mouths the tiniest bit. "I can only give you tonight."

Only tonight. One night out of a lifetime. One night to remember. Or regret. It was the scariest decision she'd ever made, but this might be the last time that this was her choice. If she went to San Francisco, she'd be bartered. If she didn't, a woman alone could not always guarantee her fate. But she could guarantee that this first time was with someone who cared and someone she cared about.

"Don't make me with child."

His gaze narrowed, his hand came over her stomach almost protectively.

"I won't."

But he wanted to, she could tell. He very much wanted to. And, heaven help her, she could imagine it, too. Turning, Shadow sat on the bed, keeping her on his lap. This was one of her favorite positions. In this position she could feel him from hip to breast.

"Why aren't you nervous?"

"What makes you think I'm not?"

She shrugged and looked away. "You have been with many women."

With an easy push, he spread the camisole open. She closed her eyes.

"But I've never been with you."

That brought her eyes open. Men said pretty things to women all the time to get what they wanted, but

Shadow wasn't throwing pretty words at her. He was giving her the truth.

She gave him a truth of her own. "I love everything you do to me."

"I can say the same."

She could feel him staring at her breasts. Part of her worried and part of her rejoiced.

"I don't know what to do with my hands."

"Leave them where they are." Where they were was on the bed beside her hips.

"If I leave them here, I can't touch you."

"Maybe I want you feeling, not touching."

He made it very easy to feel. Like the skim of butterfly wings, his fingers eased across her chest.

"You're beautiful, Fei. Like fine porcelain. All graceful curves and delicate points."

His thumb flicked her nipple. Too light to give the sensation she craved.

Arching her back, she thrust her breasts up. "I will not break."

But she could. Shadow knew he could break her so easily and not because she was fragile. In some ways Fei was the strongest person he knew, but in others… That honesty she gave him so absolutely meant she was vulnerable to *him*. He wasn't a fool. He knew she thought she was falling in love with him. He knew she weaved daydreams about what could never be. Hell, he'd woven some daydreams himself. He was a bastard for asking for a wedding night. But he wanted a taste of what others took for granted. And he wanted it with Fei.

Still, he had to warn her.

"No matter what happens tonight, you're still getting on that stagecoach with Lin. You're still going to San Francisco."

"Not your home. I understand."

"Good."

He wanted to strip off his pants and free his cock and rub it all over those sweet, pretty breasts of hers, branding the feel of her into his senses. He wanted to press them together and fuck them until he came. Then he wanted to kiss and love them until she came. He wanted to see the pleasure take her senses, see himself reflected in her gaze when she came and whispered his name. Instead, he picked up the cloth, dipped it in the cooling water and wiped it over her chest. Gently. Tenderly. Caring for her the only way he could.

And through it all she watched his eyes, his expression. No doubt looking for disappointment. There wasn't a goddamn thing about her that disappointed him. He meant what he'd said. She was perfect.

He dipped the cloth back in the basin. She caught his hand before he could wring it out.

"What's wrong?"

"I need a kiss."

Hell, so did he. She reached up. He reached down. His hand curved around her head, hers went around his neck. They held on to each other as they kissed. She kissed him with a passion he'd taught her, nibbling at his lips, licking at the corner, easing her tongue between, claiming him the way he'd claimed her but with a feminine demand that curled his toes.

"Fei." Her name came out on a sigh of pleasure. "I'm going to touch you now, honey."

Moaning, she nodded.

He kissed her chin, her cheek, her throat. His hand skimmed up her side, over her ribs, over the curve of her breasts. He cupped one in his hand and plumped it. So delicate. He flicked his thumb over the tip again. So sensitive.

"I want you naked." A little gasp and a shiver.

"I want you naked, too. I want to feel your skin against mine."

He could see it, feel it. *Shit.* She was going to burn him up.

Dragging off his shirt, he gave her what she wanted, skin against skin. Goose bumps chased over her skin. Heat raced over his as he took her nipple into his mouth. She arched, pressing more of her breast into his mouth in silent demand. He closed his lips around the soft peak, sucking gently until it hardened, keeping the pressure even until she shifted and she pulled at his hair.

"Shadow."

That's what he'd been waiting for. That breathless sigh of his name, of which he could never get enough. Replacing his mouth with his hand, Shadow switched his attention to her other breast, pinching her nipple as he nibbled at the other peak, bringing it to the same point of need. When they were both hard and rosy from his attentions, he leaned back and brushed his hair behind his shoulders so there was nothing between him and the beauty of her desire. She watched him, eyes heavy with passion, lips swollen from his kiss, her breath coming in excited gasps. He couldn't wait anymore.

"Stay just like that." Getting out of bed, he shucked his moccasins and his pants. He washed quickly. He expected her to turn away with maidenly modesty, but she didn't. She watched him with an avarice that made mincemeat of his good intentions. The water was cool on his heated cock, frigid on his balls, but the heat of her gaze kept him hard. He took the basin, jerked open the window and threw the water out into the alley below before closing the window and pouring fresh.

Fei held out her arms.

He'd accept that invitation soon enough. "Not yet."

"Yes. Now."

He loved the demand and the reasons behind it. "I haven't finished bathing you yet."

Her cheeks turned as rosy as her nipples when it dawned on her how intimate they would be. He smiled. "You're going to like this."

She held up her arms. Inviting him back into her bed, into her embrace.

"Who's supposed to be seducing whom here?"

"I think we are seducing each other."

She was right, they were.

His cock slid across the silk of her pants as he came

over her. She gasped as he settled between her thighs, letting his cock drop against her pussy. "Liked that, did you?"

She nodded. Watching her face, he did it again, and again, moaning as the friction delivered the perfect pressure. The smoothness of the silk against his cock, softness of her breasts just inches from his mouth became too much, too damn fast. He wasn't going to last as long as he wanted.

With a hard tug, he pulled off the rest of her clothes. She lay before him exposed and shy, but very beautiful.

Sliding up her body. He loved her slowly, rubbing his cock against her clit, driving them both crazy with the insubstantial contact. Her breasts swelled and her nipples hardened, straining for the touch of his tongue.

"Shadow."

He straddled her torso. She was so small compared to him. He touched the tip of his cock to the tip of her left breast, watching her eyes widen, looking for repulsion, finding nothing but interest. He rubbed the head of his cock over the tiny nipple, snuggling it into the crease.

"Oh, yeah." Lightning shivered up his spine. He did it to the other one, too, marking it as his in a primitive way that his soul needed.

"Mine."

Fei didn't argue, just watched him with that quiet anticipation that was hotter than any touch. Taking his cock in his hand, he gave her breasts a little slap before resting the heavy shaft between them. The image of his cock lying between her breasts, looking impossibly thick against her delicate torso, the head just inches from her mouth was almost enough to make him come.

"What do you want?" she asked in a whisper.

Always so giving.

"Just this." "This" was his cock resting between her breasts, thick and hard, dark against her white skin. "This is beautiful."

Plumping her breasts, he pressed them in around his cock. Her skin was damp from the washcloth, creating a bit of ease. He pumped slowly, the tension in his balls gathering. He wanted to thrust just a little farther, until his cock prodded her mouth. He held himself back. This was their first time. Demands like that could wait.

Fei had other ideas. Holding his gaze with hers, she lifted her head, stuck out her tongue and lightly touched the tip of his cock. Another bolt of lightning shot through him, jerking him forward. She didn't pull back, just opened her mouth and took him until the head of his cock rested on the flat of her tongue.

She wiggled it softly.

"Son of a bitch. You don't know what you're doing."

"I know what I so not want to miss, and that's you."

He couldn't help himself then. Fisting his hand in her hair, he supported her head while he fed her his cock with slow pulses of his hips. And she took it, wrapping her lips tightly around his thick shaft, her mouth working in a blissful suction as he pumped in and out, giving her more and more as she gave him more and more.

Shit. He was going to come. Yanking free, he angled his shaft down, coming hard, bathing those sweet nipples in hot come, rubbing it into her skin afterward, whispering her name as he left his mark on her, imagining that it'd always be there, that she'd always be his.

When he could gather a thought, he asked, "How the hell do you do that to me?"

She smiled at him and licked her lips. "I have no idea."

He took the invitation, sliding his softening cock back into that moist heat, letting her soothe the rampaging desire with a swipe of her tongue and gentle suction, as he supported her head, her desires. She didn't seem inclined to let him go.

"You, Fei Ochoa, are one potent woman."

She smiled around his shaft. He kept it up for as long as he could stand, but then very gently he eased his cock from her mouth, moaning as she gave him one last kiss.

"I liked that."

God, so did he.

"There's a lot more you're going to like tonight, honey."

She smiled and stretched. "I cannot wait."

One hard kiss on her mouth and then he was sliding down her body, returning his hands to her breasts, loving them gently, bringing her passion back up as he admired the view. Her pussy was as delicate as the rest of her. Tempting. He could see the soft inner folds peeking out in a kiss of pink. He wanted his mouth on it.

Slow down, he told himself. *Slow down.*

Going back to the basin, he dipped the cloth in water and brought it back to her. Her eyes were big, but not afraid. Thank God, not afraid. He started at her shoulder, letting the cool cloth warm up against her skin, wiping gently at her breasts, working his way down over her stomach to her hips.

"Open for me."

She did, easing her legs apart. He slipped the cloth between, wiping gently at her labia, spending a little extra time at her clit, smiling when she gasped and spread her legs farther. Perfect.

Lathering more soap on the cloth, he cleaned her gently, washing her pussy, her ass, the crease, trailing his fingers behind the cloth, gliding over the rosebud of her anus. She quivered. A tap and she shivered again. She was very sensitive there. His cock snapped back to the ready. He tossed the washcloth back into the basin. Water splashed, he didn't care. He was back at her side before she could lose the heat of his touch.

He circled her breasts in gentle kisses, bringing her passion back up as his hand went down, finding her pussy swollen and wet. "So eager."

"I can't help it."

"No one wants you to help it. This is exactly what you're supposed to be feeling. Burning like I'm burning for you."

"You are burning?"

"Yes."

"Do you ache, too?"

"Yes, for the touch of your skin on mine, for the feel of your breasts in my mouth, for the taste of your pussy. Oh, yeah. I ache."

Taste. He hadn't meant to say the latter, but he was glad he had because the night wasn't going to pass without him loving her with his mouth. He kissed his way down her torso, sliding his hands beneath her hips, lifting her to his pleasure.

He didn't kiss her pussy immediately. He admired it. The thick outer folds with their light dusting of hair opened to reveal the delicate tender flower between. His Fei. So courageous and brave. So intensely feminine. So perfect for him. He had to have her.

At the first pass of his tongue, she stiffened. At the second, she became merely tense. At the third, she relaxed, spreading her legs, arching into every lick, every nibble, moaning when he slipped a finger into her pussy, grabbing his hair when he took her clit between his lips and bit down ever so gently. When he did it again, she yanked. Hard.

"Shadow?"

"What, honey?"

"Do not make me wait anymore."

Ah, shit. "I'm trying to slow down here."

"Why, when I feel that if you touch me just once more I will explode?"

Why, indeed. Sprinkling kisses up her torso, he said, "I want it to be good for you."

Hooking her right leg over his thigh, she rubbed her pussy against his cock, her nipples against his chest. Her breath caught. A flush covered her breasts. Her lip slipped between her teeth. "It is already so good. So good."

Yes, it was. "Don't come."

"I must."

Not without him. Not this time. Pulling back, he let his cock slide down until it snuggled into the well of her vagina. This time she'd come on his cock.

"Open your eyes."

She did, clinging to his gaze as she opened that first little bit. For the first time ever, he felt the clench of her vagina around his cock.

"Fei."

"Oh, the heavens." She arched up, taking him deeper.

With a hand on her hip, he held her still. "Easy. Let it be easy."

Twisting beneath him, she shook her head. "I need you. Now."

Damn it, he needed her, too. Settling his thumb on her clit, he rubbed in time with her thrusts, pressing harder as he went deeper. He felt the barrier of her virginity. Felt it give… Watched the wonder take over as his cock sank deep.

"Shadow!"

He held still within her, feeling every ripple, every quiver as their bodies blended in a primal bonding.

His. She was his. No one else's. His balls pulled up tight. A tingling began at the base of his spine.

"All right?" he asked, his voice harsher than he intended.

"Yes, oh, yes."

"What do you need?"

Nails digging into his shoulders, she sighed. "More. Just more."

He'd give her whatever she wanted. However she wanted it. And right now she wanted him. With another whisper of her name, he braced himself above her, keeping his thumb on her clit, watching her face for the right pressure, the right rhythm. Needing her to come with him this time. Holding back when he felt her stiffen and those first sweet contractions ripple around his penis. Holding back as long as he could, but when her nails raked down his back and she thrust her hips up on a small scream, taking him all, he couldn't resist anymore. With a hoarse cry, he yanked out and came on her stomach, cock jerking, breath rasping as he kept his promise.

Pleasure with no complications.

What every man wanted, so why did he feel so cheated?

CHAPTER ELEVEN

FEI'S UNCLES WEREN'T AT ALL what Shadow expected. He'd been expecting dignified men dressed in the coarse apparel he was accustomed to seeing on railroad workers. The three men who came to the boardinghouse door wore robes of heavy silk, gold rings and a quiet arrogance that spoke of a habit of giving orders. They greeted Lin with dignified excitement, hugging her with their eyes rather than their arms. There was one worry down. Lin's family was glad to have her back. They were a bit more reserved with Fei, but not cold.

When they got to him, Shadow held out his hand. Fei introduced them. Chung was the oldest, a reserved man with gray at his temples. Dao was the middle brother. Han the youngest. "Thank you for coming so promptly."

Instead of shaking his hand, the uncles folded theirs in front of them and bowed. He bowed, too, looking at Lin for an explanation. She just shrugged. Apparently shaking hands wasn't something the Chinese did with Indians. Chung took a step forward.

"We thank you for the return of our niece."

"I didn't have much to do with it. By the time I got there, Fei and Lin had just about rescued themselves."

"They have become bold in their ways since being in this country."

Shadow glanced over to see how Lin and Fei were taking that pronouncement. Fei's fingers were clenched so tightly that the knuckles showed white. Lin merely stood there, head down, seemingly unconcerned. "Sometimes bold is necessary," Shadow replied.

That got him a lift of an eyebrow from Dao.

"It is with great disappointment that we learned of her fate at the hand of our brother," Han said.

"It was a shame how his mind went there at the end," Shadow offered, "but it could have been much worse."

Chung said something to Lin. She bowed immediately and headed for the stairs.

"What's going on?" Shadow asked Fei.

"They wish us to get our belongings."

"Can't help but notice you're not."

"It is just a quick trip up the stairs to get them."

With a motion of his hand, Chung repeated the instruction to Fei with no more success than the first time.

"Do you have a problem with these gentlemen, Fei?"

After the briefest of hesitations, she shook her head. "No. Just that it will be difficult to leave without my father."

"We were saddened to hear of his illness and subsequent death. Jian Tseng was much respected," Chung said.

Han made a motion with his hand and ordered in a voice no less commanding for it's softness, "Niece, please get your belongings."

With a low bow, Fei backed out of the room.

When she disappeared up the stairs, it was Shadow's turn to say, "Thank you."

"For what do you thank us?" Dao asked.

"For the bit about Fei's father."

"We remember our brother as a strong man with great wisdom." Chung sighed. "It is a shame that will not be her memory."

No, Fei's memory would be smoking timbers and guilt.

"I was sorry he passed on."

That much was true. Shadow was sorry because he'd like to kick the son of a bitch in the ass. How did someone who'd raised a woman with Fei's sense of honor and courage fall so low as to sell his own niece?

"With no body to bury, he will not rest with his ancestors," Han informed him.

Was that an attempt to give Shadow peace? Because he sure as shit liked the idea of the man not getting any rest in the hereafter. He had put Fei and Lin through hell. "The fire burned too hot. There was nothing left to salvage."

"We understand."

Fei and Lin came down the stairs, bags in hand, heads bowed.

Ida came into the room carrying a tray loaded with

a pitcher and glasses. "I've got lemonade for all who want it."

Shadow took the heavy tray from her. She didn't give it up right away, looking at him, then pointedly at their guests and shaking her head. Was she worried how it would appear to Fei's uncles if he carried a tray? Did she think he cared? Ida was sixty years old, long past the time she should be taking things easy. She'd done him more favors than anyone else. In her own way, she was a force to be reckoned with, and if he wanted to take a heavy tray from her, he was taking a heavy tray from her.

"Thank you, Ida."

Carrying the tray to the table in front of the horsehair sofas, he set it down.

"Gentlemen?" With a wave of his hand he indicated the sofa and beverages.

Chung declined with an eloquent lift of the hand. "No. Thank you. We have had a long journey and another yet to come."

Shadow sat. "Yeah, you do, but the stage doesn't leave until tomorrow. We have time to talk if you wish."

Another look passed between the uncles as they took seats on the opposite sofa. They said something in Chinese to Fei and Lin. With a bow, both women backed out of the room. Shadow picked up a glass and rested his arm along the back of the couch. A breeze blew through the windows, rustling the sheer curtains. There was only one reason men sent women out of the room.

"You wanted to discuss something with me?"

They glanced at Ida. "It is a private matter."

"This is my house," she said firmly. "If anyone is going to leave, it will be y'all."

"I guess that means she's staying," Shadow said.

Reaching into the sleeve of his robe, Chung brought out a small leather pouch. It clinked when he set it on the table.

"We wish to pay you for your trouble. Lin is very important to us."

No mention of Fei.

Picking up the pouch, Shadow hefted it. From the feel of the coins and the weight of the sack, about a hundred dollars. A hefty bounty. If he were still in the business.

He pushed it back.

"There's no need to pay me."

No one took the gold.

"What will happen to Lin and Fei?" he asked.

"Lin has been betrothed since birth. It is a fine family that waits to welcome her into it."

"She is all right with that?"

Chung nodded. "It is tradition. There have been many meetings, many consultations. It is a good match."

"And he'll still hold to that agreement, even though she was kidnapped?"

"She has said she was not harmed. There will be no loss of face if this is true."

In other words, they weren't going to tell her prospective in-laws about this incident. Shadow agreed with that. No sense borrowing trouble when there was nothing to be gained from it.

"And Fei?"

"We are happy to take Fei into our household," Dao said.

Interesting phrasing. "She will have a place in your home?"

All three men nodded. "Fei went to great lengths to protect her cousin. Our family will honor that. It will diminish her shame."

"Of being married to me."

It was Han who answered. "The shame of being rejected by you."

The shot hit home. "I'm not rejecting her."

"Whatever your reasons, the result is the same," Han replied calmly. "You have repudiated her."

"I'm saving her life."

It was Chung who ended the argument. "Whatever the reason, we agree with the decision."

"And we will deal with the consequences," Dao finished.

Shadow took a breath, steadying the rage within. This was Fei's family. They had her best interests at heart. It didn't matter if they thought him a bastard. "You'll take care of her?"

Chung inclined his head in a semblance of a bow. "Yes. She will have a home. Food. All that she needs."

Shadow didn't ask about husbands. He didn't want to know. This was a good, wealthy family. Lin's life would go on as if it'd never been interrupted and Fei would have a place in their home in their home. Eventually a husband. Maybe children. "Good."

"Well, that much good news calls for a drink." Ida poured four glasses and took one for herself. Shadow picked up his glass and waited for the men to do the same. They raised the glasses, took a sip before standing. Chung set his on the table. The other brothers followed suit.

"We thank you for your hospitality, but we must go. There is much to prepare before our journey."

Shadow stood, too, towering over them. He saw in their manners the culture to which Fei was born. In their clothes and status, the life to which she would return. He told himself it was good. Picking up the pouch of gold, he handed it back to Chung. "Don't forget your gold."

That earned him a measured gaze and a bow deeper than the others. "As you wish."

The men went to the foyer. Fei and Lin were waiting, sitting in the chairs, feet tucked slightly to the side, palms folded, eyes lowered. When the uncles entered the room, they stood.

"It is time to go."

Lin picked up her bag. Chung said something to her and she smiled behind her hand. They turned and headed for the door.

Fei didn't immediately follow. From across the room, her gaze met his. Shadow searched it for some sign of happiness. Relief. There was nothing there. Just that serene calm. Han motioned to the bag and headed for the door. Fei picked it up and fell into step behind him. Shadow remembered when she'd done that with him, how it had irritated him. It still irritated him. She wasn't a goddamn slave.

"You just going to let her leave without a word?" Ida asked him.

"We said our goodbyes already."

Which didn't explain why he was waiting for Fei to turn around, to look at him, to show him…something.

"In all the years I've known you, Michael, you've done some questionable things, but you've never been a fool."

Shadow waited. Just before she went out the door, Fei looked back. There was something in that look. Something important, but before he could decipher it she walked out. The door shut quietly behind her.

He wanted to pitch the lemonade across the room. "What do you want from me, Ida?"

"I expect you to do what's right."

Right was letting Fei go back to her family that would take care of her and protect her. A family that could offer her a home. Stability. A family that wouldn't get her killed.

"This is the right thing."

Ida slapped her dust rag against the furniture. "If you say so."

HE WAS GOING TO GET DRUNK. Stinking, fall-facedown-in-a-horse-trough drunk. And then if he was really lucky, he was going to get in a fight or two. Anything to let off the steam building up inside him.

The town saloon was actually rather nice. The owner, Jimmy, had owned an establishment back East and had the bar shipped out West, piece by piece. The result was a well-polished counter that sat ten on a good night, eight on any other. Shadow took a seat farthest from the door. The customer to his left grunted and shot him a look when he sat down. Shadow summed him up. Sober enough and big enough to give a good fight if the occasion arose.

Shadow tipped his hat back. "Go on, say it, asshole. Give me an excuse."

The man turned away. Jimmy came over.

"Evening, Michael."

"You need some backbone in here, Jimmy. Getting tough to even fish up a decent fight."

"Then you should simply start a fight or just work out whatever's chewing on you with whoever is doing the chewing."

"I don't want any trouble, Jimmy. Just getting a drink."

"Then why are you complaining?"

"Maybe because I don't have a drink."

Jimmy sighed. "What'll you have?"

"Whiskey."

Reaching beneath the counter, Jimmy poured him a glass. Not the rotgut he served the others, but the high-end stuff. Shadow tipped him well for the consideration.

"Leave the bottle."

"Whatever you say."

Yes, whatever he said. Everyone did whatever he said. Shadow pounded back the first two shots, grimacing as the liquor burned down to his stomach. He was doing the right thing by Fei, it just felt wrong because he was a selfish-bastard son of a bitch.

"I ain't drinkin' in a bar with no stinkin' Indian."

Shadow smiled and raised his glass to the patron farther down the bar before taking a drink. "Door's to your right, be easy enough for you to go through it."

"So why don't you hit it?"

This man didn't have the build of the first, but he had three friends who could more than make up the difference.

Jimmy came over on the pretext of wiping down the bar. "Joking over, Michael, don't go starting anything. We've got a new sheriff. He's not as understanding as the last."

"I don't need understanding. Just a drink."

"Why don't you take your bottle on home, finish it there?"

"Because I'm here and I'm comfortable." So was the bottle. Comfortable in his hand.

"They don't serve Indians in here."

He ignored the stranger's comment. The man was a fool and there was always time to get to fools, but right now he wanted another drink. He could still feel, still think, and that wasn't acceptable. He could still see that last look Fei had shot him from beneath her lashes as she went out the door. Inscrutable, but he couldn't shake the feeling that it had been disappointment.

Jimmy snapped out the bar towel and glared at the stranger. "The day you tell me who I can serve is the day you can start paying my bills, Paul. Drink up, Michael."

Shadow tossed back another shot. *Michael.* Michael wasn't who he was. Michael was just a name. He was Shadow Ochoa. Hated. Respected. Admired. Feared. But never fucking ignored. For the past year he'd been Michael, running and hiding, he'd been miserable. He'd done a lot of things the past year that he'd regretted, but none more than hiding who he was so he could be safe.

He missed his brother. He missed the men of Hell's Eight. He missed their housekeeper Tia's lectures. He missed the fights, the jokes, the camaraderie. He missed his goddamn home.

Not that he'd regretted killing Amboy. It would have taken years for the legal action to proceed. And for all those years, the man would have just kept sending assassins, and Shadow wasn't taking chances that one of them might have succeeded. Not with his brother's happiness on the line. Not with Caine's happiness on the line. They'd had so little happiness in their lives. It was worth defending.

He poured another drink, and set the bottle on the counter. A man in a black duster, brown hat and a beard that obscured his features came up alongside and reached for the bottle and asked, "Do you mind, stranger?"

Yes, he did. "You touch that and you're gonna end up bringing back a stump."

The man laughed and kept reaching.

Shadow smiled as the anger gathered in a cold, hard ball in his gut. He flexed his fingers, feeling the familiar energy running through him. This he knew. This he understood.

The man's hand touched the bottle. Shadow grabbed his wrist, twisted it up behind the guy's back and, with a flex of muscle, broke it. With a foot on his ass, Shadow shoved him across the bar. Swearing viciously, the man held his arm. His cronies came up beside him. Shadow smiled.

"It's always best to wait for an invitation."

Jimmy said, "Doc's still in his office, couple doors down."

The men nodded and hustled their friend out the door.

When Shadow turned back, it was to find Jimmy's hand on the bottle.

"Whatever's eatin' you, Michael, you need to take it home."

Shadow shook his head.

"I'm not taking a goddamn thing anywhere until I finish my drink." Inside Shadow, the smile started. This was who he was. Not some white knight, not some stable family man, but this. Shadow Ochoa. Devil. Killer. The bastard nobody messed with.

He sat back down on his stool.

The stool was hard under his ass. The bottle was hard in his hand. The men around him were hard in their ways. This was his world. This is how he lived and this was how he'd die. Maybe women coming into Caine's, Tracker's, Sam's and Tucker's lives had allowed them to change midstream, but a woman couldn't change anything for him and not just because of the price on his head. If he was half the man his brother was, he never would have let Fei go. He would have held her and been what she needed and to hell with the price on his head.

The bell sounded at the stage office down the street. The stage was coming in. When it left tomorrow, Fei would be on it and he wouldn't see her again. He'd have the memories of her softness and the illusions that had come with it, and she'd have her life. It was a fair trade.

Shadow poured another drink and tossed it back. He didn't even feel the burn this time. Always a good sign that he was well on his way to drunk. There was a tingling in his fingers. The barricade that kept the demon inside him weakened.

Four men in the corner, who'd been keeping to themselves since they walked in, glanced his way. The one with the long, dirty-blond hair gestured excitedly. The others leaned in. Their voices rose.

He spun his shot glass on the counter, flipping it over. He might get that fight, after all.

"Go home, Michael."

Michael. He'd picked the name because it sounded

normal. Michael didn't get into trouble. Michael wasn't an outlaw. Michael paid his bills, laid low, didn't cause a ruckus. Michael had had a shot at redemption. Too bad Michael didn't exist.

Chairs rattled as the four men got up. Jimmy reached under the bar for a shotgun. Shadow shook his head.

"No need, Jimmy."

"Looks like they're gonna commit some violence on you."

He nodded. "Looks like the plan."

The drinks hadn't hit him yet, but they were starting to warm his stomach. To a man, the yahoos coming at him were a hard-eyed bunch with the lined faces that came from spending too much time outside. Bounty hunters? That would explain why Jimmy was trying to get him out of there.

He turned as they got closer, resting his elbows back against the bar.

"Can I help you, gentlemen?"

"You might be able to."

He waited. They fanned out around him, blocking him in. Their ages ranged from early twenties to mid-thirties. They wore common enough brown pants and blue shirts. Their hats were equally unspectacular. But their guns were impressive. Worn low, some in single holsters, others in double. Shadow had no doubt they knew how to use them. The one on the right reached for his gun. Shadow had his out and pointed at the other man's head before it cleared its holster.

"I wouldn't do that."

"Put your gun away, Rufus. We just came to talk."

"Do you mind, mister?"

Shadow shrugged. "Talk away. Not sure how much longer I'm gonna be listening, but you've probably got a good five minutes before the whiskey hits and my attention starts to wander."

The kid on his right was still entertaining thoughts of pulling that gun.

"Get your hand away from the hogleg, sonny, or I'm going to put this bullet right between your eyes."

The kid moved his hand away from his gun.

"What do you want to talk about?" Shadow asked the apparent leader.

"Are you the guy that married up with that Chinese gal instead of dancing at the end of a rope?"

They made it sound as it were a sacrifice.

"Yeah."

"Word is, she found gold a while back."

There was no point denying it. Fei said she had brought it to the assayer's office. "I didn't stay with her long, but she did show me a nugget."

The men perked up.

The talker pushed his hat back, revealing a receding hairline. "We'd like to buy you a drink while we talk about it."

"I already bought my drink and there isn't anything to talk about."

"We heard it was real."

That rumor he didn't need to build. "I saw it."

"And?"

He spat. "If it was real, do you think I'd be sitting here in this bar drinking cheap whiskey, talking with the likes of you?"

"No call to get nasty."

"I've yet to get to nasty. Right now, I'm working on pleasant."

They exchanged glances among themselves.

"It was fool's gold," Shadow said.

"She had it assayed," the leader countered.

"Yeah, well, a little problem with that."

"What do ya mean?"

"The assayer is hot to get under her skirts. He told her what she wanted to hear and then went on to offer his services in helping her."

"She pretty?" the young one asked. Again Shadow feigned disinterest. "She's pretty enough that he was willing to put some effort into it."

"She have any more gold around her house?"

"Well, there's no house left. That burned to the ground. But, no, she was right proud of that nugget. Paraded that little nugget around like a favorite son. It's all she had. Saw it shining in the sand. Decided she'd struck gold."

"She found it on a hill?"

"Yep. Just sitting out there in the middle of the desert, pretty as anything. Went and decided she'd struck it rich." He shook his head. "Gotta tell you boys, she wasn't that bright."

Some of the interest left their faces. Gold wasn't just sitting out in a sandy desert. Gold was in rock or in streams where rock had been eroded. But gold wasn't often found sitting atop dry sandy soil.

"So it was a bust?"

"Why the hell do you think I'm sitting here drinking this bottle? I'd thought my ship had come in all because some piss-ass assayer wanted a piece of tail. Shit. I could have been having a good time elsewhere." He poured another glass of whiskey. "Gentlemen. To better days."

The leader, a man of nondescript appearance, a missing tooth and a scar on his cheek, put two bits on the counter.

"Sorry to hear that. Next drink's on me."

Shadow nodded. "Thank you kindly. It'll go a long way to soothe the disappointment."

Jimmy was still standing at the bar with his hand on the gun. Shadow eased the hammer off his revolver and lowered it.

"It's been nice meeting you boys, but now if you'll excuse me, I have drinking to do."

Turning, the men stepped away, headed back to their table and proceeded to talk among themselves.

Jimmy shook his head. "That was close, Michael."

"Not close enough."

"They're a mean bunch, those. They're always sniffing around here, looking for news that someone struck gold, and every time they leave, someone ends up dead and a claim vacated."

"Claim jumpers."

"Yes." And they were interested in Fei's claim. Damn

good thing she was leaving tomorrow, because, even though he'd put some doubt in their heads, if they were true gold seekers, they wouldn't let it go.

The door opened, more sunlight spilled into the saloon. A big man stood there. He had a gut that came from good living, but his eyes were still sharp and his hands stayed limber near his guns. Shadow spotted a badge on his vest pocket.

Shit. The sheriff.

Shadow sighed, poured a drink and chugged it. "Evening, Sheriff."

The sheriff walked over with a hard-eyed look that was meant to intimidate the men he was stalking. The sheriff moved his bottle to the side and leaned against the bar. What the hell was it with everyone touching his bottle?

"Did you break Benny's wrist?"

"Was Benny the bigoted ass with a big mouth and no common sense?"

"That'd be him."

"Then, yes, I did."

"We don't allow fighting in this town."

"Since when?"

"Since a month ago when I came in and took over."

"So you're the new sheriff in town, coming to clean it up?"

"Aye, that I am."

"You might want to start by telling the bigoted asses of this town to keep their hands off a man's booze."

"I might just do that, but in the meantime, you need to come with me."

"Where to?"

"Jail."

Shadow found it interesting that Jimmy's hand was still on the rifle. Maybe the new sheriff wasn't the straight arrow he pretended to be.

"Sorry, Sheriff. I don't like jail." The hairs on the back of Shadow's neck rose just as he caught movement out of the corner of his eye. He turned, lashing out. Something crashed into the back of his head, and the world shimmered out of focus.

CHAPTER TWELVE

"YOU'VE GOT A VISITOR, INJUN."

Shadow moaned as the voice pierced the din created by the hundred hammers inside his head, beating on his brain. A visitor. He cracked an eyelid and raised his head. Bars were all he could see. Dropping back flat, he squinted at the water stain on the ceiling. He was in jail. As soon as the hammers let up, he'd have to see about busting out.

Covering his eyes with his forearm, he muttered to whomever was trying to wake him. "I don't want any visitors."

"I don't think she particularly cares what you want."

She? Had there been a she last night? He had a vague recollection of deciding to get drunk, and looking forward to a fight, but not much else. He looked at his knuckles. No scrapes. Apparently he'd accomplished only one of his goals.

"Who is it?"

"Now, that's not any of your business. She paid for five minutes and she'll be having it."

Paid? Lifting his arm, Shadow peered at the deputy.

"How the hell can it not be my business? It's my visitor."

"It's a lady. So here."

A bucket of cold water splashed over him, soaking his clothes and the bed. Shadow sat up, sputtering.

"Clean yourself up."

Shadow hadn't been in a jail yet where a deputy or sheriff didn't run it like their own personal little kingdom, handing out humiliation as if it was the only way they could get through the day. Apparently this was no different. He sluiced the water off his face with his hands, caught a whiff of his own stench and shook his head. It was going to take more than a bucket of water to get him clean.

The door opened. A small woman, dressed in beautifully patterned silk, her mouth accentuated with a touch of red and her hair elaborately coiled on top of her head, came through the door.

Lin.

With a bow, she told the deputy, "I thank you for allowing me this time, Deputy."

The man openly leered at her. "The name's Ryan. And five minutes is what you paid for." He held out his hand.

Lin placed two coins in it. Ryan kept his hand out. Ignoring it, Lin glided into the room with Ryan on her heels, not stopping until she reached his cell. "Half before and half after, this was our agreement, yes?" she said.

"I've changed my mind. I'll need payment in full now."

Lin slipped her hand through the bars. "Would you hold this for me?"

Two dollar coins rested in her palm. Clever woman. Over her shoulder, Shadow smiled at the frowning deputy as he took the coins. "I'd be happy to."

Belatedly understanding what was going on, Ryan stepped forward. "Hey, you can't do that."

As serene as a summer day, Lin replied, "The handling of finances is a man's duty."

"He's a prisoner."

Lin inclined her head. "Behind the bars of your sturdy jail, so the money should be safe."

"Of course," Shadow goaded, "you could always take it up with the sheriff."

Ryan shoved his partial payment in his pocket and checked his pocket watch. "I'll be coming for that in five minutes."

It was a threat that made more of an impression on Lin than Shadow.

Shadow tossed the coins in his hand. "I'll be waiting."

Lin stood by the cell clearly expecting the deputy to leave. Shadow could have told her he wasn't going to leave voluntarily. The man had buck teeth, bad skin and an odor that outdid Shadow's current condition. It was a safe bet that they didn't get much in the way of female company, and company as exotic as Lin? Well, the man wasn't going anywhere. Not without some encouragement.

"I would like privacy, please."

"I can't leave you alone with him. He's a dangerous man."

"He is behind bars."

"This one's a tricky one."

"I have been alone with him before."

"You have?"

"He is married to my cousin."

That was news to Ryan. And not good news, if his expression was to be believed. "You married up with a Chinese, injun?"

Shadow took off his moccasins and poured the water out. "Who the hell I marry is none of your business."

"What the hell are you going to do about it if I make it my business?"

Just what he needed. A pimply-faced kid making a challenge. "Knock those ugly-looking teeth of yours down your throat."

"Watch your language. There's a lady present."

"I'll keep it in mind."

"You sure you want to be in here with him? A pretty little thing like you could do better."

Like him. The implication was clear. Shadow had to give Lin credit for not losing her breakfast over the thought of stepping out with that piss poor excuse of a man. Rather than puke, Lin nodded with complete composure.

"I am sure. His wife has asked me to speak to him of matters of importance to their marriage."

"*Importance,* huh?" Ryan smirked at Shadow. "Sounds to me like you're not going to be married much longer, injun."

Knocking the deputy's teeth down his throat was becoming more and more enticing. "If my wife had any sense, this marriage would have been over long ago."

From his position Ryan couldn't see the dirty look Lin shot Shadow. It didn't go with the demure dip of her chin and her softly voiced entreaty. "Please, I have given you your money. These are private matters."

Ryan hiked up his pants. "I understand, but a woman like you needs protection."

Lin was shaking her head before Ryan finished. "My father would not approve of me speaking before an audience."

Shit, Shadow thought, if Ryan gave any thought to anything beyond the happy feeling in his pants, he'd realize Lin's father wouldn't approve of her being here at all.

Ryan tucked his thumbs in his waistband and rocked back on his heels in a clear emulation of the sheriff. "That much privacy will cost you more."

The deputy's gaze traveled from the top of Lin's head down to her toes and then back up again, lingering in the middle. "Of course, if you're short on cash, I'm sure we can work something out."

Lin gasped.

Shadow had had enough. "Get your ass out of here,

you little puissant, before I tell the sheriff how you're profiting off your prisoners."

Ryan spat. "The sheriff doesn't give a shit what I do."

"Maybe not, but I bet he cares about not getting his fair cut."

Ryan swore and stomped through the door, leaving it open. Shadow didn't imagine he went far.

Lin reached over and pulled it closed. Ryan immediately shoved it back open. "Rules are, it has to stay open."

"Please, just for a few minutes. I will pay a dollar more."

Ryan held our his hand. "Money up front."

Reaching into her glove, Lin produced the coin. Rolling it between his fingers, the deputy left them alone.

The meekness dropped from her demeanor as soon as the door closed. With a quick smooth of her skirt, she stepped toward the bars and studied the dried blood on Shadow's forehead.

"Are you all right?"

"Just a slight disagreement as to whom the bottle belonged."

"Did you win or lose?"

"I don't remember."

"You all right in there?" The door opened and Ryan looked in. Apparently satisfied with the distance between Lin and the bars, he nodded.

"Call me if you need me."

Lin bowed. "I will."

"Sure you don't want to charge for *that?*" Shadow sneered.

Ryan just grinned and closed the door. Shadow gripped the bars and glared at Lin. He felt like shit and Lin wasn't the woman he wanted to see. "Don't you have a stage to catch?"

"It leaves in an hour."

"And your uncles let you out and about?"

"They do not know I'm here."

"They don't do a very good job keeping track of you."

"They trust in my obedience."

"Obviously a mistake. So why are you here?"

"We need to talk."

"Is everything all right?"

"I am fine."

He couldn't help wondering why Fei hadn't come.

"Did Fei stop to dress up, too?"

"Are you making fun of my dress?"

"No, you look pretty. Real pretty. I think the deputy is going to be dreaming about you for years to come."

She wrinkled her nose. "I would prefer not to be part of his dreams, but I did want to distract him."

Holding the edge of her sleeve in her hand, she brought it across her nose. "Were you wrestling cows last night?"

"Something like that. What brings you here, Lin?"

"Fei."

"So you said. But what exactly, pertaining to Fei?"

"You threw her away."

"The hell I did."

"I want to know why."

"I don't know how much Fei told you about me, Lin, but I'm not exactly the most upright of citizens."

She waved that away as if it wasn't relevant. "You could go somewhere else."

"I've got the whole U.S. Army on my ass and quite frankly I'm tired of running."

"And this is why you did not tell my uncles of your marriage?"

"I told them."

She looked surprised. "Oh." A pause. "You did this to protect her."

"Yes."

She lowered her sleeve from her nose. "Do you know the life that waits for her, Mr. Ochoa?"

He cut a glance to the door. Lin's voice was pretty low, but it was possible the deputy had heard. The last thing he needed was for the sheriff to know who he was.

"My name's Michael."

She blinked and then nodded. "My apologies. I forgot. Mr. Michael, what do you think is the life my cousin will enjoy when she leaves here?"

"I think she's going to have pretty dresses like the one you're wearing. I think she's going to find a nice man of her culture, and I think she's going to forget all about the time we spent together except as a smile in her voice when she talks to her grandchildren about the adventure she had when she was a young woman."

Lin shook her head. "You have no knowledge of our culture."

She said that with a great deal of disgust.

"I know you take care of your own."

"Yes, but what is our own is very specific."

"What does that mean?"

"It means that purity of blood is highly valued. Fei is not Chinese. She is only half. I do not know how it is among your people, Michael, but among the Chinese, a woman of mixed ancestry has limited options."

"You mean she's not going to marry a prince?"

"She will not marry at all. There are many levels of belonging for women of our culture. As I am pure Chinese and of good family, I will marry a man of prominence. The marriage will be arranged for me. I will likely be first wife."

"First wife?"

"I have heard it is not uncommon among many Indian cultures to have more than one wife."

"I was raised white."

"Oh. Well, in Chinese culture a man is allowed more than one wife and many concubines. All have a place in the household, but their status differs. I will be first wife. First wife is a position of great respect and, over the years develops much power, as long as I produce a son. This will be my destiny, because I am of pure blood and good family."

"Fei is of the same family."

"But not of pure blood."

He didn't like what he was hearing.

"My influence right now is small, but I can try to find Fei a position of concubine—"

"That sounds like a mistress."

"It is similar. As I was saying, I can try to find her a position of concubine within my household so I can offer her protection, but my future mother-in-law may not like this. She could see the two of us in the same house as a threat to her power, so I can make no guarantees."

"Just because Fei's mother was American?"

"Yes. Perhaps if Fei were properly submissive and strived more to please, it is possible that she could be second or third wife to a lower-ranked family, but it would not be a happy time for her. Always, she would be taunted because of her blood. And her children, if she were allowed to have any—"

"What the hell do you mean 'if she were allowed to have any'?"

"First wife may decide that such children should not be born so as not to bring shame to the family."

"Son of a bitch."

"No culture is perfect, Mr. Ocho—Michael." She paused. Then, "Fei is not made for such a life. She enjoys her adventures and longs for more. She has always been this way. Even as a child."

I have decided to embrace my American ancestors.

He could see why now.

"Then why did she go with you?"

"You made it clear there was no place for her in your life. The same pride that will not allow her to be concubine will also not allow her to be a beggar for your attention."

"Why the hell didn't she tell me this?"

"You repeat yourself."

"Likely because I'm pissed." He hadn't sent Fei to safety. He'd sent her to hell.

"Where is Fei now?"

Lin looked at the door and then back at him.

"You might as well tell me all of it."

"She ran away last night. I know not to where. She did not leave a note."

"Because she didn't want to be found, or because she was stolen?"

"I saw her leave."

"You saw her leave and you didn't tell your uncles?"

"My uncles are burdened with anger because of my loss of face."

"Nobody knows about your loss of face."

She smiled. "And it will stay that way. But still, they know, and their knowing I am afraid may cost Fei."

So she let her go.

"It's a dangerous world out there for a woman alone."

"Yes."

"And that explains why you're here."

She nodded again. "I know Fei argues and has strong opinions."

"I rather like that in her."

"This I know, too. I came to ask you, Mr. Ochoa—" he didn't bother to correct her this time "—how much room there is in your heart for Fei?"

"A lot of people will tell you I don't have a heart."

"And a lot of people will tell you that Chinese are dumb like mules. Saying something does not make it so."

"No, it doesn't."

"You evade my question."

"Probably because I don't have an answer."

"You do not care for her?"

He cared too damn much. "I kinda stopped myself at the knowledge that she wasn't for me."

"You did not stop yourself from her bed."

That was definitely censure.

"I'm not a saint, Miss Yen, and Fei is a very tempting woman."

"Yes, she is, and only a fool would let a woman like that leave his life."

"I don't recall there being any 'let' about it. She was just as clear about how I wasn't for her."

"Because she is afraid."

"Of what?"

"Of being under a man's thumb. I have no doubt, if Fei were a full-blood Chinese, she would be the empress of our country, so great are her skills. But because she is not, she is held back. In our world, she cannot be what she wants to be. The only way she sees that she can be that woman is to have no one else in her life. It is a wrong thought, but it is the one that she holds."

"And what do you expect me to do about it?"

"I expect you, Mr. Ochoa, to be the man you declared yourself to be."

"And who is that?"

"Hers. For better or for worse, I think are the words of the ceremony in your country."

She looked at him, from head to toe, making him vividly aware of the state of his clothing, his lack of hygiene.

"And right now, I do not think it gets worse for either of you."

With a bow she turned and knocked at the door. And that fast, the competent woman who'd just politely read him the riot act was gone and in her place was the demure proper lady. "That's a nice trick."

She glanced at him over her shoulder and, for once, she didn't hide her smile. "Yes, it is."

SOON AFTER LIN LEFT, Shadow heard the front door of the jail close, followed by heavy footsteps running down the wooden walk outside the jail.

Shit. That couldn't be good. Getting off the bunk, Shadow tested the lock on the cell door. There wasn't a lot of give. Next, he went and tested the window. There was a bit of weakness in the concrete around the bars, nothing a few months of digging couldn't work loose. But the way the deputy had bolted out of there, Shadow had a feeling he wasn't going to get a few months to work on it.

Ten minutes later there were more footsteps along

the walk and then the front door to the jail opened. From the sound of it, the deputy had gone and fetched the sheriff.

"I told you it was him. I heard her say his name and I looked it up."

The statement only confirmed his fear. The door opened and the sheriff came in holding the flyer. Shadow had seen the flyer before. The picture wasn't that flattering.

"You're Shadow Ochoa, aren't ya, boy?"

"I haven't been a boy in a long time."

"Then let me ask you this. How long has it been since you've been Shadow Ochoa?"

"What's the date?"

"June twenty-seventh."

"A year, four months and three days."

The deputy started calculating on his hands. "That'd be about right, Sheriff."

The sheriff shook his head. "He's not disputing who he is, Ryan, or the date of his crime."

"Oh." For a blessed minute Ryan was quiet. And then, "Does this mean I get the reward, Sheriff?"

"We split it fifty-fifty, just like it says in your contract."

"How much is it?" Shadow asked. It'd been a while since he'd checked.

"Two thousand."

Shit. The army was pissed. It might have been a mistake to play those tricks on the colonel, but he'd discovered that living without Hell's Eight didn't leave him with much purpose. And since dead was dead, he'd figured it didn't matter how much angrier the people charged with sentencing him got. But now he'd met Fei, and she was out there somewhere alone, and he couldn't afford to be in jail.

"You and the deputy are going to be rich men."

"And you're going to be dead," Ryan gloated.

The sheriff tapped the flyer against his palm. "You should have had more sense than to pick a fight when you're wanted by the law, Ochoa."

He should have had more sense about a lot of things. "If sense was my strong suit, Sheriff, I wouldn't have killed a man in front of half the U.S. Army."

The sheriff grunted. "You've got a point. I've sent a wire to the nearest army post. Colonel Daniels will be here in two days."

Two days wasn't much time. "Do me a favor?"

"What makes you think I owe you a favor?"

"You don't owe me, but you might want to do this one anyway."

"What?"

"Send a telegram to my brother, Tracker Ochoa. Let him know where I am and what's going on."

"What? And bring Hell's Eight down on my ass? I don't think so."

"My brother's a law-abiding man. So are the rest of Hell's Eight. Texas Rangers through and through. You don't have much to worry about, but it'd mean a lot to Tracker to get a chance to say goodbye."

"And why should I care whether your brother gets what he wants?"

Shadow leaned against the bars. "It's always good to have Hell's Eight in your debt."

"You're being awfully calm."

"Sheriff, there comes a time in a man's life where he just gets tired."

"You're damn young to be tired."

"It's been a damn life. I'm ready to have my trial, to stop running."

"They'll string you up."

"Maybe. And maybe Caine Allen can pull some strings and I'll go to jail."

"That would take a hell of a lot of strings."

"Hell's Eight are owed favors by a lot of people. It's not often it works the other way."

The sheriff drummed his fingers on his thigh.

"I don't think we should listen to him," Ryan interrupted. "Hell's Eight have got a reputation for taking care of their own. You don't get much more 'their own' than a brother."

"They've also got a hell of a reputation for upholding the law." The sheriff pushed his hat back. "Where do you want me to send the telegram?"

Shadow gave him the address, then stuck his hand through the bar.

"Thank you, Sheriff. I'm in your debt."

The sheriff took it. "A hell of a lot of good that's gonna do me. You're gonna be dancing at the end of a rope by the end of the month."

"Maybe."

"Of course, you could just get away with rotting in a jail cell."

But it was also possible he'd escape. Stranger things had happened.

CHAPTER THIRTEEN

HE'D RUN OUT OF TIME. Shadow looked out the window of his cell at the gallows, specially constructed for his hanging. He had to say, the town hadn't spared any expense. The wood was solid, the rope thick, the height sufficient and the angles true. Leaflets had been passed around heralding the event. There was going to be a box social and dance afterward. Someone was trying to rustle up fireworks. His hanging was going to be the event of the season for Barren Ridge. Shopkeepers' only complaint was the lack of time to order souvenirs. The speed of the trial was going to cost them money.

Shadow wasn't sure what strings Colonel Daniels had pulled to get his trial run the way he had, but somehow the bastard had made it happen. Last Tuesday afternoon, right on schedule, the colonel had shown up at the jail. He'd walked through the door, in full uniform, not a speck of dirt on him. He'd stood in front of Shadow's cell and grinned. Just long enough for Shadow to get close enough to reach him through the bars. Nothing more. Just gave him that one-sided grin that made him look like a ghoul, touched his hat with two fingers and left. Three days later, he'd been officiating at the trial that had convicted Shadow. Tomorrow, he'd be standing on the gallows, giving the call that would have Shadow hanged by the neck until dead, and the sanctimonious bastard would likely still be grinning. Shadow gripped the steel bars of the window. He should have gutted that crooked bastard right alongside Archie.

He ran his fingers through his hair, grimacing at the feel. One of the deputy's petty tyrannies had been to deny him a bath. As a method of irritation, it was working. Shadow was pissed. And impatient.

The jail was deserted, as it always was this time of day. Shadow looked through the barred window, down the street. Nothing stirred in the shadows and the only movement in the alley was the meanderings of an old tomcat. No sign of any of Hell's Eight. Not surprising. It would take a week of hard riding to get there from Hell's Eight land. If the sheriff had sent his telegram as promised, on the day he'd promised, and if anyone had been at the ranch to receive it, and if the riders didn't run into any difficulty along the way, Shadow could reasonably expect help to arrive about a day after they put his body in the ground. The rough metal of the bars cut into his fingers. Son of a bitch, the colonel was clever.

Just how clever, they hadn't realized, when they'd been searching for the man who'd been hiring assassins to kill Desi and Ari—Caine's and Tracker's wives. They'd known Archie had accomplices. There was no way Archie could have known what he needed to do without some help, and they'd been sure some of those accomplices had to be high up. But they hadn't suspected Colonel Daniels. He'd been that good at hiding his involvement. It was only after Shadow had killed Archie and been labeled an outlaw that his suspicions had been aroused. There'd been too many similarities between the attempts on Shadow's life and the attempts on Desi. Colonel Daniels had been one of Archie's accomplices, which explained why Desi and Ari's wagon train, a train carrying a wealthy and influential family, had been so ill protected when crossing Indian territory. And why it had taken the army three weeks after the attack to even begin searching for the two abducted girls. Oh, the blame could be shifted through the layer of lower ranks to look like just "one of those things," but it would be easy for Daniels to orchestrate the necessary scenarios. A miscommunication here. A delayed order there.

Shadow let go of the bars and wiped the rust from his hands. The colonel was clever, no doubt about it. But while Shadow was certain that his unorthodox trial would somehow be explained to the higher-ups, the colonel had to be getting nervous. Hell's Eight might be Texas Rangers, but Daniels knew them well enough, or rather he knew Caine well enough, to know there wasn't a prayer in hell that Caine was just going to sit back and let one of Hell's Eight get strung up by a crooked son of a bitch posing as an upstanding member of the military. Rigging the trial would guarantee Shadow's death, but it would also guarantee his own. There was no way Hell's Eight would let that slide.

Even if the other members were inclined to overlook the colonel's actions, Tracker wouldn't. Shadow might not be around to exact revenge, but Tracker would hunt Daniels down, no matter how long it took, and when he found him, no rank, no amount of political influence, would save him. Tracker would find him and Tracker would kill him. Slowly and painfully. Shadow smiled. This time the colonel's arrogance was going to be his downfall.

The deputy came around the side of the building carrying a bulky sack in both arms. Shadow watched as Ryan struggled to haul the heavy load up the stairs to the gallows. He paused at the top, leaning back before dropping the sack. It hit with a loud thud. The tie came undone. Rocks spilled onto the freshly built wood. Ryan swore and quickly looked around to see if anyone had noticed. Shadow shook his head. The deputy would do better finding employment in a mercantile. He wasn't suited to the law. He quickly gathered up the rocks, stuffed them back in the sack and then tied the sack to the end of the rope dangling from the overhead arm. Standing by the lever he looked toward Shadow's cell window and called, "You there, injun?"

Shadow didn't answer.

"You aren't going to want to miss this."

Ryan pulled the lever. Slick as shit, the door opened and the rope snapped taut. Shadow winced as the sack swung on the end of the rope. No doubt he'd swing just as lively tomorrow. He took a breath, recalling vividly how it felt to have a rope slipped around his neck and the air choked from his lungs. He'd prepared himself to die at the end of a knife or at the point of a gun, but hanging had never been in his plans. And tomorrow he was going to do it a second time in one month. More proof God had a sick sense of humor.

"See that, injun?" Ryan crowed. "Tomorrow that's gonna be you dancing and kicking at the end of this rope."

The hell it was. God might have a sick sense of humor, but the devil was in the details and Shadow had a few details still left to see to. Like finding Fei. "I see."

"The great Shadow Ochoa." Ryan spat. The glob landed just behind where the hangman would stand. Where the colonel would likely stand. "Baddest man to ever come out of Texas. Just goes to prove talk is cheap when it comes to a man's reputation. You're nothing more than a drunk who doesn't have enough common sense to stay out of trouble."

A couple of passersby slowed at the exchange. Shadow waved. They hurried on, no doubt to embellish the exchange until it elevated to the level of him being a violent lunatic. The local newspaper did need its headlines.

"Hell, you didn't even put up a fight."

"Doesn't look like it."

The pissant was enjoying gloating a bit too much. Shadow leaned against the bars and glanced up the street. Still no sign of life. “You planning on having a reputation after this, boy?”

“Sure do.” He hauled the bag of rocks back up through the opening to the floor of the platform. “I’m the one who caught the infamous Shadow Ochoa.”

Shadow shook his head. No doubt Ryan had already put that story out there, and no doubt how the capture had come about had nothing to do with the truth. “So you’re the one they’re going to come gunning for, then.”

Ryan froze in the process of untying the rope. “Who?”

The little pipsqueak deserved that spook. “All the men who were once gunning for me are now going to be gunning for you.”

“They don’t have anything against me.”

“Most of them don’t have anything against me, either, son. They just want my reputation, and once I’m gone, they’re going to want yours.”

Even from this distance, Shadow could see Ryan grow pale. “Didn’t think about that, did you, dumbass?”

“Shut up.”

“Rather than playing with those rocks, you’d better get to practicing your quick draw.”

Ryan drew his gun and pointed it at Shadow. “Shut up!”

“Scared?”

“Get away from the window and shut up!” It came out a screech. Shadow chuckled and stepped back.

“Fool.”

"Still scaring little children, Shadow?"

The deep baritone came from behind him. There was only one man with a voice so similar to his. Only one man who could get into the jail in broad daylight without the door scraping or the hinges squeaking, or someone calling a warning.

"Tracker." Shadow turned around. His brother looked tired. More weary than a week's ride warranted. "Good to see you. Thought you were going to miss the big event."

Instead of pushing his hat back, Tracker settled it farther down on his head, the way he did when he was pissed. No anger sounded in his tone, though. "I missed your first hanging. Ari would never let me live it down if I missed the second."

Tracker's wife had been through hell and back. Last time Shadow had seen her, she'd been healing but still fragile. "How is she?"

"Doing a lot better." Tracker walked over to the window that was perpendicular to the cell and looked out at the street. "She's going to make you an uncle in a few months."

An uncle. Shadow shook his head and smiled. Damn. "Well, now I know what took you so long to get here."

"It would have helped if you'd had the good sense to get caught closer to home."

"I wasn't planning on getting caught at all."

"How *did* you get caught?"

"A slight misunderstanding."

"The same kind of misunderstanding that had your neck stretched just a couple weeks ago?" Tracker asked, looking pointedly at the fading bruising.

"How'd you hear about that?"

"I did some checking after I got the telegram you sent in regard to your *wife*."

"Ah. So that's what got your attention."

"Yes. Considering I didn't even know you were near the state, hearing you got married was quite a surprise."

He hid the truth in sarcasm. "I got homesick."

"Then you should have gotten your ass home," Tracker retorted.

"You know I couldn't do that."

"No, I don't."

"Then you should have."

Tracker looked around the cell. Shadow knew what he saw. One threadbare blanket, a wooden bench and the remains of last night's dinner rotting on a plate on the floor. Ryan was enjoying his role as king of the jail.

Coming back to the cell, Tracker asked, "So, where is your wife?"

"Gone."

"Her doing, or yours?"

"She's not the kind to cut and run."

Tracker nodded, sending his long, black hair sliding over his shoulders. "So, your decision."

"Hey, injun, you're going to miss the next test," Ryan called.

"Are you just planning on standing here and chatting all day until the sheriff and deputy come back in?" Shadow asked.

"No, I thought we'd bust you outta here in a spell."

"You couldn't have done that before the trial?"

The front door opened. Caine slipped in. Right behind him came Sam followed by Zacharias. Zacharias didn't come into the cell area. Instead, he nodded to Shadow and took up a defensive position by the outer door. Of all the Hell's Eight men, not counting his brother, Shadow felt the strongest kinship with Zach. They both had the same darkness inside. The same cold practicality when it came to getting the job done. The same drive to right all wrongs. The same drive to protect.

"No. The trial was necessary," Sam offered from where he was searching the sheriff's desk.

"How so?"

"Can't get you a pardon if you're not convicted," Caine pointed out.

"You got the governor to give me a pardon?"

"Working on it. It's an election year. He's worried about how being associated with Hell's Eight will look to the voters."

"He wasn't too worried about how it was going to look when we got him out of that bind with that prostitute who was blackmailing him in regard to the boy he'd been dallying with."

"Yeah, well, politicians have convenient memories."

"Unfortunately," Caine explained, opening the chest by the door and taking out Shadow's gunbelt and knives, "the governor and his wife have an understanding. She doesn't comment on his sins and he doesn't comment on hers."

"So she'll cover for him?" Shadow asked.

"With as many alibis and excuses as he needs to walk away smelling like a rose."

"Mighty nice gallows they built you out there," Sam interrupted, looking out the window. "Don't think they're taking any chances with the rope breaking."

"Yep," Caine concurred. "That's definitely a rope to do Hell's Eight proud."

Shadow couldn't help the smile. Damn, it felt good to spar with his brothers. "Go to hell, all of you."

And they *were* his brothers. It might have taken a year of being cut off from them for him to understand it, but he got it now. Sam, with his blond hair, easy smile and intense way of looking at things, and Caine, with his green eyes, brown hair and deadly calm, might not look anything like him, but they were as much his brothers as Tracker was. He'd never accepted that, always thinking that it was blood that made family, but there was a connection there. He'd die for any of these men. And they'd die for him.

"Looks to me like you've already been there and brought some of it back with you." Caine shook his head as he got closer. "Don't they give you a bath in here?"

"The deputy is right considerate. Once a day I get doused with a bucket of cold water."

"Is the deputy that pissant out there, thinking he's

got a sense of humor?" Tracker asked, looking through the window.

"Yup. I think it makes his morning."

"Uh-huh."

Shadow knew what that *uh-huh* meant. Tracker was taking notes. That didn't bode well for the deputy.

"Notice you got the sheriff to send the telegram," Sam said.

"You sound surprised."

"I just never suspected you had sweet talk in you."

"I've hung around you long enough to pick up a few tips."

"Maybe his new wife taught him something before he kicked her out," Zacharias called.

"I didn't kick her out."

"Hell, Tracker, you're right," Sam mocked. "He probably doesn't even realize he does it."

"What's that?"

"Kick people out of your life under the pretense that you're protecting them."

"The hell I do."

"Didn't take you long to get rid of us after you killed Archie," Tracker stated quietly. There was something in his brother's tone that snapped Shadow's head around. He studied his scarred face. Hell, since when did Tracker get hurt?

"I'd just murdered a man in front of the army."

"We could have handled the army," Caine said.

"The hell you could."

"Not after you ran."

"You wanted me to stick around for the hanging?"

"We had a plan," Caine snapped. "You didn't even give us a chance to enact it."

"I have trouble watching the people I love die."

"But you expect us to watch you die," Tracker cut in.

"I don't."

"You do."

"You have trouble being beholden," Zach said from the other room.

Shadow bit the inside of his lip. This he hadn't missed.

"So what've you been doing the last year, Shadow?" Caine asked.

"This and that."

Sam grinned, gathering up some papers from a drawer. "We heard some of your 'this and thating.' Did you really get caught in bed with the mayor's wife up there in Cheyenne?"

"I wasn't technically in her bed."

Folding the papers, Sam tucked them into his shirt. "It's not like you to be unaware of your surroundings."

"You haven't seen the mayor's wife."

"Beautiful women were never your downfall."

"Doesn't mean they couldn't be."

"What I'm more interested in is how you got your own horses stolen from you," Caine interjected.

"I had a bit too much to drink."

"So you decided to steal them back?"

"I had a bit more."

"And you got caught?" Caine asked with the relentless way he had of getting to the truth.

"That was the end of the bottle."

"Hell, Shadow. What's happened to you?" Sam asked.

"I killed a man."

"You've killed plenty of men."

"Unfortunately, I killed the one who had the ability to take it all away."

Tracker stilled. "All what away?"

It was harder than he had expected to admit it. "My purpose."

"You always had purpose, Shadow."

No he hadn't. He'd had a code he had lived by, pain he had reacted to and anger he had fed, but none of that was purpose.

"Time to go," Zacharias interrupted. "Ida's here."

Shadow went to the window and looked out. Sure enough, Ida was coming around the corner. She pushed a cart laden with covered plates. "What has Ida got to do with this?"

"Ida is going to keep folks busy for us while we slip you out."

"You involved Ida?"

"No. Ida involved herself. As soon as she saw Tracker, she demanded explanations and then demanded to be allowed to help," Sam corrected. "She likes you. And believe it or not, she considers it her right to help you."

"I don't want her involved."

Sam snorted and took the keys off the wall and tossed them to Tracker. "Get his sorry ass out of there before he does something else stupid."

Shadow covered the lock with his hand. Tracker looked up, his expression impassive.

"There's no going back if you do this."

The muscles in Tracker's jaw clenched and the scar on his cheek turned whiter. Tracker shoved his hand aside. "There's no going forward if I don't."

Tracker had a beautiful wife and a child on the way. A future. If it were ever discovered he'd broken his brother out of jail, it would all disappear.

"You've got a family."

A muscle in Tracker's jaw twitched. "And you're a part of it."

"Not like this."

The key turned carefully in the lock, making minimal noise. "Any goddamn way it comes, you're my brother."

What the hell was he supposed to say to that? The door opened with a soft creak. Shadow didn't step through it.

"What about the deputy?" Shadow said.

"Let him play with the gallows while he can," Tracker said. "He's gonna have a rough day tomorrow when he has to explain why the guest of honor's gone missing."

"How *is* he going to explain that?"

"I don't give a shit," Tracker answered.

"You should." Shadow didn't want Tracker hurt because of him.

Shadow stayed put. Tracker glared at him, that stubborn set to his shoulders. Shadow wanted to hit him. Tracker had achieved the one thing they'd given up hoping for. A loving wife. A home. A place where he belonged. Security. And now he was throwing it away.

"I'm not worth it, brother."

Tracker grabbed him by the arm and yanked him out, shoving him toward the door. "Shut the fuck up."

Shadow spun around. "What the hell is your problem?"

Tracker matched him glare for glare. "You."

Caine stepped between them, slamming his hands into their chests, separating them. "Now is not the time for this."

He was right. Shadow reentered the cell and grabbed his hat and jammed it onto his head.

"Anybody see you come in?" Shadow asked.

"Nobody that'll tell," Caine said.

That didn't mean anything. "They're gonna suspect."

Caine handed him his revolvers. "Can't convict a man on suspicion."

"Have you met the sheriff here? I'm not so sure."

"He'll be paid off."

Hell's Eight always paid their debts. Shadow fastened his belt, feeling more himself as he tucked the end through the buckle.

"What's the first thing you're going to do when you get out of here?"

He could tell Tracker was worried it was going to be "get a drink."

Taking his sheathed knives from Caine, he answered, "I'm going to get a bath."

"And then what are you going to do?"

Fei's image came to his mind so vividly that he wanted to reach out and tuck her hair behind her ear, wrap his arms around her shoulders, kiss the worry from her eyes. From beyond the door, he could hear Ida yelling. The distraction had begun. He slid the last knife into the top of his moccasin.

"And then I'm going courting."

SHADOW HAD TO WAIT two days for the bath, and it looked as if it was going to be even longer before he could start courting. Colonel Daniels was not taking his escape well. After two days of riding in circles eluding the posse that wouldn't quit, they'd finally camped for the night in a hollow about a day's ride south of Fei's claim and a day's ride east of Barren Ridge. Rolling up his bedroll, Shadow looked to the east. Dawn was finally coming. The men were sitting around the fire in various stages of readiness. Sam was leaning back against a rock, hat pulled down over his eyes, eking out a few more minutes of sleep. Zacharias was sharpening his knife on a whetstone. Tracker and Tucker were repacking their saddle bags. Caine was sipping coffee. And Shadow was coming out of his skin. Somewhere out there was Fei. Alone and vulnerable, no doubt trying to attempt the impossible.

"Son of a bitch."

"You say something, Shadow?" Caine asked.

Shadow yanked the rawhide tight around the blankets. "Just thinking out loud."

Caine nodded. "Had a few of those moments myself." He took a sip of his coffee, grimacing before spitting out some grinds. "So this woman we're about to hunt down, what does she look like?"

"Last time I saw her, she was about this high." Shadow put his hand to just below his breastbone. "Slender, almond-shaped green eyes with flecks of amber, small nose, lush mouth, long, thick black hair—"

"Hell," Tracker interrupted, glancing over at Caine. "He's a goner."

Shadow stood and kicked dirt over the fire. "What? I can't notice a woman?"

"Oh, you might notice a woman, but string that many words together about her?" Sam shook his head. "That's a dead giveaway."

"I just had to hear him use the word *lush,*" Caine said. "Not sure I'm going to survive that shock."

Zacharias's knife scraped across the stone loudly in an abrasive interruption. "Does your Fei have any special skills she might be using for a job?"

"She's an expert with dynamite."

Zacharias glanced up at him from under his hat brim, his expression inscrutable. "And she didn't blow your sorry ass up?"

"She happens to like my sorry ass."

Tucker tipped his hat back. "Liking your ass aside, it's doubtful she could use a skill with explosives to get a job."

"She has before." When everyone looked at him, Shadow explained, "She pretended to be her father when he took ill."

Caine quirked an eyebrow. "She posed as her father?"

Shadow shrugged. "No one gets too close to the explosives. Put on a big hat and the right clothes, and as long as the job gets done, who's going to question it?"

Caine picked up his rifle and brushed some dust off the sight with his thumb. "True. But that still takes guts."

"Fei's long on guts."

"So, a brave woman who might have changed her appearance?" Zach surmised. "She might not be easy to find."

Shadow ran his hand around the back of his neck. "Probably not."

"And why would she want to change her appearance?" Caine asked.

Shadow dropped his hand to his side. "She has a habit of pissing people off."

Sam tipped his hat up. "Like who?"

"Culbart thinks she stole from him."

The shadow from the flames danced across Tracker's face, alternately hiding and defining the deep scar on his cheek, taking him from handsome to vicious in a subtle fluctuation of light as he asked quietly, "Did she?"

"Literally or technically?"

Caine braced his rifle against a fallen log and withdrew his revolver from the holster. "Let's start with technically."

"Her father sold her cousin to him. Fei took her back."

"A woman who understands family," Sam observed. "You could take lessons from her."

Shadow had about had it with Sam's digs. "Do you have a problem with me, Sam?"

Beneath the brim of his hat, Sam smiled that itching-for-a-fight smile he was famous for. "Nothing that can't wait."

Shit. He didn't have time for this.

"Where do you think she'll go?" Caine asked, cutting off anything else Sam had to say.

"To her claim."

"Claim?" Zach asked.

"She found gold, which is why she married up with me in the first place. She was desperate."

Sam laughed. "Shit, she really did marry you in the middle of a necktie party? I thought that was just shine on the back of a tall tale."

Shadow wished. "You and me both."

Tracker asked the question Shadow could read in everyone's eyes. "Why?"

"She needed the gold to buy her cousin back, but she

couldn't get the gold out of the claim without protection."

Both Caine's eyebrows went up. "And she thought the hangman's noose was a great character reference?"

Shadow couldn't explain that himself. "Somewhere between the rope going around my neck and the hanging, she decided I was the dragon she'd been waiting for."

The steady rhythm of Zacharias's sharpening faltered. "She thinks you're a lizard?"

"For your information, in Fei's culture, a dragon is a noble beast. A warrior. Defender of the weak."

"She thinks you're her hero," Tracker said quietly.

"Yes."

Tucker slapped a mosquito on his neck. "Have you seen the gold?"

"Yeah."

"Hard to move gold around without somebody knowing," Zacharias observed.

Shadow nodded. "There are some claim jumpers circling around her already."

"Do you think she got the gold out yet?" Caine asked.

"I don't think she's had enough time."

"But if she did, where would she be headed?"

"San Francisco."

"Didn't she run away to avoid going there?"

Shadow had told them all he knew about Fei. Including how they'd parted.

"Yes."

"Then why change her mind?" Sam asked.

"To free her cousin."

Caine slid the revolver back in the holster. "Does her cousin want to be freed?"

"I believe Fei's going to offer her something she's never had."

"And what's that?"

"A choice."

Caine got to his feet and dumped out the rest of his coffee. "Well, then, I guess it's time we find Fei and her pot of gold."

CHAPTER FOURTEEN

A FRESH START WASN'T as easy as Fei had hoped it would be. Walking down the street of Simple, a town two stops along the railroad route west of Barren Ridge, checking windows for help-wanted signs, Fei began to consider the possibility that she'd made a mistake leaving when she had. She'd been worried about being lost in San Francisco, of being swallowed up by the crowds as she started over. Of being in a place where her skills had no value. But in small towns, a woman alone stuck out, she was discovering. Employment was also scarce and her skills had no value.

Was this what you wanted to protect me from, Father?

It was galling that her skills had no value not because there wasn't a need for explosive experts. There was a big need, but because no one believed a woman could actually do the job, she couldn't get a chance. She paused at the edge of the walk, waiting for a buckboard to pass. Humiliation burned over her anew as she recalled the way the railroad crew chief had laughed in her face, refusing to even allow her to demonstrate her skills. She'd wanted to light a stick of dynamite and stick it down his pants. Instead, she'd had to stand there and listen to him offer her another job, that of camp girl. She stepped down off the walk into the street. In fact, the only employment around seemed to be that of camp girl, but she wasn't desperate enough to take that position. Yet.

It was on the way back from that interview that Jewel had been stolen. Fei had only left her for a moment. Just long enough to pick some berries to ease her hunger. She'd heard a startled whinny. By the time she'd gotten free of the brambles, a man was galloping away with her horse. Without her horse, she couldn't get to her claim. Not only would it be a two-day walk, but once she collected the gold, it would be too heavy to carry out by hand. As she stepped back up on the walk on the other side, she discreetly checked the small cloth purse tied to her hip, hidden by her long tunic. When she'd left Barren Ridge four days ago, she'd had to wrap the coins to keep them from jingling. Now, with only three coins left to pay for lodging and supper, she could walk down the streets with no fear of detection. Money did not go as far as she'd thought. Just one more eye-opening realization she'd discovered on her road to independence.

Stopping, she took a breath, trying to soothe the panic. There was only enough money to pay for tonight's lodging, but not tonight's supper. She had no prospects. No hope. She fingered the coins as she passed the telegraph office. No options. The rhythmic *tap-tap-tap* of the telegraph machine followed her down the walk, lured her back. Looking through the window into the dim interior, she watched as the man tapped out the code that sent messages across the distances, connecting families in wondrous ways. Such a marvelous machine. It could be the answer to her problems if she were willing to accept the life someone else deemed right for her. It would be so easy to send a message to her uncles. So easy to sit on this bench and wait for them to come. And they would come for her. It would be a loss of face not to.

They likely would lecture her, too, mostly because it would be a loss of face not to. It wasn't that they were bad men. Her uncles loved her in their way, and wanted the best they could give her. They just didn't understand why she wasn't happy with what was, in their mind, proper. They'd found her a very respectable match. Second wife to a firstborn son of a good family that owned several small grocery stores in San Francisco. His business was set to expand. The uncles said he was of good temperament, very fond of his first wife, who was of delicate health. It was because of his love for his wife that he was looking for a second. He wanted to ease her burdens. It was, actually, an excellent match.

Sighing to herself, Fei sat down on the iron bench set up in front of the office. So why couldn't she jump at it? It sounded as if her prospective husband was a kind man. One who would likely make minimal demands on her. Marrying him would provide her with a secure life. Not a perfect life but a good one. Why couldn't she see it as anything but prison?

Shadow's face popped into her mind. Handsome, strong and resolute. He'd sent her away without a word of apology, his jaw set in that way that said there would be no arguing. And she'd gone without a fight, partly because that's what she'd been raised to do, to follow a man's orders, and partly because she hadn't known how to fight such a wall of resolve. And she regretted it. She should have fought. She'd wanted to fight. But she hadn't and now she was left with frustration and regret, whereas he…? She sighed and forced herself to accept the truth.

Shadow was probably hundreds of miles away from here by now. In another town. With another woman. Moving forward with his life. Enjoying a future that didn't include her. Moving on in ways she couldn't. Grabbing tightly to the handle of the bench, Fei clamped down on the pain and forced herself to admit the truth. She hadn't asked and he hadn't promised. Their marriage had ended the way it had begun, spontaneously, without a lot of discussion. She would have begged if she thought Shadow would have listened. She would have argued his belief that sending her to a life she abhorred would be better than whatever time she had with him. Would have. Could have. They plagued her. Why hadn't she at least tried?

Shadow had told her going away was for her own good. He'd told her she would be happier elsewhere. He'd told her, and she'd listened, as if he knew it all.

And yet he hadn't even asked her what was waiting for her in San Francisco. How she felt about it. He'd been so arrogant, believing that his right to take care of her was greater than her right to take care of him. And she'd allowed it. She should have at least told him what a crock of bull it was. There was a lot she could have done, including telling him that if he wanted another woman, she'd get her father's cooking knife and castrate him.

Fumbling in her pocket, she searched for her handkerchief before the tears could fall. She'd done a number of stupid things, but bawling in the middle of the street did not have to be one of them. How could he even think of being with another? She couldn't. Not as wife. Not as concubine. Not even as convenience. In her heart, she was Shadow Ochoa's wife. In her heart, he was her husband. She just didn't know what to do with that. Stay. Go. Accept. Fight. A tear escaped her control. Her handkerchief escaped her detection. Would nothing go right this day?

"Looks like you could use this."

A crisply folded white handkerchief was pressed into her hand. She took it as a second tear joined the first. The handkerchief smelled of bluing and wool.

"Thank you."

"You're welcome."

She looked up. The man was not overly tall, nor overly broad. The most prepossessing thing about him was his dark blue uniform. It was well dyed, beautifully cut and sported an assortment of braid and medals.

She motioned with his handkerchief. "I will have it laundered and returned."

The man smiled, a one-sided stretch of his lips. "Keep it for as long as you need."

Despite the friendliness of the words, the smile made her uncomfortable.

"May I may be of assistance?"

"No." She shook her head, sniffing back another tear. "I will find the answer."

"Are you sure? I'm not without some influence."

Fei looked at his uniform again. Likely he did. A belated sense of caution kicked in. "You are a military man?"

"Around these parts, I am *the* military man."

Shadow's enemy. Did he know who she was?

Lowering her gaze, she stood and bowed.

"I am honored to be assisted by such an important man."

"I assure you, ma'am, the honor is all mine. Now, if I cannot help you, could I at least have the pleasure of your company for lunch?"

Her stomach chose that moment to rumble.

"Would that be a yes?"

She shook her head. She chose an obvious excuse. "My family would not approve."

"What objection could they have?"

"I am Chinese."

He slipped his gloved finger under her chin and lifted her face. The touch was coldly dispassionate.

His gaze became assessing. With his thumb, he tilted her head to the side. “Not fully.”

She jerked her face free. Even though he wasn’t a large man, he was still much bigger than she. And something about him made her think of coiled snakes in tall grass. He made her nervous.

“No, I am not.” She took a step back and bowed, effectively escaping his touch. “I must go.”

“Before you go, is there someone I can speak to?”

“In regard to what?”

He reached into his vest pocket and pulled out a piece of paper. With a smile, he handed it to her. “I’d like you to be my guest to the box social in Barren Ridge tomorrow.”

Barren Ridge was four hours away. Why would he invite her there? She took the paper. “I do not understand.”

“I’m told this is the most exciting event that has happened around here in years.”

Looking at the flyer, she felt the blood drain from her face. Centered at the top of the page was a sketch. It was both clever and horrific. It was Shadow, yet not. A demon caricature of him. In the drawing, he was portrayed as a knife-wielding monster with a head larger than the rest of his body. Around his neck was a spiked noose. The caption read: Caught At Last.

They were going to hang her Shadow. At the bottom were instructions on how to enter a basket in the box social. And they were going to have a dance afterward. She wanted to throw up.

"Shadow Ochoa has been terrorizing the state for years now. It's going to be quite a celebration."

"Why do they call him a savage?"

"He's half Indian."

And she was half Chinese. That meant nothing. She touched the sneer the artist had etched into Shadow's face. They'd made her dragon a demon and were planning on dancing on his grave. That could not happen.

She handed the flyer back to the man. "I do not even know your name."

"Colonel Jeffrey Daniels." He bowed. "And what's your name?"

Keeping her gaze lowered, she allowed a hint of distress to enter her gaze. "I am sorry." She looked down the street is if she feared being watched. A proper Chinese woman would never be seen in the company of any man, unescorted. Least of all a white man. "I must go."

Any hope she had that he would just let her walk away died the moment he fell into step beside her. She glanced up the street again, as if fearing to be caught. "Please, you must go."

Instead of moving away, he inched closer. When she would've slowed and let him go by, his hand curved under her elbow.

"I'm afraid, ma'am, that I'm going to have to insist on accompanying you."

She stopped dead. "Why?"

He stepped in front of her, hemming her in.

"Because you have something I want."

Slipping her hand under her tunic, she grabbed the purse and yanked it from the belt. She held it out. "This is all I have."

He didn't take it. "I think you have more than that."

"I don't understand."

His "You will" lingered in her ears. With pressure on her elbow, he forced her back down the sidewalk. A woman in a black dress and a perky, feathered hat approached. Fei wanted to cry for help. Pain shot up from her elbow, crippling the impulse. The woman, oblivious to Fei's distress, nodded as she drew even. "Good day to you."

The colonel touched his fingers to his hat and nodded back with a slight smile, maintaining the illusion that they were a couple out for an afternoon stroll. "Good afternoon."

Fei nodded and walked, her mind racing. She had to help Shadow. She had to help herself. She had to escape.

They came to an alley. Instead of crossing, the colonel pushed her into it. She stumbled a few steps before stopping and planting her feet. Again, he stepped in front of her, so close that his cologne stung her nostrils. Keeping her gaze down, she asked, "What do you think I can give you?"

"Shadow Ochoa."

"He is in jail." She waved in the direction of his pocket. "They are going to hang him tomorrow night. It says so on the paper you showed me."

"It seems Mr. Ochoa did not like our accommodations."

"He escaped?" Relief put a quaver in her voice. Hopefully, he would think it fear.

"For now. I'll get him back."

"I won't help you."

"Yes, you will. Mr. Ochoa is very fond of you."

She dipped her head lower, not having to fake the shame. "He used me."

He reached out. She stepped back. He was quicker than she had expected. His gloved fingers slid behind her neck, a parody of the caress that Shadow so often used, but it didn't excite when this man did it. When this man touched her, a chill went down her spine.

"You didn't spend that much time in your marriage getting to know your husband, did you?"

"It was a very short marriage. It ended when he threw me out."

"I highly doubt that."

Tipping her coin purse, she spilled the contents into her palm and held it up to his face. "This is all there is between me and starvation. If Shadow loved me, I would have more."

Daniels shook his head. Clearly, he did not believe her. "Shadow Ochoa has a habit of disposing of those he loves. He tells himself it keeps them safe."

"Well, if it is true, it is not working very well."

"I want him back."

She gave up feigning calm. "So do I, but I don't think either one of us is going to get our wish."

"You may be right." His thumb stroked her neck. "As a matter of fact, I'm going to let you convince me you're right, which means I'll need a different form of compensation."

Rape? He was going to rape her. Fei looked around. There was nothing in the alley except a couple of crates, tossed to one side. Nothing stood out as a weapon.

"No."

She jerked away. He pulled her back. From the street end of the alley came men's voices. The colonel pushed her up against the building. His forearm hit the wood above her head. His body pressed into hers while his hand came around her throat. His mouth lowered to her ear. From the corner of her eye, she could see the men passing, laughing. Just ten feet away. Ten impossible feet.

His fingers tightened on her neck. "If you cry out, I'll cut your throat."

She believed him. "What do you want?"

"Shadow or the gold. Either one."

SHE WOULDN'T GIVE HIM SHADOW. Even if she could, she wouldn't. He read the answer in her eyes.

"So I guess it will be the gold, then."

"Why do you think I have gold?"

"I see a copy of every assayer's report that comes out of this state."

"But I only found the one nugget."

"No, you didn't."

"How do you know?"

"You don't lie well."

Yes, she did, but that would be another thing she would work on. Lowering her eyes, she whispered, "We will need horses."

He eased his hand off her throat and straightened. "That's not a problem."

"I will also need my things."

"You're not hoping that someone's going to rescue you when you get to the hotel, are you?"

"No. That is not one of my hopes." Being able to get what she needed out of her room without him noticing? *That* was one of her hopes.

He took her elbow. "Let's go."

The whole way to the hotel, she held on to a wish, almost a belief, that someone should notice she was being held captive. At least they should look at them twice, but nobody looked at the army officer and the Chinese woman. In reality, nobody looked at her at all, but they all looked at him and she had to admit, he did cut a striking figure in his uniform. Part of it had to do with how he carried himself. The rest had to do with how well his uniform fit and the utter cleanliness of it. She looked at his gloves. There wasn't a smudge in sight. The colonel was a very precise man.

"How did you find me?"

"There aren't many women who look for jobs as explosives experts. Word gets around."

She cursed herself. She hadn't even thought of hiding that.

They arrived at the hotel without incident. It was a simple three-story structure with modest decor and a clean interior. They catered to families. An unmarried woman alone was suspicious, so she wasn't surprised when, as soon as they entered the lobby, the clerk called her over. Daniels stayed with her, his hand on the middle of her back. As if she needed the warning.

Bowing, she greeted the clerk. "Hello, Mr. Brown."

Keeping his voice low, the clerk informed her, "I'm sorry, Miss Fei, we don't allow gentlemen up to our female guests' rooms."

She didn't need the colonel's painful grip on her elbow to know he didn't like that.

"You do not rent rooms to men?" she asked.

The challenge was slapped down. "This is not a saloon. We do not allow fraternizing above stairs."

The gentleman in the corner reading a newspaper folded the top to look at her. A woman coming down the stairs ushered her son out the door faster than was necessary. Fei's blush was not feigned.

"Oh, my."

She didn't know what to say or to whom.

Daniels's lopsided smile gave her the shivers. "I'm sorry, darling, it wasn't my intention to ruin your reputation when I suggested we come get your trunk."

"We didn't mean any disrespect, sir, but this is a decent hotel for families," Mr. Brown said.

"I understand."

"If the lady needs help with her trunk, we have a bellboy who could assist, if that would be acceptable?"

Fei's "That won't be necessary" was overridden by the colonel's "That would be appreciated."

"Of course." The clerk rang a bell on the desk. A middle-aged man came out of the back.

"Miss Fei will need help with her trunks."

The man nodded and waited. Daniels reached out and stroked the back of his fingers down Fei's cheek. "Don't take too long, darling. We've got an appointment in ten minutes."

She kept her expression demure and her eyes downcast through sheer force of will. "Of course."

Her room was on the second floor. She took the stairs as quickly as she could. The bellhop lagged behind, likely not in a hurry as he knew he was going to have to wait on her anyway. Reaching her room, she quickly entered and closed the door behind her. She didn't have much time.

Dumping out the trunk, she lifted the false bottom. Four sticks. She only had four sticks left. Tearing at a petticoat, she started ripping strips of material off the bottom. Grabbing two sticks of the dynamite, she tied them to the outside of her right thigh and then two to her left. Putting on the petticoats over her clothes, she tied them before pulling her blue cotton dress over her head. Buttoning it quickly, she stuffed the sulfurs in the pocket. In the other one, she stuffed her map. Smoothing her skirts, she checked her appearance. The dynamite wasn't noticeable. On the floor, amidst the shirts and dresses, was her gold nugget. Her good-luck charm. She picked it up. For a moment she just stood there holding the nugget, inner panic flaring.

The colonel would kill her as soon as he had what he wanted. She had no doubt of that. She assumed he was telling the truth when he said Shadow had escaped. Maybe he was telling the truth about the other, too. Men tended to know more about their enemies than about their friends. And Shadow was an enigma to her. It had always felt like love when he touched her, but then he'd step back and the feeling would be gone. So the colonel could be telling the truth or he could just be spinning her a lie because he needed her to believe it so he could recapture Shadow. And quite frankly, she was tired of guessing.

A knock came at the door. With minimal fuss, she tossed a pair of pantaloons, a new shirt and skirt, stockings and a sweater into her pack. The rest she shoved back into the trunk. Then she hurried over to the door, vividly aware of the dynamite strapped to her thighs, the chances she was taking. Fingers on the doorknob, she stopped and took a breath. Catching a glimpse of herself in the mirror by the door, she smoothed her hair. Everything looked to be in place. It was time to go. She opened the door.

"Your trunk?" the bellhop asked.

"I have decided I only need a pack."

After a second, he held out his hand. She gave him her bag. He motioned her out the door.

On the way down the stairs, she discovered that deciding it was time to do something was a long way from being comfortable with doing it. When she got to the landing, her knees were weak and her hands were shaking. There was no time to give in to panic. The colonel was waiting at the bottom, one foot on the first step, one hand on the railing.

"I was just coming to look for you," he informed her as she descended the stairs.

"It took longer than expected," she told him when she got to the bottom.

His pale blue eyes went from her to the porter.

"Where's your trunk?"

She halted on the step in front of him. "I decided all I needed was the pack. We are coming back, aren't we?"

"Of course."

He was lying.

The porter handed him her bag. The colonel's smile was a false stretch of his lips as he handed the man a coin. "Thank you." Adding several more, he said, "And please see that the lady's room is held for the next week."

So much money spent on an illusion that didn't matter. Why did he bother? she wondered.

"Of course," the desk clerk said, motioning the porter over and collecting the coins.

Fei reached for her pack. The colonel smiled and tucked the pack over his shoulder. "I'll carry that, my dear."

Of course he would. Holding the front door open for

her, he waited for her to pass through. As soon as she was level, he said, "You changed your clothes."

The comment snapped just behind her ear. She jumped. His hand came down to the center of her back, touching lightly, letting her know he was there. That he was in control. It was hard to swallow.

"It is uncomfortable to ride in my tunic and pants," she lied. She needed the skirts to hide the dynamite. "The material is too thin."

"I'm not complaining. I don't approve of that heathen garb anyway."

Heathen. He was calling her heathen and he was the one doing the kidnapping. Instead of spitting out the truth, she kept her gaze down and her hands meekly folded. Her ancestors had known one thing, men relaxed around a woman they thought submissive.

"While you were gathering your items, I sent a boy to have our horses brought around."

He motioned to the rocking chairs. "Please sit."

It wasn't a request. It was only the illusion of choice. She gave him the illusion of gratitude. With a bow so shallow as to be an insult, she said, "Thank you."

"I can see what Shadow liked in you. It's a nice change to have a woman around who does as she's told."

"A woman's place is cherished at her husband's feet."

He sat beside her. "Maybe later we'll test that out."

Maybe by then she would be gone. The dynamite felt heavy on her thighs. She could only hope it didn't slip. Had she tied it tightly enough? Had she tied it too tightly? The only way she would know was if it fell off, or if her legs got numb. Waiting to find out just put a finer edge on the night. The colonel reached into his vest. She stiffened.

"No need for nerves. It's just a journal." He held it up. He opened the cover and she knew immediately there was nothing "just" about it. There were dates and columns and precise areas of structured writing.

He took a pencil out of the spine and turned to a page three-quarters of the way through.

"You write in this book?"

"Yes."

"Why?"

He closed the book and tied the leather flap down. With equal precision he tucked the pencil into the spine. "It's good to have a record. There will come a time down the road when people will need to know what I've done. I don't want the newspapers and the biographers creating fiction because they don't have fact."

"It is your life story?"

He turned so fast she jumped back. "Do not refer to my life's work as a *story*."

"I am sorry."

"People don't always understand why leaders have to do what they do."

"You wish to be understood?"

"Of course."

"Do you put all in the book? Good and bad?"

"How else would there be context?"

She had no idea.

Three men rode up the street leading two saddled horses. Daniels stood as the riders approached.

"Colonel."

"Men."

The men did not have the colonel's neatness of appearance. They looked like what they probably were, opportunists. Men who did whatever they needed to for coin.

Daniels glanced down his nose at her. "Do you need assistance?"

Getting out of the chair, no. Getting up on the monster horse they brought her, likely.

"I do not know."

"Well, since daylight's burning…"

Grabbing her by the waist, he tossed her up onto the big chestnut. She clung to the saddle horn, glad she hadn't strapped the dynamite to her waist. *"Xei-xei."*

"I do like the way you say that."

"I will remember." *And never say it again.*

He smiled, grabbed her horse's reins and turned them south.

"I just bet you will."

CHAPTER FIFTEEN

BY THE TIME THEY REACHED the claim, their number had grown to twenty and Fei had run out of fear. Not that she hadn't started out with a fair share, but every hour they'd ridden she'd watched, prayed and hoped. But no miracles had occurred. No heroes had appeared. After twelve hours, she'd decided she would have to save herself. By the fourteenth hour, she had a plan. By the fifteenth hour, she was prepared to enact it. The horses plodded into the clearing.

"We're here."

The men looked around. "I don't see anything."

The colonel pulled out his revolver. "Playing games now would be very foolish, my dear."

The revolver didn't scare her. They wouldn't kill her until they knew for sure they had the claim. "It is here."

She slid off the horse.

"Where are you going?"

She walked stiffly up to the boulder. "The way is through here."

The men dismounted and tossed the horses' reins over a bush. The horses immediately ducked their heads to eat. It had been a long ride. "Where?"

She slipped behind the boulder. The colonel grabbed her arm and hauled her back out.

"Oh, no, you don't."

"But this is the way…"

The man called John came over. "Damn narrow space. Do you think it's a trap?"

"Send her in first and see."

John gave her a push. Daniels yanked her back. "Not without some guarantee we can get her back."

"What do you suggest?"

He grabbed some rope. "Fix it so we can reel her out." He tied the rope around Fei's waist and knotted it tightly in back. John tossed him a thinner rope. Daniels used that to tie her hands in front of her, and then to secure them to the thicker rope at the back of her waist. She stood, waiting patiently. She couldn't implement her plan until she was in the cave. The colonel stroked her hair off her face. "You look very pretty like that."

She bowed her head, giving him the impression he wanted.

"Just get her in there. This place gives me the creeps."

With a shove, Daniels sent her into the cave.

THE CLAIM WAS EXACTLY as she and Shadow had left it. The bag of food tins they had brought still sat by the mouth of the cave. The saddlebags for carrying out the gold were on the far wall. The blankets and pillows she'd started to lay out were neatly bundled ten feet apart on either side of the fire pit. It was as if it was all waiting for her, eagerly anticipating the time she'd pick up the threads of her original intent and fix all that had gone wrong since she'd disobeyed Shadow's order to stay put and stay safe.

The claim was the same, but everything else was different. *She* was different. She wasn't scared any longer. Not of making a decision anyway. Daniels and his men were not going to have her claim. They weren't going to have Shadow. And they weren't going to have her.

Behind her, she could hear the colonel and his men struggling to pass through the opening. Once they succeeded, she wasn't going to have much time. Rummaging awkwardly through the food sack, she located the knife and cut through the rope that bound her wrists and then sawed through the one on her waist, the pieces falling to the ground. She took the sulfurs and map out of her pocket and stepped out of her dress and petticoats.

From beyond the rock entrance, she heard the colonel curse when the tension left the rope. "Fei Yen!"

Her heart leaped to her throat. It was now or never. Lighting the lantern, she moved farther into the cave. She set it on a rock and looked at the map. She focused on small scribbles that looked like pebbles. It'd been two months since she'd checked the explosives her father had laid out. She needed to be very sure where the connections were. She wasn't going to have much time once the series started. The narrow entry to the cave was only a delay, not a solution.

"Goddamn it, girl, your ass better be there!"

It was, but it wasn't going to be there for long. Her hands shook. One way or another, she was leaving.

"Get the hell out of the way, John," she heard Daniels order.

"Why? So you can get the gold for yourself?"

Fei picked up the lantern. The flickering light cast grotesque shadows along the wall, highlighting the dug-out areas and the shored-up tunnels. There was fresh dirt around the openings. The claim was less stable than before.

"Take off your gun belts, and strip down, goddamn it," she heard the colonel say.

It was time to go. Following the marks on the map, she walked around the perimeter of the cave, checking the fuse connections at each of the three tunnel openings that led deeper into the cave. The left one led to the waterfall. The center one was a dead end. The third narrow, ramshackle tunnel *looked* like a dead end but actually snaked around behind the waterfall. Getting to it was the key to her plan. If the explosions started from there, she could escape out the back of the cave, leaving the men trapped in the center. Buried. She shivered at the horrific image. Her stomach turned, but she buried the weakness. These men had killed others. Would kill her and Shadow. They needed to be stopped. She could stop them—she couldn't think beyond that.

Fei finished checking the front section and headed into the left tunnel to the back. She hated the back of the cave. There were steep ledges that crumbled to deep drop-offs along the carved-out path. When placing the charges, she'd almost fallen to her death when a narrow part of ledge had given way under her feet.

Putting the memory out of her mind, she picked up the sack of gold she'd reserved for herself months ago and dragged it close to the ledge. She searched the floor, looking for the connection. She couldn't find it and began to panic. She took a deep breath and looked again. There was a spill of pebbles on the ground that didn't look natural. She gently pushed them aside and found the connection, but she didn't remember laying out pebbles like that. She sat back on her heels. Her heart pounded in her throat, her breathing stuck in her chest. She also didn't remember tying those wires together.

"Fei!"

She jumped at the loud echo of her name. Daniels and his men had made it into the cave.

"Where are you?"

She didn't answer, just quickly moved on to the next location.

"Shit," she heard one of them mumble. "There's no gold here."

Something was dumped on the floor. "The hell there's not. Look at this!"

They'd found the gold she'd collected before she'd gone to free Lin. Good. That should keep them busy. The next connection was the same as the first—the wires connected and covered with pebbles. She knew she hadn't done that, which begged the question, who had? Her heart started racing an the sick feeling in her stomach grew.

There was a hoot when the men found her supplies. Cans clunked against stone as they emptied the sacks out on the ground. She had to hurry. The gold pulled on her shoulders, dragging her down.

"Follow the stream. I think I hear a waterfall back there."

"Usually do find gold in rushing water." She thought that might be John.

"Nature's shovel is what I call it."

It made it easier for Fei to find the other connections now that she knew what she was looking for. Her muscles burned as she strained to carry the weight of her load as she went from point to point. A little voice inside said *leave it,* but she couldn't. It was her fresh start. Shadows danced on the walls as she passed, rocks scraped under her feet. *Too much noise. Too much noise.* She tried to walk more carefully. Instead of silence, she started a little landslide. Sound reverberated around the cave. Pressing against the wall, she watched the ceiling, expecting it to come down any minute. It didn't, but she'd drawn the attention of the men. She heard them closer. It wasn't a bad thing.

"I think I have her!"

"Where?"

"There's a light down here."

"Is it the woman?"

"Damn, I hope so. I haven't had me a decent woman in a coon's age."

Fei sprinted to the waterfall. Grabbing nuggets out of the water, she tossed them on the bank. She needed greed to hold the men in place. Just for a little while longer.

Fei checked her sulfurs. They were dry and ready to go. Taking a breath, she nodded confidently. So was she.

She set the lantern behind her, letting the light illuminate the spot, drawing in the colonel and his men. "There she is," someone hollered.

As if he were inviting her to dinner, Daniels called, "Why don't you make it easy on yourself and come here, my dear."

My dear. He made the endearment an obscenity. Adopting a calm she didn't feel, Fei held the dynamite, listening to the soothing hiss of the fuse, and didn't answer. The men advanced, making obscene comments, telling her what they were going to do with her body. *Just a little more. Just a little farther.* Something flew past her ear, drawing a small scream past her resolve. The man who'd just uttered the most vile comment dropped, a knife in his throat. His last obscenity ended in a gurgle.

From the shadows she heard a deep rumble of sound, "A man ought to know how to talk to a lady."

Oh, my God. Someone else was in here. *Who are you?* She couldn't get the question past the knot in her throat. The immediate question of friend or foe was answered by the stranger's next question, "You ready to throw that yet?"

Her heart started beating again. Friend. He had to be friend. "Almost."

Daniel's men crouched and drew their guns.

She stood there, giving them a target.

"Get the hell down!" the stranger ordered.

She shook her head. Heart thundering in her chest, she stood stock-still and started counting. She needed them to stay where they were.

Five.

Four.

Three.

Two.

One.

By the time they recognized what was flying through the air at them, Daniels and his men had no time to react. The walls shivered and groaned, the explosion reverberating with a deafening thunder. A hand latched onto the back of her shirt and lifted her off her feet, knocking her down behind a boulder. She had a vague impression of long hair and broad shoulders before the stranger picked up the lantern, grabbed her hand and dragged her with him as he ran faster than she could ever run by herself.

"Wrong way," she gasped.

The stranger either didn't hear or didn't care. Just before he reached the back side of the waterfall, he took an immediate left, navigating the treacherous paths with precision, circumventing the men between them with the shortcut. She knew he'd had to have been inside her claim a while to know about this shortcut back to the front of the cave. When they got to the chamber to the right of the entry, he set the lantern down, grabbed her by the waist and tossed her across the narrow ravine as if she weighed nothing. Pebbles and small rocks pinged off her shoulder as rocks rolled and crashed. Rolling to her feet, she glanced back over her shoulder, getting her first good look at the man as he prepared to jump. And gasped.

He wasn't just big, he was massive. Tall and broad shouldered, he wore a black vest with no shirt, displaying the thickly slabbed muscles of his abdomen. He had the powerful arms and chest of a blacksmith, but he moved with the grace of a warrior. His skin was dark. His shoulder-length, black hair flared back from his rugged face as he ran toward the ravine. Just before he jumped, a rock fell from above.

"Look out!"

It was too late. It hit his head. His shadow flared up on the far wall in a dramatic crescendo as he fell to his knees, inches from the ravine. Beyond the entry, a dog barked.

The choice of what to do was taken out of her hands. She couldn't leave him. Getting a running start, she leaped back over the ravine. She checked his pulse. Alive but unconscious. Grabbing his legs, she pulled him away from the edge. The muscles in the back of her thighs burned and ached, but she'd only managed to move him a foot.

From the sound of the angry voices, the colonel and his men were disoriented but regrouping. It was doubtful they'd find this chamber. From their perspective, the entrance was at the edge of what looked like a small dead-end tunnel. The men's voices faded. They'd turned down the dead end. She turned the lantern down to a flicker. That would give her time, but they'd be back. She needed to get around to the left to set off the dynamite on that side first. That was the plan. To keep them in the middle as the whole claim came crashing down around them.

It was a well-thought-out plan. Her father's plans always were. But nowhere in it was the need to move an unconscious giant. From the back of the tunnel, the dog barked again. It had to be from the second entrance. Was there help out there? Friends of this man? She had to risk calling for them. She couldn't move the man herself and she couldn't fight off Daniels, sitting in this chamber. Hidden though it was, they would find it eventually if they kept looking. And they would look. These men would not leave her claim until they'd searched every nook and cranny. Greed made men thorough.

"Hel—"

A hand slapped over her mouth. The palm tasted like dirt. She looked down. The man was looking up at her. At least he was awake.

"Fei Yen?"

He knew her name? Cautiously she nodded.

The stranger removed his hand. His drawl was low and deep, not as compelling as Shadow's, but somehow soothing. It said that here was a man who could handle anything. "We've been looking for you."

"Who are 'we'?"

"Hell's Eight."

That was Shadow's family. Relief made her giddy. Definitely friend. "Who are you?"

"I'm Tucker McCade, ma'am. Shadow sent me for you."

"He is alive still?" More relief flooded over her.

Tucker sat up and touched his head before pulling his hand away and looking at it. Blood coated the surface. "Yes, ma'am."

She closed her eyes and thanked the ancestors.

"Where'd you pick up the colonel?" he asked in the same hushed baritone.

"In Simple. He tracked me through my search for employment. I didn't know… I was upset, he offered me a handkerchief…"

Tucker nodded, pressing his fingers to his head again.

"And next thing you knew, you were his prisoner."

"Yes," she whispered. Everything in her told her *shut up, leave, detonate the dynamite,* but Tucker was still woozy from the blow. She had to wait. Had to find patience while inside her the clock ticked. "How did you know?"

"You don't have to tell me about the colonel, ma'am."

"How do I know you're Shadow's friend?"

"You saying I'm lying?"

She licked her lips. Nobody in their right mind

would call this man a liar, even if he said it was night in the middle of the day. "I want you to prove you're his friend."

"You and your cousin Lin killed a wild boar by supposedly tripping and falling on it."

She sighed and shook her head. It was not her most womanly moment. "That *would* be the thing Shadow would tell you."

Tucker chuckled and pressed his hand to his head. "Shadow doesn't just tell it, he brags on it."

"He is proud of such a thing?"

Tucker smiled. "The man thinks the world of you, Mrs. Ochoa."

Inside Fei, a little of the coldness warmed. Shadow had bragged on her, and he'd claimed her as wife to his family.

"He is not ashamed of me."

Tucker cast her a sharp glance. "I'd say just the opposite."

She closed her eyes to fight the bite of bittersweet tears. "Thank you."

"Don't cry."

"I won't." It was just good to know. If the plan failed and she died, she had that knowledge to add to the memories.

The men's voices were getting louder. The colonel and his men were finding their way back. They needed to move. "Can I trust you?"

"Do you want to?"

She wasn't sure, and she was running out of time.

"Will it make it easier for you if I tell you my wife says I'm cuddly?"

Cuddly? This man? "You are married?"

"Don't sound so shocked. And yes, to an opinionated little pacifist."

She took in all that muscle, accentuated with scars that had to have been accumulated through years of battle. She remembered how he'd thrown that knife. "You are a pacifist?"

"I'm working on it."

"Then what good will you do me?"

He smiled and held out his hand, helping her to her feet before getting to his. His smile transformed his face. Taking it from austere to…kind. "Today, I'm not working on it that hard."

"I'm not sure I should trust you."

"Because of the gold?"

She nodded. He shrugged. "If I wanted your gold, I could have taken it long before now and there isn't anything you could do to stop me."

She jerked her chin in the direction of the approaching voices. "I could sic them on you."

Daniels and his men had grown bolder since there were no more explosions. They were almost back at the waterfall.

"Yeah, you could, but there's nothing they could do to stop me, either."

It wasn't a boast. He said it the way Shadow said those kinds of things. As if it were a matter of fact.

And it probably was. If all he wanted was the gold and escape, he could have done it long before now.

"Besides, you're planning on blowing up their asses."

"Yes." She cocked her head to the side. "You're the one who connected my fuses."

"Couldn't help myself. Sweet pattern you laid down there. Got them all corralled in. Beats picking them off one by one."

"It was my father's pattern, but I need to finish it."

They couldn't get out without finishing it. There were too many of the others. He nodded. "Yeah. Between the men here and the snipers outside, they've got us pinned down."

"Snipers?"

"Shadow and the others are handling the snipers, but it's not likely that they'll get them before these yahoos force our hand."

She swallowed and nodded. She understood. Her situation hadn't changed much. It was still them or her. "Shadow is all right?"

"Just worried about you. If he didn't have such a dislike of small places, he'd have been the one scouting in here. As it was, Caine had to force the issue." He held her gaze. "He wanted to be with you."

She was glad he wasn't. The chances of her plan succeeding were not good. "I think I see the way out!" someone called.

"You go and run," another snapped. "I'm not leaving without some of this gold."

Tucker looked at her knowingly. "They're right where you want them."

"How do you know?"

"Gold nuggets don't just pile up like that in a stream. Someone salted it for a reason."

She didn't know what to say. Apparently, Tucker didn't require anything. He was back to studying the map.

"How are you going to get back to light the fuse?"

She pulled out her map. "There's a tunnel to the right that circles around to this spot behind the waterfall."

He studied the layout. "You need to set off the front first, for that to work."

She nodded.

"I'll handle that."

"You'll be trapped."

He tapped the paper. "There's a bigger opening now, just a bit farther down."

"The air hole?"

"There was no way I was getting out the back way so I expanded it. Hope you don't mind."

He would have needed to. For the first time since she entered the cave, hope flared. She just might survive this. "I do not mind. What about the snipers?"

"It won't be the first time I've ruined a sniper's day."

The gold would not distract them forever. It was now or never. Tucker covered her hand with his, bringing her gaze to his. "Are you sure you want to do this?"

There was no question. "The gold is not my destiny."

"Just your fresh start."

"Shadow talks too much."

Tucker chuckled. "Can you make it to here?" He tapped the map at the location of the other detonator.

"Yes. They will not see me."

"I'm going to need a distraction."

He was right. His detonator was in sight of the salted streambed. She took the dynamite out of her pocket. "I will provide it."

"Take the lantern." She picked it up. "And, Fei?"

She stopped and turned back.

"Be careful."

She nodded. She was always careful. Especially now when she might have a future. She just needed to get to that one spot. The terrain was tricky, full of loose rocks and drop-offs, but it was where she needed to be. There was only one place the dynamite would be effective. If Daniels got past it, Tucker would be trapped. Not that the explosion she was planning would kill them. It would just block them from the front exit and send them back to the middle of the cave. The charges she'd planted two months ago would take care of the rest.

Across the way, she saw Tucker move into place. Partially hidden by rock, he gave her the thumbs-up. She lit the sulfur. Daniels's men turned at the flare of light.

"There she is!"

"Get her!"

She shook her head, touching the match to the short fuse on the dynamite. She needed them to stay where they were.

Five.
Four.
Three.
Two.
One.

CHAPTER SIXTEEN

TUCKER HAD DONE HIS JOB. The explosions came one right after the other. One man standing near a charge was catapulted through the air like a doll. Another swore and dived for cover. Only the colonel didn't panic. With unswerving determination, he came running toward her as rock crashed down on rock and dust billowed thicker than smoke. It was hard to hear, hard to breathe, hard to think. She hadn't realized how loud it was all going to be. How devastating. It was as though the world was ending. Turning, she sprinted for the back of the cave. She didn't have much time. The cave was rigged to blow in sections. It was her last-resort plan. And now that it was set in motion, there was no stopping it.

"Goddamn you!" Daniels shouted above the blasts. Looking over her shoulder, she saw he was gaining. The lantern he carried swung wildly, throwing a garish light. His revolver was in his hand.

"No!"

She turned and threw her lantern at him. It thudded to the ground to his right. Oil spilled and lit in a steady creep of fire that added a touch of hell to the chaos. Amidst the horror of the cave-in and spreading flames, he laughed. He was insane.

Faster! her mind screamed, but no matter how fast she ran, the colonel ran faster. Behind him the cave began to collapse. The next two explosions came quickly. There was a shout behind her. Looking over her shoulder she saw the colonel on his knees, rocks pounding his body.

Good.

She made it to the waterfall. After rounding the corner, she stopped by a small pile of rocks. Shoving the debris off the top, she exposed the fuse beneath. Digging in her pocket, she searched for a sulfur. For a second she hesitated. There'd be no going back after this. No gold. No future. No fresh start. The colonel came around the corner, bloody and furious. She struck the sulfur. Nothing happened.

"Where are you, you bitch?"

No more threat to Shadow.

Light. Light. The chant went through her head. The sulfur flared. Sheltering it in the cup of her hand, she touched it to the fuse.

The fuse hissed and sputtered. She wasted precious seconds to make sure it stayed lit. The colonel spotted her. No more time. Half crawling, half running, going by feel, she made it to the narrow ledge that led deeper into the cave. It was dark there, very dark. Keeping her hand against the wall, she got to her feet and ran recklessly, desperately. At this point, there was only the slightest chance she'd escape. If the fuse burned just a bit slower than it was designed, if she ran just a bit faster than she thought she could… There was a chance.

Something struck her from behind. The sulfurs went flying out of her hand as she slammed to the ground, her nose hitting a rock. Stunned, she couldn't move.

"You goddamn bitch." The curse roared in her ears. "That's my gold blowing up."

Rough hands turned her over. There was nothing neat about Daniels now. His hair was covered in dirt and sticking out in clumps. Blood ran in rivulets down his face, carving out demonic-looking paths in the dust that glowed eerily in the faint light of his discarded lantern.

"I'll kill you."

He was still wearing her pack on his back. There was still hope. All around them the cave shook as if caught in an earthquake. She'd placed the dynamite well. The cave-in was imminent.

"Let go of me!"

She gouged for his eyes. He knocked her hands aside. She kicked at his legs and punched at his face. He swore and grabbed her by the throat. Slapping at his face and grabbing at his hands, she tried to dislodge his grip, but it was useless. He had the strength of a demon, squeezing her throat as she choked for air. Her hand slid off his cheek and bumped against something bulky and square. *The book.* She might have lost the gold with which to buy Shadow's freedom, but there was still Daniel's book. With her right hand, she fumbled for it. With the left, she struggled to reach the pack. Daniels squeezed harder. Pain exploded in her neck, panic pounded at her mind, but in a strangely detached way, she worked apart from it, shielded from the horror by purpose. Her index finger hooked in the pocket of the pack. The small knife she used for everyday things wiggled into her reach just as the edges of her vision went black.

"No!" It was a gasp from her heart. She could not lose now. She was so close. To the opening. To her life.

Shadow. His face filled her mind's eye. Beloved. Determined. His hand reached out and curved around her nape, his thumb caressed her cheek. So real she could feel it. Rough skin caressing her in the tenderest of touches. Beyond the foulness of the colonel's face, Shadow's eyes burned into hers with a message she could not read, his lips formed syllables she couldn't hear.

"Shadow..."

Just saying his name gave her strength.

The colonel leaned in, hissing in her ear, "Fuck that Indian and fuck you!"

Live!

The order leaped into her mind as the knife popped into her hand. She flicked the sheath off with her thumb. Staring straight into the colonel's eyes, she plunged the knife into his neck with the last of her strength. Jerking back, he grabbed at his throat. She placed her foot in the middle of his chest and pushed. He fell to the side as the ledge crumbled. His feet went over. She scrambled back. He reached out, his fingers wrapped like vises around her ankle, and then she was sliding with him toward the abyss. Digging in her feet, she fought gravity. The edge came closer, the chasm loomed, swallowing Daniels. His maniacal laugh filled the cavern as they went hurtling over the edge.

"Shadow!"

Her scream was lost as one last explosion rocked the cavern.

THEY HEARD THE EXPLOSIONS before they reached the cave.

"Shit!"

"That sounds like dynamite," Caine said.

"You did say your new wife was handy with the stuff, didn't you?" Tracker asked.

"Could be Tucker," Zach offered. "The man loves to play with the stuff."

But it wasn't Tucker, Shadow knew. He kicked Night into a gallop, plunging down the slope toward the mouth of the cave. "It's Fei."

Tracker came up along one side. Zach the other. Bending down, Tracker grabbed Night's reins and pulled him back as Caine took the lead. Protecting him, Shadow realized.

"We don't know what we're getting into," Tracker snapped. "Use your head."

Shadow didn't care what was ahead. If Fei was blowing the cave, she was in trouble.

Shadow!

Fei's scream was a whisper of sensation in his imagination, blending with the urgency inside.

"Breaking your neck isn't going to help her," Sam shouted.

"Neither is wasting time." Slipping the knife from his boot and leaning over Night's neck, Shadow cut Night's reins off between Tracker's hand and the bit. The horse stayed game, taking the descent at a gallop even with the shift of weight. Tracker lurched to the side with the release of tension. Zach held steady, his dark face splitting in a grin and touched his fingers to his hat as Tracker dropped the useless pieces of leather.

"As you wish."

Tracker swung back into position on his right. Caine fell into position beside him, Sam covered the left, all four riding as hard and as recklessly as he was. The horses hit the plateau with a grunt and surged forward. There were no questions. No arguments.

Shadow was off the horse and running even before Night came to a stop. Caine was right behind him, followed by Tracker, Zach and Sam.

It was obvious within seconds that the opening was impassable. Slapping the boulder with the flat of his hand, Shadow cursed.

"Where the hell is Tucker?"

"In there, if Fei is," Sam answered. Dynamite was still exploding. The colonel's horses tied to the trees stomped their feet in agitation. Their riders wouldn't be coming for them.

"Over there."

Looking to where Caine pointed, Shadow spotted a plume of smoke.

"There's another entrance!"

"Not for long, from the sound of things."

It would be long enough. Shadow wouldn't let it be any less. Vaulting back onto Night, he kicked him back into a gallop. The gelding gave him what he asked for, running too fast through the rocky terrain. It wasn't fast enough. The explosions stopped. As Shadow's feet hit the ground, the earth stopped shaking and the plume was just a slight puff. If they'd arrived a minute later, there wouldn't have been any sign at all.

Hold on, Fei.

"Still think she's in there?" Tracker asked.

Shadow had no doubt. "Yes."

"We're going to have to widen that opening. While it might be big enough for a woman, we're never getting through," Sam said, dismounting.

Shadow grabbed the shovel tied to the back of his saddle. "Then let's get to it."

The others did the same.

"Must have been a hell of a fix for her to bring the whole place down around her," Zach said.

"Could it have been a mistake?" Tracker asked.

"No."

"Dynamite could have been unstable," Sam observed.

Shadow remembered how Fei had stood that night with the dynamite in her hand, utterly confident as she bluffed. "It's not a mistake."

He started digging. The ground was hard and rocky. He didn't do much damage on the first push. His gut went cold. Fei. He held her image in his head. Not as she might be—bloody and broken under tons of rock—but as she'd been that last night they were together. Wild and sweet and giving. His Fei.

Live!

Three other shovels hit the dirt and rock beside his. Together they chopped and dug, widening the opening.

"I sent her away to keep her from this."

"Dying?" Tracker asked.

"Yes."

"You thought sending her outside your protection would guarantee that?"

"Yes."

Tracker tossed a shovelful of dirt to the side. "You are an arrogant ass."

"Not now, Tracker," Caine grunted.

"Where's Zach?"

"Covering our asses, as always."

"Quit talking and dig," Shadow ordered.

"Just trying to distract you."

"I don't want to be distracted."

"You never do," Tracker snapped. "You just latch onto an idea and cling to it like it's the only way, whether it is or not."

"What the hell does that mean?"

"Not now, Tracker."

"If all you're going to do is irritate, then get the hell up on the ridge with Zach."

"No."

Sam grabbed a large rock and pulled it free of the hole, muscles straining with the effort. "In case you haven't noticed, Shadow, we're all in a mood to kick your ass."

The rock came free. The opening was wide enough to fit through.

"You can give that a shot later."

Caine struck a sulfur and lit a lantern. Sam handed him a rope. Shadow tied it to the lantern and lowered it down into the hole. It was only three feet deep. Rock and dirt scattered the floor. Dust still roiled. It was a very small opening.

Sam unbuckled his gun belt. "I'll go in."

Shadow grabbed his arm. "No. I'll go."

"It's tight. I've got the better chance."

"It's unstable in there."

"You think it's going to be less unstable for you?"

"You don't like caves."

"She's my woman."

"That makes her important to all of us."

He knew that. Shrugging out of his weapons, he let them drop to the ground. But he was still the one going in.

Tracker's eyebrow went up.

"You must be in love if you're treating your weapons like that."

"Shut up."

Sam put his hands on his chest, stopping him. "I said I was going."

Caine interceded. "Let him go, Sam."

"Why?"

"Because, if it was Bella in there, you wouldn't let anyone take your place, either."

Putting his hands up, Sam stepped back. "Do what you need to."

"Thank you. I thought I would."

"Do it without the sarcasm," Caine advised.

Sam tossed the rope around Shadow's waist and knotted it behind his back. "You give us three tugs on this and we'll haul your ass out of there so fast it will make your head spin."

"Got it."

Tracker handed him the lantern. "Be sure you come back in one piece."

"I will."

"Good, because I'm going to kick it when you get out."

"What the hell are you so pissed about?"

"You're Hell's Eight, Shadow," Caine said.

He knew that. "So?"

"That means you're family."

"No shit."

Tracker checked the knot before grabbing it and jerking to get his attention. "That means we get to protect you, too."

HE WAS CRAWLING THROUGH his grave. The thought wouldn't leave Shadow's mind as he inched along in a crouch in a tunnel four feet high and three feet wide, heading deeper and deeper into the cave in a slow, tedious process that involved shoving the lantern forward, crawling to it, then repeating the process. Sweat broke out over Shadow's body. Not just because the air was stiflingly close, but because, with every foot he went in, the mountain above him seemed to weigh more. Son of a bitch, he hated tight spaces.

The tunnel seemed to groan. Pebbles sprayed over him. Dust hovered in a thick cloud. He coughed and closed his eyes, waiting for it to settle.

"Shadow, you all right down there?" Sam called.

"Yeah. Just dandy."

"You need to come out. This whole side could collapse."

"Not yet."

"Look around. Does it look like she could have survived?"

It didn't look like anything could have survived.

"I don't know."

"I'm pulling you out."

"No."

"Yes."

Reaching in his boot, Shadow pulled out his knife. Without another thought, he severed the rope. Two seconds later when Tracker realized what he'd done, the curses started. "Goddamn it, Shadow."

He wasn't leaving there without Fei.

Ahead, all he could see was a solid pile of rock just into the curve of the path. Damn. Biting the knife between his teeth, he crawled toward it. Fei was beyond the rock. Somewhere. He wiped the sweat from his eyes and started shifting the rock to the side. One small boulder at a time, lining the tunnel around him, trying not to make the space too impassable as he did.

"Hello?"

The greeting came to him, muffled by the rock, but recognizable.

There had never been a sweeter sound. "Fei?"

"Yes."

Very carefully, he moved more rock, only to have the hole immediately fill with debris from above.

"Where are you?"

"I'm down here."

"Where's 'down here'?"

He managed to get a small hole through.

"On the ledge."

Shit! It was a struggle to keep his voice calm. "How far down?"

"Six feet, maybe."

Which meant, if he got to her, he could probably reach her.

"You have to hurry. The cavern could collapse any time."

He'd noticed. "Are you hurt?"

"No, I'm not. But this is not good."

No, there was nothing good about being buried alive.

"I'm going to get you out."

"No. The path is gone. It will take too long. The air isn't good."

Just what he needed. More bad news.

"You must save yourself."

"Working on it." Right after he saved her.

"Tucker said you do not like small places."

She'd seen Tucker. "Tucker talks too much."

Another rock moved to the side. Another two inches of space gained. It was something.

"I see the light."

"Good."

"What happened, Fei? I told you to stay with your family."

"You cannot send me away and expect to control me."

She was still on that. "You know what my life is like. I didn't want you in that."

"Yet, it still touched me."

"What the hell do you mean?"

"Your colonel found me."

"Daniels? Son of a bitch!"

"Yes. Son of a bitch. He made me come here. He wanted the gold."

"Why didn't you just give it to him?"

"It is my fresh start, not his."

"So you decided to blow it up?"

"No, this I decided when he decided to kill me. I'm glad he hasn't succeeded."

I do better with bluffing than killing. He remembered when she'd told him that. "What the hell does that mean?"

"He is still trying."

Shadow froze. "Does he have a gun on you?"

"I think he is dead."

That explained the tightness in her voice. "Don't think about it."

"I cannot help it. I am sitting on him."

Sitting on him? "How big is that ledge, Fei?"

"Not big. And getting smaller with every tremble."

"Can you shove his body off the ledge?"

"No."

"Can you…"

"Shadow, I can do nothing but sit here and lose my mind."

"You're too stubborn to lose your mind."

"It is all I have left to lose."

The hole was big enough to get his arm through. There was only a slight bit of level ground until he reached air. She was right—the path was gone. From what he could see, where the path should have curved around had collapsed, resulting in a straight drop-off. Twisting about, he reached down. "Can you reach my hand?"

Her fingers brushed his. He lunged forward and grabbed, holding on tightly when she almost slipped away. He closed his eyes; relief flowing through him with debilitating force at the contact. "Goddamn, Fei!"

Then her fingers slipped away. He yanked his arm clear and shouted through the hole, "Fei!"

"I am sorry. It is hard to balance on…him."

Jesus Christ. She was trying to balance on a body on a ledge just to touch his hand? "I'm sorry, honey. I didn't think. It's not the time for hand-holding anyway."

"No, that time has passed."

"Fei…"

"You broke my heart, Shadow Ochoa."

The catch in her voice devastated him and cracked the wall he'd erected around his emotions to protect her. The sob that followed spread that crack into a crevice. Pain seeped into his concentration, disrupting it.

"Don't cry, honey."

"You had no right."

It was like a puzzle, trying to figure out what part of the slide he could move without disturbing another.

"Now is not the time."

"There is no better time. I am very good at what I do. I blew this cave, so it would be no more. Whatever hasn't caved in yet will shortly."

He'd rather talk about how he'd hurt her. "I just wanted you safe."

"That was not your choice."

"The hell it wasn't."

Something poked him in the hip.

"What the hell?"

"She's got a point."

"Sam?"

"We thought you might need something to support that mess. Found this stuff outside."

Shadow reached back and felt a plank poking his hip. It was about the length of his arm. "I'm going to need about two feet to get her out."

"Got it." There was a pause and then, "Good thing

she's a small woman, otherwise I don't think we'd have a prayer."

Shadow put his hand on the rock pile, imagining he could feel Fei's hand on the other side. "We'll have you out of there in just a minute, Fei."

"No, you won't, but it is all right. I have had more than I expected in my life."

"I don't want to hear this."

"I didn't want to hear you tell me goodbye. We do not always get what we want."

Sam came back. "If it were me, I'd humor her."

Shadow swore and took the post Sam slid up along his side. "What did you have that exceeded your expectations?" She didn't answer. "Fei?"

"I've known great passion. I have loved. I made my fortune and I had a fresh start."

Her passion had only been for three days. Her love had sent her away, her fortune would never be spent and her fresh start had gotten her kidnapped. He only addressed the latter.

"Some fresh start. It only lasted five days."

"It didn't have to last, it just had to be. And it was more than I would have had, had I stayed where I didn't belong. Where you tried to send me back to."

Shadow wedged the post against one side of the hole. Even to his untrained eye, it looked shaky. He went to work on the other side. "We've already been over that."

"No." A rock came hurtling through the hole and bounced off his shoulder. "*You* went over it. *You* decided. You made it happen so it was good for you. You did not care that it broke my heart. You did not care that you could have been hanged and I would not have known. You didn't care."

Son of a bitch. She was crying. "I cared," he said.

"If you cared, you would not have sent me away."

"What could you have done?"

"Many things. Some foolish, some smart, but I would have had the choice to do something."

"You would have tried to break me out."

"Maybe."

"Honey, the dynamite would have been flying for sure."

She continued as if he hadn't interrupted. "Or maybe I would have sat with you and held your hand while you waited for the trial. And maybe I would have sent a message to your family. And maybe if they hadn't come, and nothing I tried worked, maybe I would have stood in the front of the crowd, holding your soul with my heart until the last, not letting you go alone to meet your ancestors."

"Goddamn, Fei. I wanted to spare you that."

"And maybe," she continued, beating him up with the force of her truth. "Maybe, if you had allowed me my right, I would not hate you so much now."

"Fei."

"Do not talk to me anymore, Shadow. I do not want my last emotions to be ones of anger and regret. I want to remember what was, before you decided I did not matter."

"Nothing but you *does* matter."

"Pffft!"

Sam slid another plank forward. "That woman has a brutal way with words."

Shadow took it. "She's upset."

"She's also right."

"I have a right to protect the people I love."

"But not to the point where it's all about you."

He wedged the first plank in to the opening of the cavern and hammered it in with his fist. "It's never about me."

"You'd better work on your listening skills, because when we get that woman out of there, you're going to have a long haul to get back in her good graces."

Shadow forced the second plank into place. The opening was less than two feet. It would be tight. "I don't want her hurt because of me."

"Yet she was, despite all your sacrifice, and now she's sitting on a ledge on the dead body of the man who tried to kill her, breathing foul air, listening to you tell her you're right and she's wrong."

"Sam."

"Bella taught me that you can't claim to love if you don't know how to accept it." Sam patted his leg. "I'd rather face twenty Apaches on the warpath than go through that 'accepting' thing again."

"Bella loves you."

"Maybe Fei loves you."

Shadow flinched away from the knowledge. "She thinks I'm a hero."

"I do not. I think you are a jerk," Fei interjected.

Sam laughed. "There you go."

"Shut up, Sam." Shadow pushed the top brace in. The side threatened to fall.

"Watch it!" Sam stretched, but couldn't reach the post to help.

"Christ, it's tight in here."

"Yeah."

"Turn on your side and let me see if I can get in there to steady this one."

"Shit." Shadow waited until Sam seemed to have a grip before letting go. "Got it?"

"Sort of."

Another avalanche of rock tumbled down, but the makeshift bracing around the hole held.

"It held," he called to Fei. "I'll have you out in a bit."

"Shadow," she called back. "It is time for you to leave."

I hate you.

He wasn't leaving with those words between them.

"I'm taking that holding as a good sign," Sam grunted. "You clear out as much of that rock as you can, and I'll go get the rope."

"Done." Sam left. In his wake there was only silence.

"Fei? Talk to me, honey."

"Why?"

"So I know you're alive."

"I am alive."

"Good."

Moving the debris wasn't as easy as he'd hoped. Because of the tight confines of the tunnel, the debris had to be distributed down its length in such a way that it wouldn't block progress. And every time Shadow crept back and forth, more of the tunnel wall seemed to disintegrate.

Sam came back. "Caine says to get a move on. You can see up top where the ground is sinking."

"Shit." Knotting a loop in the rope, he fed it into the hole and over the drop-off.

"Fei. I'm lowering the rope."

"All right."

From deep in the cave, there came a rumble. Fei screamed. Shadow could hear the rock falling down. "Grab the rope."

The order was for Sam and for Fei.

From above, Tracker called, "Move!"

"What's happening?" he shouted.

"It's collapsing from the other end!" Caine shouted back.

"Fei, get that rope around you."

She didn't answer immediately. "Fei?"

"I've got it."

"Pull!" Shadow shouted up the hill.

"Slow and steady," Sam corrected, backing up, giving them room.

Shadow stretched into the hole, fighting back the horror as the wooden braces cut into his side. As long as he was in this hole, Fei had a way out. And Fei was getting out. He felt the touch of her fingers. The brush of her hand. Locking his fingers around her wrist, he breathed a sigh of relief.

"I've got you."

Her fingers locked around his. "And I've got you."

For a second they hung like that, him holding her, her holding him. Shadow couldn't see Fei's face, but he could feel her pulse beneath his thumb. It was racing.

"I won't let you go."

"You have before."

"Never again."

She shoved something at him over the lip of the ledge. "What's that?"

"A book Daniels kept, documenting all his schemes. He was a very vain man. He saw himself as a hero. It will free you."

"Stop pushing that thing at me."

"It will free you."

"What I want free is you."

"Shadow—"

"Give me the damn thing."

"Do not lose it—"

Stuffing the book in his shirt, he cut her off, "Brace your feet against the wall and try to keep straight until you can see the hole, then lie down and we'll drag you through."

"I want to tell you."

"Tell me when we're clear."

"But I wish you to know—"

"You hate me. I heard you."

"I don't—"

"Pull," he hollered before Fei could say more.

He inched backward along with the rope, staying in the hole as long as he could, unwilling to leave her exposed any longer than possible. The scariest moment he ever lived was the one when he had to let go of her hand.

"Don't let go of that rope, Fei. No matter what."

"I won't."

"Back on out now, Shadow," Caine called.

"Pull," Shadow called, pressing back against the wall, holding the lantern above his head. It was a tight fit, but she'd make it.

"Goddammit, Shadow, get out first!"

Not without Fei. "Get her out of here."

The rope pulled taut. Inch by inch, Fei came over the ledge. Above them, the cave groaned loud and long. A death cry. There was no more time.

"Haul her out now!"

They did. Fei went, speeding by him like a stick riding a hard current.

For a brief moment he saw her eyes and the accusation there, before her shoulder hit a rock and she turned the other way.

He told himself it didn't matter how she felt. She was safe. She'd get over it. He'd done the right thing. It didn't help.

"We've got her," Sam hollered. "Now haul your ass out of there."

He started working backward. Rock sprayed down, first small and then bigger. A sprinkle to a torrent, pounding him with the force of fists. Dirt and debris slammed his skull into the ground and began filling in the holes around him, beginning to entomb him in a slow steady trickle. He couldn't move.

"Shadow!"

Fei. His Fei.

"Someone grab her! Don't let her back in there," he heard someone shout.

"Goddamn! She's quick."

Something touched his leg. Grabbed his ankle.

"Shadow, move!"

Fei? She wasn't supposed to be there. "Get out."

A rope slipped around his ankles.

"Pull!" she screamed.

"You first," he whispered, pushing back with his hands. "Get safe."

Fei didn't answer. He didn't know where she was. Was she out?

Get out.

The tugging at his feet increased and he slid along. He tried to twist around. He caught a glimpse of her at his feet, guiding the rope. He saw the crack start to break across the ceiling. Saw the end coming.

Pushing up on his hands, he lunged for her, kicking as hard as he could, knocking her through the opening and into the light.

Live.

CHAPTER SEVENTEEN

THAT NIGHT, SHADOW STOOD at the window of one of the hotel rooms they'd rented. Pulling back the curtain with two fingers, he watched the street below. There was nothing untoward. No men lurked in strategic locations. No women hung in windows. All there was were the normal comings and goings of a sleepy town on Sunday evening. Which was good. From the looks of things he'd have time to rest and heal up.

A twinge in his shoulder had him rubbing it and rotating it in a small circle. There wasn't a muscle in his body that didn't ache. He was bruised from head to toe, and would likely be stiff for several days, but as it was a miracle he wasn't dead, he wasn't complaining. The memory of being in that cave would be with him a long time. The moment when the cave collapsed and Fei had been in the path of all that falling rock would haunt him to the grave.

There were moments in a man's life that defined the right and wrong of his grasp on the world. That moment had been one for him. He'd always thought himself a cold-blooded killer. A man in whom the softer emotions had long since been beaten out, but in that moment when he'd watched the ceiling crack and known Fei would die if he didn't get her out, he'd seen with crystal clarity his one thing. He loved Fei. For a man who'd thought he was empty inside, it was quite a revelation. It also scared the shit out of him.

He wasn't sure what Fei saw in that moment, but in the aftermath, she'd been madder than a hornet. As soon they'd pulled him out and she'd been certain he was alive, she'd spun on her heel and demanded to be taken home. When she'd learned they couldn't take her home until they knew what mischief the colonel had left in his wake, she'd huffed and demanded to be taken to a hotel. Away from him.

She'd gotten half her wish.

They were in a hotel a day away from Barren Ridge. Four days away from Hell's Eight. Fei had studiously avoided him on the ride, seeming to gravitate to Tucker, riding with him, and talking to him to the point Shadow had felt a bite of jealousy. Another new emotion and one he'd never felt before. He didn't particularly want to feel it right now when his emotions felt like raw meat sizzling on a fire. She hadn't even said thank you. Then again, neither had he. He ran his fingers through his hair. Maybe he was a little one-sided at times with how he saw things.

Movement in the street below caught his eye. A familiar figure dressed in black drew his attention—Fei. He'd recognize that demure bring-on-the-world walk anywhere. She was supposed to be resting in her room. What was she doing out? She was moving at a fast pace, looking nervously over her shoulder as she stepped up onto the wooden walk on the far side of the street, heading toward the…saloon?

Where was Tucker? He was supposed to be watching her. Disregarding the impact to her reputation, there was no end of trouble Fei could get into in a saloon. Just when he was about to head down and drag her home and to hell with the risk of being recognized by someone, she came out. Her step seemed lighter. And that might have been a smile on her face.

What was she up to?

She crossed the street and disappeared out of sight unto a storefront. He couldn't see what kind of shop it was from here. If he remembered correctly, it might just have been a dry-goods store. He waited for her to come out, scanning the surroundings constantly for any threat. His patience wore thin when ten minutes passed and there was no still sign of her. He pounded on the wall. "Tracker!"

After a moment, Tracker entered the room, bare-chested, stretching and yawning. Clearly he'd been asleep. He stopped inside the door. "You pounded?"

Shadow continued to look out the window. "Fei is out."

Tracker cocked an eyebrow at him. "And?"

"She's up to something."

"She's not a prisoner."

Shadow checked the street again. Still no sign of her. "She gets into trouble."

"She's a grown woman."

"That just means she gets into bigger trouble."

Tracker leaned his shoulder against the wall. "She seemed to handle herself just fine with Daniels."

Shadow let the curtain drop and turned around. "She blew up a damn cavern while she was in it."

Tracker shrugged. "And walked out alive."

"If we hadn't been there she wouldn't have."

"But we were there. And isn't it the Hell's Eight motto that any plan that ends with us walking out alive is a good one?"

"It's not hers."

Tracker sat on the bed and leaned back against the headboard and just shook his head.

"What are you staring at?" Shadow demanded.

"You. You've really got it bad, don't you?"

"What?"

"Love."

Panic flared in Shadow's gut. "Don't say that."

If it wasn't said, fate couldn't feel tempted and she wouldn't be hurt.

"I am not in love with Fei."

"Bullshit."

Shadow set his jaw. "She deserves better."

"Where do you think she's going to find that?"

"Her uncles have found her someone."

That gave Tracker pause. "Her uncles?"

"Yes."

"Found? As in 'we went shopping for canned goods and look what we found for you along the way'?"

"Arranged marriages are tradition among her people."

"So is kidnapping among ours. Doesn't mean I hold with it."

"Just drop it, Tracker."

"I don't think I will. You dragged me out of a good sleep for this parlay, so I think I've got some room to ask questions. The first one being just what exactly makes this man so desirable?"

"Her uncles said he's of good family, owns several dry-good stores and is generally stable." He left out the part about Fei being second wife.

"He sounds as boring as hell."

"Fei will be safe there."

Tracker laughed out loud and shook his head. "Have you met your wife, Shadow? The woman plays with dynamite."

The nudge of truth was unwelcome. "She probably isn't my wife."

Tracker sat up a little straighter. "Did you sleep with her?"

"That's none of your business."

"I'll ask a different way, then. Are you using her?"

"Hell, no."

"Then she's your wife."

And yet it touches me.

Fei had been miles from him, and his past had found her, putting her in danger. Married, it would be a constant way of life. "No promises were made."

"How convenient." Tracker's drawl deepened with

disgust. Not something he was used to hearing in his brother's voice when it came to him.

"Son of a bitch, Tracker, she doesn't want to be married!"

"I don't blame her. A woman likes to know her husband knows his own mind."

"I know my mind."

Tracker went back to leaning against the headboard. "Part of it anyway."

Shadow was in no mood for this. "What the hell are you implying?"

There was a long pause. Tracker ran his hand through his hair. Something he only did when uncomfortable. His lips thinned and his gaze narrowed the smallest bit. "We should have talked about this long ago."

It was Shadow's turn to push his hair off his face. "No."

"Yes." Tracker shook his head. "It doesn't do any good to pretend it's not there."

"We were kids."

"And now we're not, but sometimes I think the old man is still there behind me, belt in hand, ready to tear apart the smallest good I find."

Shadow took another step into the center of the room. Another step toward Tracker. "Stop it."

Tracker stood then, the same legacy of hate in his eyes. "I was there, Shadow. I know exactly what it's like to wonder why your father hates you. To try not to love because you know whatever it is will be hurt.

I know that feeling of failure that settles into your gut when you loved despite yourself and he found out. The inability to save what you loved. I remember the beatings, the hate. Hell, I took beatings for you and you for me. Beatings we got for no other reason than we wouldn't turn on each other. We survived and we've both got the scars to prove it."

Shadow hated the child he'd been then. Too weak to save his brother, his dog, his cat, his mother. He'd sworn never to be that weak again.

Tracker took a step forward. Close enough to touch. Shadow couldn't bring himself to reach out, bridge that gap.

"That was a long time ago."

Tracker put his hand on Shadow's shoulder. "Yeah, but sometimes when I wake up in the middle of the night, I'm still there."

Shadow took a step back, away from the comfort that felt like weakness. "The old man has a long arm."

"It's getting shorter."

Not in Shadow's experience. "Why?"

Tracker folded his arms across his chest and dropped the name like a challenge. "Ari."

His wife. The woman who'd brought the sun to Tracker's world and the darkness to his. A lot had changed between them when Tracker had found his wife. A lot had been lost.

"She does love you."

"You finally believe that?"

"I wouldn't have killed Amboy the way I did if I didn't."

"Uh-huh."

Tracker dropped his hands to his sides. The easy camaraderie that was always between them frayed under the strain of the changes of the past year and a half.

"I want to thank you for that gift, and then I want you to take it back."

Well, Shadow didn't want this. He wanted his brother the way he used to be. "Is this where you tell me you're going to you kick my ass?"

Tracker's eyes narrowed. "I wasn't planning on it, but you're fast changing my mind."

Shadow ran his hand though his hair and shook his head. He was too tired to fight tonight. "Just tell me what this gift is you want me to take back...get it over with."

"You killed Amboy to give me Ari."

He'd killed Amboy so his brother could be happy. "Happy birthday."

Tracker's mouth thinned. A sure sign he was about to start swinging. Some part of Shadow took perverse satisfaction at getting under his brother's skin.

"I want you to take it back," Tracker said.

"Amboy will be stinking to high heaven by now. Sure you want me digging him up?"

"No." An expression Shadow'd never seen before crossed his brother's face. Utter weariness, mixed with...defeat? Shit, nothing ever defeated Tracker. He was a fighter. The one Shadow could always count on to knock heads rather than glasses. By rights, Shadow should be swallowing teeth.

"Tracker?"

Tracker shook his head, cutting him off with a wave of his hand. "I don't give a shit about Amboy, but if you can find where you buried my brother, I'll take him back any way he comes."

Shadow stood there as Tracker turned away, feeling his pain like a new cut as it mixed with his own. It'd always been he and Tracker against the world, even within the camaraderie of the Hell's Eight, they had been a separate entity. Tracker had been his anchor and he Tracker's. Until Ari. When Tracker found Ari, that had all changed. It was no longer Tracker and Shadow. The bond had shifted, broken. He didn't begrudge his brother his happiness, but he wasn't going to get in the way of it.

"You have Ari now," he called, stopping Tracker before he reached the door.

"Yes." Tracker didn't look back.

"You're happy with her."

"Yes."

"Good."

"It is." This time Tracker turned. His expression was as impassive as Shadow had ever seen it. "And not to pop your swelled head, but there's nothing you could do to ruin that."

"Really? She seemed a bit testy when I was around."

"You know her history. You know why. You just

didn't stick around long enough for her to stop being afraid. You ran."

He was getting damn tired of people accusing him of running. "What do you want from me, Tracker?"

"I want you to understand it's not either-or, Shadow. Any choice like that is unnatural, but if push came to shove and I had to choose between you and Ari, I'd choose Ari."

Shadow flinched at the blatant truth. "Of course."

Tracker opened the door and glanced back, holding Shadow's gaze, letting him see his pain and frustration. His anger. "The exact same way you'd choose Fei."

THE EXACT SAME WAY you'd choose Fei.

The truth hit Shadow with the force of a sledgehammer. Tracker was right. If he had to choose, he would choose Fei because she was his future, his better half. Because that was the way it was supposed to be. But loving Fei didn't mean he loved his brother less. He toyed with the understanding, poking it from different angles, checking it against what he'd always assumed. Whenever he tried to take Tracker out of the equation, it didn't add up. The same thing happened when he tried to take Fei out. They both belonged in his life. They were both necessary. And he understood. Adding Fei to his life was like adding another room to the house. It didn't ruin the structure, just created more space to be enjoyed.

It's not either-or.

No it wasn't. It'd just taken him a lot longer than most to realize.

He rapped on the wall. Tracker didn't rap back. Shit. He pulled on his shirt. It was going to be up to him to mend this fence. Before he could leave, a knock came at the door. Palming his knife, Shadow leaned back against the wall beside the door.

"Who is it?"

"Fei."

He opened the door. Fei stood there dressed in a pretty white dress with blue flowers. Obviously new. She blinked as she took in his open shirt. Her gaze dropped to his pants and they widened. She licked her lips.

Following her gaze, he saw his pants were unbuttoned. "Sorry."

Her hand came over his. "Don't button them on my account."

He didn't know what to make of that. "Tracker just took me to task for taking advantage of you."

"Your brother needs to mind his own business."

"I'll tell him you said so."

"Please do not."

She was just a little afraid of Tracker. He smiled.

"May I come in?"

He stepped back. She breezed in. She had that same bounce in her step that she'd had leaving the saloon. He scanned the lay of her dress for any betraying bulges. She didn't appear to be packing any dynamite. "What are you up to, Fei?"

"What makes you think I must be up to something?"

"What were you doing in the saloon?"

"You were spying."

"I was just watching the street."

"I ordered a tub for us. One big enough you can soak. It was the only place that had one."

Son of a bitch. The woman never stopped surprising him.

"What did you think I was doing?" she asked.

"I had no idea."

She took a step closer. "But you worried?"

"Yes."

"Why?"

There was no hope for it. The woman had ordered him a tub. He had to fess up. "Because last time we talked you said you hated me."

She sighed. "I tried to correct that, but you wouldn't let me."

"I was busy."

"And I was mad."

"Why?"

"You don't listen."

"I listen. I just don't agree."

"If the only words you hear are the ones you agree with then you do not listen."

She had him there. "You're right."

She blinked. "I am?"

He nodded. "I've recently come to the conclusion that I can be a pigheaded—"

"Ass?" she finished for him.

"Yeah." She smiled and smoothed her hand up his forearm. "I have decided you cannot help it. You are very protective."

"Is that what you're calling it?"

"Yes. To the point you protect the ones you love from yourself."

"Uh-huh."

"But, Shadow?"

"What?"

She took that step in that brought her thighs against his. She placed her palms against his chest, connecting them. "I do not want to be protected from you."

He should push her away. Instead, he brought her closer, sliding his fingers through her hair, savoring the feel of her body against his, opening his senses to the feel of her, the scent of her. The reality of her. "You should."

"Only if you want to be protected from me?"

Hell, no. "Not a chance. What other woman is going to march into my room and tell me to leave my pants unbuttoned, invite me to take advantage of her and inform me that I love her?"

"I did not tell you you loved me."

"You implied it."

"That is not the same."

"Very true."

She waited. He knew what she wanted. The words clogged in his throat. Smoothing his thumb over her lips, he shook his head. "I'm sorry."

Her smile faltered. "You cannot say it?"

"I want to."

"Why?"

He didn't want her to know that part of his past. That ugly part of him. "No good ever came of it."

"Are you telling me I am wrong?"

He didn't know how to answer that.

She touched a bruise on his chest, tracing the shape with her fingertip. Her tongue peeked out between her teeth. Her head cocked to the side as she looked into his eyes, everything she felt inside visible in her expression. Desire. Uncertainty. Love. So much love.

"If you cannot tell me, can you show me?"

"Oh, hell, yes." He could show her. With pressure on the nape of her neck he brought her up on her toes. "Come here."

Her hands slid up over his shoulders, wrapping around his neck pulling him down. "Gladly."

The passion surged as always, hard and demanding almost angry in its intensity. *Can you show me?*

He stopped. Could he? He knew how to show Fei passion. Could he show her love? Closing his eyes, he willed the lust back and sought the emotion beneath, finding at its core the softness. The lush center.

Gently, as gently as he could, he touched his lips to hers, bringing that lushness to the heat, fitting the edges of his lips to hers, pressing lightly, lingeringly, holding the moment as long as he could before doing it again. Just as softly, just as lingeringly.

She sighed and melted against him as sweet as a

summer breeze, her breath fluttering against his cheek as he turned his attention to the side of her neck.

"Oh, my."

He'd never heard that combination of wonder and bliss in her voice before. He liked it. He liked knowing he was the one who put it there.

"Can you feel it, honey?"

"I think so."

Think wasn't good enough. He wanted her to know it. "I guess I'll have to try harder."

She tilted her head to the side. "Please do."

He chuckled and nibbled a bit, still keeping it light. Beneath the surface, lust writhed with impatience. He pushed it back, because this was new for him, too. He'd never consciously made love to a woman before. The first time should be with Fei.

"Shadow," she moaned as he caught her earlobe between his teeth and bit down just enough to send that shiver down her spine.

"Yes?"

"I can't stand while you do this."

He did it again, just to check if she was telling the truth. Her knees collapsed. He caught her easily. With a laugh he swung her up in his arms.

"The door."

He kicked it closed. She smiled and ducked her head. "Thank you."

"You have a beautiful smile, Fei. Don't hide it from me."

He sat her on the bed, resting one knee by her hip

before easing her back, following her down as she went, smiling the whole way.

Goddamn, he loved her. “Fei.”

Cupping her breast through her dress, he found her nipple. With a light pass he brought it to life. She gasped.

He did it again. “Do you like that?”

“Oh, yes.”

“Tell me how it feels.”

“Like a wonderful door opening to something better.”

“I like that.”

“So do I.” Cupping his face in her hands, she whispered, “My dragon.”

“What is it with you and dragons?”

“They are magical mythical creatures that fill me with wonder.”

She said those things so easily. Exposed her heart so easily. “As you do.”

“Fei.”

“What?”

He shook his head. “Just…Fei.”

Her smile broadened. “Kiss me again.”

He did, gladly, the desire working past his control, demanding more than light touches, adding fire to the softness. Burn to the heat. He wanted her breast in his hand. Her skin against his.

“I need you out of these clothes.”

“Oh, yes.” Her hands beat his to the buttons on her dress. One by one they popped open. He traced the ever widening V with his fingers, following the lapel to her breasts as she spread them open, lingering on the peak of her breasts, circling the nipple before following the same path back and repeating the procedure on the other side. Teasing her until she shifted and arched, moaning himself at the sweet presentation.

"Shadow?"

"Yes?"

"Just that." She smiled and ran her hands up her torso. That smile did all sorts of crazy things to his insides. Still smiling, she pulled her camisole down, exposing her breasts to his hungry gaze. "And maybe this."

His cock throbbed and his control slipped further. "Honey, I'm not going to be able to give you what you want if you keep that up."

Cupping her hands under her breasts, she plumped them to his gaze. "I told you, Shadow, I do not want you to protect me from yourself."

"It's not protection."

She pinched the nipples lightly, sighing as goose bumps raced over her skin. His fingers closed in envy.

"Then what?"

He didn't know how to say it. "I want you to hear me."

Her eyes opened. "I've always heard you. Even when I didn't like what you had to say."

"You love me, Shadow, as I love you."

"Son of a bitch."

Catching her hands, he brought them up around his

neck, feeling the smile start deep inside blending with the heat to something new. Something good. Something better.

"Come breathe your fire on me, dragon," she whispered in his ear.

Shadow took her at her word, sliding his arm under her back, arching her up, taking her nipple into his mouth, closing his lips around it, sucking gently then harder, whipping his tongue over the receptive surface, keeping her put when she would have twisted away, giving her what she asked for. All the fire she brought out in him.

"That's it," he encouraged as she wrapped her fingers in his hair, holding him to her as she cried out with pleasure. "Burn for me."

"I am."

Out of the corner of his eye, he could see her other nipple, plump and pouting. Needing. He transferred his attention, with a soft growl capturing the soft bud in the heat of his mouth, loving it until it was as hard as the other.

"Shadow. Oh, my God, Shadow."

He knew how she felt. He ached right along with her, needed right along with her, desired right along with her. He touched the tip of his finger to the tip of her breast, pressing gently. "Just a little more."

"I can't take any more."

"Yes, you can."

With a tug he transferred her hips to the edge of the bed. Pushing the material of her skirt up and out of the way, he untied her pantaloons and slid them off her hips. For a second he just admired, touching her pussy with the tips of his fingers, tracing the crease down, his finger gliding easily along the slick folds, testing until he felt the bump of her clit. Dropping to his knees, he brought her legs over his shoulders. Her scent surrounded him. His mouth watered. His cock throbbed. His heart pounded in his chest. His blood thickened in his veins. She smelled of soap and sweet desire. So sweet.

"Very pretty."

Fei grabbed her skirts and yanked them over her head. "Don't look."

"Honey, nothing could keep me from looking."

She moaned in protest.

He laughed and didn't care. All he needed was splayed before him in a delectable feast. Pink, swollen and eager. He kissed the soft pad. She squealed and gasped. Her thighs fell open. Very eager.

Parting her with his thumb and forefinger, he blew gently across her moist folds. She shivered. Her fingers twisted in his hair, pulling him in. She didn't have to worry. He wasn't going anywhere. Not for a long time. The first pass of his tongue had her gasping. The second stiffening. The third holding absolutely still.

"Right there?"

"Oh, God."

Nuzzling in, he lapped at her pussy, swirling his tongue through her juices, finding her engorged clit easily, capturing it between his lips, holding it for the rasp of his tongue, the swirl of the tip.

"Oh, yes! Shadow!" Her hips bucked. Her fingers tightened. Easing his hand between them, he tested her vagina. She was tight, wet. Ready. He slipped his finger into the slick channel, groaning as it immediately clamped down, imagining all that feminine heat clasping his cock in an intimate embrace. Sucking at her clit, he brought her higher, pumping his finger in and out of her tight channel, keeping the rhythm steady, pacing it to the lift of her hips, the pant of her breaths.

"Shadow!"

As she quivered and arched, he changed his mind. He didn't want her coming like this. He wanted to feel her come on his cock, wanted to enjoy those hard contractions before they mellowed to pleasant ripples that hugged him as tightly as her arms. To feel her sigh of satisfaction against his skin as he held her in the beauty of the aftermath.

He couldn't wait any longer. With a last kiss to her clit, he drew back. Pushing down his pants, he lodged himself between her thighs. His cock nestled in the well of her vagina. With a slow push, he entered that first little bit. The delicate muscles clenched in a kiss of welcome. She was sweet. So sweet. So wild. So his.

Bending her knees, she cradled him to her. With a lift of her hips, she invited him in. "Look at me, Fei."

Her lids lifted slowly. Weaving his fingers through hers, he pinned her hands beside her head. "Let me see it happen."

With a slow push, he forged in, savoring the sensation of the silky walls caressing his cock, holding her gaze as she held his. Watching her breath catch and her pupils dilate, knowing she was watching him just as closely.

She'd asked him to show her and he didn't know how else to let her know how it felt to have her in his life. The smiles she brought. The peace she brought. The happiness. She took him all, squeezing him deep within her, shivering with the desire that always arced between them.

Whispering with tenderness, "My Shadow."

Leaning down, he kissed her lips the way they'd begun. Sweetness in fire. "My Fei."

"Yes. Yours."

"Always."

Her legs wrapped around his waist, her heels pressed into his hips.

"Son of a bitch." She was stealing his control.

"Please, Shadow. Love me. Now."

"I am."

"I love the sweetness, but—" she leaned up and nipped his chest "—I need the fire. I love your fire."

And that fast the flames burned out of his control. She ground up. He ground down, giving her all he had, taking all she gave. Wanting more. Needing more. Freeing one hand, he brought it between them, centering his thumb on her clit, rubbing firmly as she cried out.

"Oh, my God!"

His balls pulled tight. A tingling grew in the base

of his spine. He wasn't going to last, but he wanted her with him. Always.

She thrashed beneath him in an agony of pleasure. So close he could tell. So close. He continued to rub her clit. "What do you need?"

"You," she moaned.

"How?"

"Hard." Digging her heels into the mattress, she thrust up. "I need you hard."

Hell, he needed that, too.

"Deep."

"Yes!"

He drove in. She cried out, digging her heels into his back, arching up with her hips, pulling him down with her arms, begging for his kiss, begging for more. He gave her all he had, loving her hard and deep, matching her kiss for kiss, taking her cries as his, her breaths as his, giving her back his moans, his whisper of her name. Giving her everything he had in an explosion that shook him to his core. His Fei. His life.

And then in a whisper only she could hear, he gave her that last piece of himself he'd thought lost so long ago.

"Goddamn, Fei. I love you."

CHAPTER EIGHTEEN

WHEN THE SOFT KNOCK came at the door, Fei didn't know whether to curse or cheer. It had to be the bath she'd ordered. After several hours of lovemaking she could use a good soak, but soaking meant breaking the tender peace between her and Shadow. There was so much they had yet to discuss. Things that were bound to make him angry. She sighed and snuggled her cheek into his shoulder one last time. The world never wanted to stay away for long. The knock came again. When she would have slid out of bed, Shadow lightly covered her mouth with his hand. Turning his head, he whispered in her ear, "Stand to the left of the door and ask who it is."

A voice came from the hallway. "You ordered a bath, ma'am?"

Fei slid out of bed, taking the quilt with her to cover herself. The room was registered to her. It was logical they would assume only she was in it. She whispered to Shadow, "It is our bathwater."

Shadow's expression remained tense, on guard. "Do as I say."

Her bow was an instinctive response to an order, which annoyed her, but not to the extent she would foolishly disregard Shadow's precautions. She'd seen for herself how innocent-looking people could be evil. Doing as told she called out, "Who is it?"

"You ordered a bath from End of the Trail?"

"This is the saloon?"

"Yes, ma'am."

There was nothing in the man's voice to elicit suspicion. She looked at Shadow. He stood by the bed, pistols in hand.

"Unlock the door and step back," he whispered.

Out of the line of fire, she realized. The hairs on the back of her neck stood on end. "Coming."

She quickly lifted the bar and moved to the left, against the wall next to the nightstand.

Another glace at Shadow. At his nod, she called, "Come in."

The door opened without fanfare. A man came in carrying two buckets of steaming water. He barely spared her a look as he turned and backed the last couple steps in. "Bring that tub in, boys, and be careful you don't nick the walls while you're at it."

Two boys, not yet old enough to be sprouting beards, carried in a massive copper tub. Excitement leaped in Fei for a completely different reason. It had been so long since she'd had a real bath.

"Where do you—" The sight of Shadow standing there in nothing but pants and pistols clearly gave the man pause, but not for long. Not taking his eyes off Shadow, he finished, "Where do you want it, ma'am?"

There was only one place where it would fit. "Where you are standing."

"You heard the lady."

The boys set the tub down with a bang. "Son of a bitch, if you dent that tub, Jimmy is going to have your asses skinned."

The boys jumped back. The man poured the first bucket of water into the tub. "Now go get the rest of the hot water up here and don't be spilling it on the way."

The boys rushed out of the room.

"It'll just take a few trips to have this full," he added in a much softer tone to her.

She bowed before she could catch herself. *"Xei-xei."*

The man's eyes narrowed. His expression changed in subtle ways. The sound of a pistol cocking snapped his head around.

With a flick of one of the muzzles, Shadow indicated the door. "My wife would like that bath sooner rather than later."

The respect that had slipped quickly came back to the man's expression. "Of course."

He poured the second bucket of water into the tub and left.

As soon as the door closed, she said, "He did not find it so shocking a white woman was with you."

"I imagine he sees all kinds of things."

"But when I revealed my ancestry, he lost much respect."

"People get fool notions."

"Shadow?" she said, coming to his side.

"What?"

She liked the way he set one pistol down on the table and immediately tucked her in. "I am not hurt, I am annoyed."

"Ah. Want to borrow my pistol?"

He was smiling. She could hear it in his voice. Looking up, she could see it on his face. Her Shadow was smiling. Not an ear-to-ear grin. He was too contained for that. But a genuine smile that showed off his nice teeth, that showed the man he could have been if the past had been different. She couldn't help but smile back. "I would rather fetch my dynamite."

"Hell, no," he swore as he tipped her face up. "You'll blow a hole in the tub and the thought of a real bath is too tempting to pass up."

She feigned disappointment as his hair fell around her face in a silken caress. His lips brushed hers. The sulfur to her fuse. "But I would enjoy it."

Sliding his fingers through her hair, he tilted her head slightly, smiling differently as she shivered with anticipation. She so did love his kisses. "You'll enjoy the bath more," he promised with a growl that just made her shiver again and wrap her arms around his neck.

"You are probably right."

HE WAS RIGHT. FEI DID enjoy the bath more, both the lovemaking and the soak. And this moment, she decided, snuggling deeper into his embrace, she liked even better. Sitting before him in the tub, resting back against his chest, feeling his arms surround her with the same thoroughness of the water, feeling the peace around them both. This was a moment of heaven.

"Mmm." Cupping her breast in his hand, Shadow sighed contentedly. "This was a damn good idea, woman."

"Thank you." His thumb passed over her nipple, stirring memories of the passion just spent. It was her turn to sigh.

"You always make me feel so good."

His grip tightened slightly. "I could say the same."

Water sloshed in gentle waves as Fei turned on her side to better see his face. His expression was a revelation. "You are nervous."

"I can hear a *but* tucked inside all that contentment."

She was not surprised. There were many worries on her mind. "It scared me when you had me answer the door."

"Just a precaution."

She slid her hand up his chest. "A necessary one, I understand, but what if there had been problems? What if you had been hurt? Where would I go?"

"Hell's Eight."

"This place that even you will not call home? How would it be a home for me?"

"Tia would make sure you were welcome."

"Who is this Tia?"

"Tia saved our asses. Without her we would have starved to death or been shot for stealing."

Another strong woman in Shadow's life. Shadow

hadn't said, but she had the impression his mother had not been so strong.

"How did this happen?"

His big hand cupped her shoulder. "Now's not the time for sad tales."

"I would know you, husband."

"You know all that's worth knowing."

"I do not know this."

He cocked an eyebrow at her. "Stubborn little thing, aren't you?"

She didn't answer, just held his gaze until he gave her what she wanted. The smile left his eyes.

"The Mexican army invaded our town."

"Why?"

"Because it was ripe for the picking. Because they could. Because they had an urge to spill a little blood. Take your pick."

She winced and rubbed her hand over his chest, the old scars abrading her palm in a reprimand. This was painful for him. "I am sorry. I will not interrupt again."

Shadow caught her hand and brought it to his lips. "I told you this wasn't the time."

She had a feeling there would be no other. "The time is fine. It is my interrupting that is wrong."

"Fei—"

She cut him off. "I would know this of you."

"Then listen up because I'm not telling it again."

She nodded.

"The army came one afternoon. Tracker and I were

out hunting. There was no warning. They just rode in and started killing."

"How old were you?"

His face set in hard lines. "Eleven. Twelve. Old enough to kill."

A child fighting men. "You were brave."

"We were pissed, bravery didn't come into it. By the time we worked our way to the Allens', it was too late."

An emotion crossed his face she didn't understand. "Too late for what?"

"To do a goddamn thing."

Guilt. The expression on his face was guilt.

"You were a child."

His eyes were old and haunted when they met hers. "She was good to Tracker and I."

"Who?"

"Mrs. Allen. Caine's mother. She was always good to us, never asking questions, just always there with food and medicine. And hugs." He shook his head as if that were the most amazing thing. "She always gave us hugs."

"You were perhaps a very sweet boy."

He looked at her as if she'd lost her mind. "Hell, Tracker and I were little better than animals then. All we knew how to do was get mad and kill."

She doubted that. The man she knew was not created for nothing.

Thank you for seeing his softness. She sent the prayer to the unknown woman who had been so much to an unwanted child. To Shadow she said, "And love. You loved her."

"Did we?"

She had no doubt. "It is in your voice."

"Maybe. I carried around a whole lot of anger back then." He shook his head. "The woman was good to everyone and they raped her and gutted her like an animal, leaving her in the dirt like she was nothing."

"You found her?"

"I don't remember who did the finding. Just the promise."

"What promise?"

"To make them pay."

The warm water couldn't prevent the shiver that raced down her spine. "Who made the promise?"

"Those of us who survived."

"Hell's Eight," she whispered.

He lifted her out of the tub. "Yes."

She grabbed a towel. "And Tia?"

He stood in the tub unabashedly naked as water dripped down his hard body. "We found Tia on our way to keeping that promise."

"She was good to you?"

Shadow laughed. "At first, she threatened to skin us alive."

"I do not understand."

"For all our big talk, we were just kids, and we hadn't much in the way of weapons, or food. The Mexicans had laid waste to the area. No one wanted to take in eight boys with a hell of a lot of anger and appetites to match."

"Except Tia," she guessed.

"Except Tia. She kept us civilized."

"She gave you a home."

"That, too."

"You love her."

There was a pause as if to confess such a thing was bad luck, and then, "Yes."

Handing Shadow a towel, Fei guessed, "She is one of the reasons you won't go home?"

He stepped out of the tub and rubbed the towel across his chest. "She's always been good to me."

The same words he'd used to describe Caine's mother. The other woman he'd loved. The one who'd been murdered. Picking up the other towel, she dried herself with deliberate care, before saying, "It wasn't your fault what happened to Caine's mother."

He threw the towel into the chair with enough force to make her jump. His expression was harder than she'd ever seen and for the first time, she felt the force of his anger. "What the hell do you know about it?"

He wanted her to back away, to leave him with his anger. To leave this wound untended. She took a step forward instead, placing her hand on his chest, feeling him flinch in the jump of his skin. Such an old wound to be so raw. "I know you did all that you could, my husband. I know you fought with force and honor to defend those you loved. But I also know a child cannot stop an army."

His fingers wrapped around her wrist. "The hell we couldn't. We could have warned them. We saw the signs. With a little more warning—"

She cut him off, resisting the pull on her arm. She would not let him sever this connection. Looking up into his face, braving his pain and anger, she laid out the truth. "They still would have died."

"Goddamn it—"

She shook her head. "You cannot control the world, husband. Good and bad will happen as it wills. The how and when is not under your control."

"The hell it's not."

He needed to accept this. "You sent me away to save me. Instead, you sent me into your enemy's hands."

"I sent you with your uncles."

"You tried to force me into a life you thought would suit me."

"I wanted you safe."

"And I wanted to live."

"I made a choice."

"Yes. Which you forced upon me. Was the result as you wished?"

He ran his fingers through his hair. His grip tightened on her wrist to near pain. She didn't move, watching the anger inside him ride his frustration to greater heights. "Only because you didn't stay put."

"Because you didn't listen to what I wanted."

"Goddamn it, Fei!"

It was a dangerous game she played now. She only had her belief in the man that said he would not lash out at her. "God does not damn me. *You* do with your belief that you can control everything that cannot be controlled."

His grip reached pain. "I can control you."

She glanced pointedly at her wrist. "As you control yourself now?"

He dropped her arm as if it was fire, and took a step back. The wall he put between them was supposed to keep her from following. She stepped through it, braving his anger.

Placing her hand on his chest, she whispered, "You said you loved me, Shadow."

"My kind of love you don't need."

"I disagree."

He grabbed her hand, tilted her wrist up. The marks of his fingers branded her skin. "This is who I am."

He wanted her to run. She left her hand in his. "No, this is you fighting who you are."

"And who might that be?"

She took that step closer that brought them skin to skin. "A man who has seen too much. A man who loves. A man who would shelter those he loves from the bad of what he's seen."

"Shit."

He was no longer pulling away. Did he think she had learned nothing of him during their time together?

Sliding her hands up his chest, she whispered, "I would not change that part of you, husband. I would just change the belief you have that if you can control everything, if you take all the risk, then nothing bad will happen to those you love."

"I've been doing fine until now."

She shook her head. "Everyone has their destiny. You cannot shape it for them. You can only decide how much you want to be part of it."

"Is this your father's belief?"

She nodded, accepting the pain of his loss, choosing to remember how he'd been years ago. "Before illness took him, he had much wisdom."

"Uh-huh."

Now he was just being difficult. "My people believe that in all things there must be balance. The power of love goes both ways. You cannot be to the only force."

He immediately bristled. "You're saying I can't protect those I love?"

"I am saying you cannot deny those that love you *their* need to protect you."

"I don't need protecting."

Fei shoved him backward to the bed. Surprise alone gave her the advantage. She pressed on, climbing onto the bed, pushing on his shoulders until he lay back on the mattress. It was a measure of his love that he allowed her this moment of power. It was not in Shadow's nature to be vulnerable, she knew. Straddling his hips, she braced herself on his chest.

"Being protected does not mean you are weak."

"What the hell would you have it mean?"

She wanted to cuff him upside the head. Dragons were the most stubborn of creatures. She kissed him instead, hard at first as frustration paced ahead of desire. Against her hip, his cock rose. Against her chest, his heart beat. His strong, loyal passionate heart. Inside her, tenderness welled, pushing out the frustration.

"It means you are loved." Such a simple truth he fought so hard against.

"Shit."

That fast his anger left. And that fast she was on her back with her husband looking down at her with the same combination of frustration and love she'd felt a moment before. And just as had happened with her, she watched the love take over, softening his mouth, his expression.

"What do you want from me, Fei?"

A question, not a demand. A gift to her. She cupped his face in her hand. Such a strong man. A giving man. *Her* man. She drew her thumb over his lips the way he did to her. His eyes narrowed and his cock jerked. He liked it, too. "I want you to promise to try to remember love must flow both ways to survive."

"You don't ask much."

"I only ask that you try."

His eyes narrowed and his gaze dipped to her breasts. A tingle went through her. A glance down revealed her desire showed in the hard tips.

"Anything else?" he drawled.

"Yes." She shifted on the mattress, arching her back, drawing her nails lightly across his nape, hearing his catch of breath with an internal smile. She loved that he found such pleasure in her. "After you promise, I want you to make love to me."

The bed dipped as he changed position, propping himself beside her. His big hand cradled her breast, squeezing lightly, sending rivulets of sensation trickling through her in a lazy prelude to the fire he commanded so easily.

"I can do that."

Slipping her hand between her nipple and his mouth, she asked, "Do I have your promise?"

"Yes. Damn it. I'll try." He pushed her hand aside before growling against her breast, "Now come here."

She went, as she always would. With love.

THEY DIDN'T KNOCK, JUST SLIPPED into the hotel room like ghosts in the calm of predawn. Three, maybe four, intruders. Shadow eased Fei to the side and palmed his knife from under the pillow.

A hand came over his, pinning his arm to the bed. "Uh-uh."

He knew that voice. "Tucker? What the hell?"

"You won't need that."

Pressure on his wrist forced his hand open. Glass rattled as someone struck a sulfur and lit the lamp. The scent of kerosene tainted the air as the room filled with a warm glow. Tucker's expression was grim as he relieved Shadow of the knife.

"What's going on?"

"Shadow?" Fei asked, huddling shyly into his back

and pulling the quilt up over her shoulders. "What is happening?"

"I don't have a clue."

"Nothing to be scared of, ma'am," Zach said, tipping his hat. "We've just got to get something settled."

Tucker pulled him to the side of the bed. Sam tossed two pieces of rope from hand to hand.

"The only question is, are you coming willingly or are we going to have to use force?"

Shadow glanced at his brother. Tracker stood by the door, arms folded, watching. Not saying a word. Beside him Sam and Zach stood, watching, as well.

"Do I at least get pants?"

Caine scooped his up off the floor and tossed them across his lap. His "thanks" was wry. Sitting on the bed, he pulled them on.

"So, what needs settling?"

Fei scooted up behind him on the bed. Against his back he felt the bunching of the sheet and the softness of her skin. Her touch on his shoulder was gentle. Soothing. A direct contrast to the tension emanating from the others.

"Where you go from here," Caine drawled.

"I thought I'd take Fei to San Francisco."

"No," Fei gasped.

"To see your family," Shadow told Fei over his shoulder. "Not to stay."

"Told you he'd run," Zach observed.

"Going for a visit is not running," Shadow snapped.

"I don't want to visit," Fei countered.

"Your family is important."

Fei scooted higher. "So is yours." She was as determined as the expression on Tracker's face.

"He's done with running," Tracker stated in that low, no-nonsense tone that meant business.

"Have you forgotten? I'm a wanted man."

"All the more reason to come home."

Home. The word hung between them. Tempting. Forbidden.

"You know that's not possible. I can't endanger—"

Fei kissed his shoulder and slipped her hand over his mouth, surprising him into silence. He could feel the shake of her head in the rocking of her lips against his skin. "He really cannot help it," she said over his shoulder to Caine. "It is not that he does not love you all. It is just that a dragon cannot change who he is."

With a nip, he freed his mouth. Catching Fei's hand in his before she could jerk it away, he pressed a kiss on the back. "I can handle this."

"I was just—"

"What he is is Hell's Eight," Caine interrupted.

Sam and Zach nodded.

"Never said I wasn't."

"Wouldn't know it from the way you act," Tracker growled.

Fei's nails bit into his shoulder.

The power of love goes both way. You cannot be the only force.

Sitting here looking at the men who were his brothers in battle and life, he could begin to grasp the importance of those words. If it was Tracker who was being hunted by the law, and he had the compound of Hell's Eight to rely on, Shadow would want to be by his side. Where he could protect him.

Being protected does not mean you are weak. It means you are loved.

Shit. How had he not understood before now?

"Hell's Eight is where Shadow belongs."

"The army is going to disagree with that," Shadow pointed out.

Caine smiled that cold, bring-on-the-world smile that was a battle cry in itself. "And if the army has a problem with that, they're welcome to come discuss it." His hand dropped to the butt of his revolver. "At any time."

Tucker and Zach dropped their hands to their knives. Sam cocked his rifle. "Any time."

"Any arguments?" Tracker asked, his eyes meeting Shadow's.

Quite a few, but none that would be accepted. "If you harbor me, you'll be declaring war on the United States," he pointed out, trying for logic.

Sam pulled Colonel Daniel's book from his pocket. "I see it as a disagreement started by a colonel who's taken too many battle wounds."

"You really think you can sell that?" Shadow asked.

"Shit." Tucker handed Shadow back his knife. "Sam could sell kindling in a forest fire."

"And the government needs us here more than they need you dead," Caine finished.

That was true enough. And with more settlers coming out here stirring up trouble with the Indians and tensions building with the southern states, the government needed all the help it could get in the West.

"Hell's Eight's a mighty handy friend to have right about now," Tucker added. "And if we manage to come back in a few months, salvage some of that gold out of Fei's claim, we can sweeten the pot."

"Yes," Fei agreed. "It should be used for a fresh start." Sliding around his body, clutching the sheet to her chest, her heart, her hope a silent plea in her beautiful eyes, she said, "Your family wants you home, my husband."

He looked at the men of Hell's Eight. Men he'd grown up with. Fought with. Survived with. Big men, scarred inside and out by the battles they'd waged. Men who'd go to hell and back for those they loved. Men who'd known the worst, and never expected better. Their bond had been forged in youth amidst pain and blood. A year and a half ago, he'd made the decision to sacrifice himself for two of those men. He'd made that decision alone. Without consulting anyone. He'd done it because it'd been the right thing and because he hadn't seen a future for himself. He'd do it again in a heartbeat. But if he *had* to do it over again, he wouldn't have just left without a word. He wouldn't have left his family with such worry.

Sliding his fingers through Fei's hair, Shadow stroked his thumb along her mouth.

"So I see."

A year and a half ago he hadn't thought love was for him, let alone grasped how much a smile could mean to him, but now Fei kissed his thumb and tucked herself into the curve of his body where she belonged, next to his heart. Now he was loved, by a woman as wild and reckless in her own way as he was in his. He remembered the moment when the tunnel was caving in on him and he'd thought it was the end, the grip of her hand on his ankle when he'd thought she was safely out. The terror that grip brought. The hope. The love. It'd all crashed in on him in one blinding second of realization, ripping down the wall he'd built between himself and the world, leaving him with certain knowledge that he wasn't in control. It'd scared the shit out of him. It still did.

Everyone has their destiny.

Accepting that was going to take a lifetime, but he'd made Fei a promise and he had to start somewhere.

"So what are you going to do about it?" Tracker asked, the very blankness of his expression communicating how much the answer meant to him.

Holding Fei in his arms, holding his brother's gaze with his, Shadow pried himself loose from the knee-jerk response of the past. Fei was right about destiny. No matter what the future held, he was Hell's Eight. That's how he'd lived and that's how he'd die. He stood. Fei scooted back, her gaze burning into his back as he pulled on his pants.

"Well?" Sam asked.

"Shadow?" Fei whispered.

He turned at the uncertainty in her tone, and ran the back of his fingers down her cheek, seeing the same uncertainty in her eyes. "Would you like to see my home, honey?"

Her smile shook just a little and he understood how much she'd still feared he'd turn, backward, away from her. Damn, he had some bridges to mend there. Fortunately, he had a lifetime to make it right. Shit, when had he become a man who thought in terms of lifetimes?

"Very much."

Touching his thumb to her mouth, he steadied her with a soft press. "Good, because I want it to be yours, too."

Her breath caught a second before her smile broke over him like sunshine. "That would make me happy."

He knew the exact place he'd build their home. The level spot just above the main house. He always felt as if he could see the world from up there. His world. The one he wanted to share with Fei.

"We could get married in the garden."

Her breath caught again. "We are already married."

He shook his head. "I want a ceremony I know damn well is legal." He leaned down and kissed her mouth because he couldn't not and then whispered for her alone, "And this time I want the memory of your vows said with that same softness you say my name after we make love."

She blushed a fiery red, but his Fei wasn't a woman to run away from her dreams, and for some reason he didn't understand but would always be grateful for, she'd decided he was hers. "Oh, yes. I would like that memory, too."

If his family wasn't here, he'd lay her on the bed and make the sweetest love to her. They way he always planned to but never managed to make happen. Maybe on their wedding night. For now he only had words. "Damn, I love you."

It came out harsher than he'd intended. Fei still looked as if he'd handed her the purest gold. Maybe she really did understand him.

"I love you, too."

Her lips shaped the words *My dragon,* so only he could see. And it was his turn to smile. However she saw him, it was good.

"Guess that means we won't need the shackles," Tucker cut in.

"Or those chains," Zach added.

Shackles and chains? Shadow turned back to the others. "Son of a bitch, just what exactly were you planning on doing if I said no?"

It was Tucker who answered. "Whatever it took."

"Shit." Shadow believed him. He looked to Caine for confirmation.

Caine just shrugged. "You've been gone long enough."

"Place just isn't the same without you stirring things up," Sam added.

Fei held the sheet around her and came to his side, reminding him with a touch of all that was important.

His Fei. His destiny. Pulling her close, he looked to Tracker. His brother nodded.

"It's time."

Yeah, it was. Time to let the past find its peace. Time to move forward with a new direction.

"Then let's go home."

* * * * *